Too much temptation

The way he felt right now. Alive. Aware. Of Lily. She made his arms ache to wrap around her, to pull her to him and feel every curvy inch of her pressed up against him.

She would fit perfectly against him, he knew, could feel it by the way they stood so close, their bodies almost swaying together.

She felt it, too.

Max couldn't do a damn thing except brace himself in that moment. Her voice filtered through him. He could inhale her subtle scent. Feel the graze of her hands on his skin. Sense the warmth of her body radiating between them. Imagine the way her body would melt into his.

Max knew. He could feel it in his gut where it counted, and he had to force himself to take a step back by sheer effort of will, force himself not to do exactly what he ached to do—pull her into his arms.

Because that would change everything between them.

Dear Reader,

After I wrote *Her Husband's Partner*, (Harlequin Superromance #1635) I suspected the folks in Pleasant Valley wouldn't stop living simply because I typed *the end*. They didn't. After all, who *wouldn't* want to live in such a wonderful place?

Lily Angelica, for one.

She had bigger plans for her life than her tiny hometown had to offer. But while she has been off chasing her dreams, she's lost something along the way. And that *something* is an important part of being happy.

Max could have told Lily her priorities were mixed up. He learned the hard way not to take life for granted and is making the most of every moment with his young daughter. But it turns out Max's journey back from grief has skewed his priorities a bit, too, so when this unlikely pair get together to plan a wedding, they find that, sometimes, the journey to someplace better brings them right back where they started.

Ordinary women. Extraordinary romance.

That's Harlequin Superromance! I hope you enjoy Lily and Max's love story. Let me know at www.jeanielondon.com.

Peace and blessings,

Jeanie London

No Groom Like Him
Jeanie London

TORONTO NEW YORK LONDON
AMSTERDAM PARIS SYDNEY HAMBURG
STOCKHOLM ATHENS TOKYO MILAN MADRID
PRAGUE WARSAW BUDAPEST AUCKLAND

Recycling programs
for this product may
not exist in your area.

ISBN-13: 978-0-373-71739-2

NO GROOM LIKE HIM

Copyright © 2011 by Jeanie LeGendre

www.Harlequin.com

Printed in U.S.A.

ABOUT THE AUTHOR

Jeanie London writes romance because she believes in happily-ever-afters. Not the "love conquers all" kind, but the "we love each other so we can conquer anything" kind. It's precisely why she loves Harlequin Superromance—stories about real women tackling life to find love. The kind of love she understands because she's a real woman tackling life in sunny Florida with her own romance-hero husband, their two beautiful and talented daughters, a loving and slightly crazy extended family and a menagerie of sweet strays.

Books by Jeanie London

HARLEQUIN SUPERROMANCE

HARLEQUIN BLAZE

*Falling Inn Bed...

**HARLEQUIN SIGNATURE
SELECT SPOTLIGHT**

For the real Max.
You're the stuff heroes are made of. Definitely!

And special thanks to Beth Fairweather, who always makes coming up with brilliant ideas so much fun ;-)

CHAPTER ONE

All About Angel blog
Wedding Angel or Antibride?

After a string of matrimonial messes, wedding watchers around the globe are wondering if the Wedding Angel—founder and CEO of a widely celebrated destination-wedding agency that shall remain nameless—has reached the end of her luck.

Consider how her engagement ended when the paparazzi caught her fiancé—an international bridal-show producer, also nameless—in flagrante delicto with a Brazilian runway model.

Now consider this weekend's fiasco of A-list actress Emmelina Belle's Polynesian nuptials. Celebrity and wedding bloggers alike have been reporting that this much-maligned diva was seeking public redemption with her wedding to Drew Hatcher, the leading man she hooked up with last year on the set.

Stealing *Axis's* Sexiest Man of 2010 from his television-actress wife devastated Emmelina's career, but maybe she should have reconsidered her choice of event planner. Or maybe the Wedding Angel should have washed her hands of this messy client after her own run-in with infidelity. While it's true the event was already in the planning stages when the Wedding Angel's engagement went bust, a woman touted

as the Martha Stewart of matrimony should have recognized Emmelina's bid for favorable press. (What
some folks won't do for attention!)

The ceremony took place during the magical moments before sunset. The media swarmed the island
in helicopters, in Jeeps and on foot, scouring every
corner for celebrity sightings, given carte blanche
by Emmelina to publicize to the ends of the earth—
or the farthest reaches of satellite coverage.

While no one could expect the Wedding Angel
to control the weather…Mara'amu shouldn't have
been a surprise.

This easterly trade wind is known to gust
through the islands in winter, so one would expect
contingencies to be in place for an outdoor wedding.
But when Mara'amu swept across the beach during
the fire dancers' tribal performance, the wind sent
flames toward the highly flammable bamboo tents.
The ensuing conflagration sent panicked guests
fleeing in every direction. Emmelina wound up
treading water. (Score one for karma! Drew's ex-
wife is probably still laughing.)

As firefighters and local emergency personnel
contained the flames, Emmelina emerged from the
surf, steaming from both ears while the paparazzi
documented everything—including the groom's
reaction. He took one look at his ranting almost-
wife (check out the photos at *CeleBrats* for the best
shots—you can see when he makes up his mind to
escape) and seized his chance for freedom, leaving
Emmelina dripping wet at the fiery altar.

The paparazzi caught Drew at the airport an hour
later, threatening an airline clerk to find him a seat

on the first plane off the island...and said clerk politely suggesting Drew swim to the mainland.

So, thanks to the fiancé fiasco and Emmelina Belle, bridal bombs dominate the tabloids and internet, leaving wedding watchers all over the globe wondering: Wedding Angel or Antibride? Cast your vote!

All About Angel blog: the latest buzz for brides!

"ARE YOU THE Wedding Angel or the Antibride?"

That one question stood out over all the voices rushing Lily Angelica as she disembarked the private jet. She hadn't expected to find the press awaiting her on the tarmac, and even if she had, she definitely hadn't expected *that* question.

Coming to a halt, she set down her purse and laptop case, buying herself time for a deep breath. She would use the exit stairs as a makeshift podium since she was obviously conducting a press conference. Exactly what she hadn't wanted. Not with her nerves shot and the dark circles under her eyes.

Reflex had her fixing a smile on her face. She straightened and scanned the crowd.

"Lily, any comment on Emmelina's wedding?"

"Will you confirm the rumor Worldwide Weddings Unlimited contracted the former president's daughter?"

"Are you in town to hide from what's being written on the All About Angel blog?"

Mention of the All About Angel blog had Lily searching their faces to see who was rude enough to bring up such nonsense. A tabloid reporter, no doubt.

When more press rushed across the tarmac—including a cameraman—she didn't get a chance to identify any one individual.

Who had leaked her arrival? She hadn't realized the area had so many media outlets. This was Pleasant Valley, for goodness' sake. When she'd grown up here, the place had been nothing but villages orbiting towns defined by how long a drive it was to civilization.

Five minutes into the Valley.

Fifteen minutes into Poughkeepsie.

A half hour to the mall.

Two hours to the city—Manhattan and definite civilization.

"No comment on Emmelina's wedding." She projected her voice and the reporters quieted. "And, yes, I'm pleased to announce that Worldwide Weddings Unlimited is contracted for Kate Cochran's event. That's breaking news since we went to contract right before I left the Manhattan office an hour ago. And do you really think I'd hide from an anonymous blogger who can't be troubled to sign his or her name to erroneous posts?"

Posts that appeared to have no purpose other than casting doubt on Lily's reputation? She hadn't expected legitimate media to give credence to such nonsense. "I'm sorry to disappoint you, my friends, but I've come to town for a family wedding."

"Haven't heard anything about a family wedding on the wire services. Are you attending or planning the event?"

She spotted the reporter who had asked the question. *Poughkeepsie Journal.* She'd answer. "Both actually. Can't have a wedding planner in the family without asking for input. Not if there's to be peace at the event, anyway."

Laughter erupted from the crowd and camera shutters clicked wildly.

"Will you comment on the All About Angel blog, Lily Susan?"

Lily Susan.

The only people on the planet who used her first and middle names together were family, so her gaze automatically zeroed in… Her breath caught as she saw the familiar man standing half a head above the crowd. *Not* family. And how had she missed him? Despite the two dozen people huddled around him, suddenly, *he* was all she could see.

Max Downey.

The same glossy dark hair. The same chiseled face. The same fast smile.

Had the inquiry come from anyone else, Lily would have offered a quip these reporters could milk in print for all they were worth. But Max owned the *Mid-Hudson Herald,* a legitimate media corporation, even if his questions hadn't sounded like it—not when he was asking about the All About Angel blog.

From *him* the question took her so off guard she could barely think let alone quip, with her heart pounding too hard. Their gazes met across the distance….

All these years and his piercing green eyes still tied her tongue in a knot.

But Lily wasn't the same young girl who had nursed a crush on her big brother's best friend. Max's flashing dimples and deep voice could no longer take possession of her reactions and make her blush like a teenager.

Especially when he asked such idiotic questions.

"Last I heard you owned the *Herald*, Mr. Downey. Don't you have professionals on staff who know the difference between relevant and irrelevant questions?"

More laughter. More clicking cameras. The video was rolling, too.

Max cocked his head to the side and glanced at her with an expression that was amusement and arrogance rolled into one. "Yes to both questions."

"Both?" She arched a quizzical eyebrow.

"Yes, I have professionals on staff and, yes, I have a relevant question." Wealth and privilege radiated from him, in his matter-of-fact tone and his confident manner. There was no mistaking that he was a man used to getting what he wanted.

Lily knew it was coming before he even opened his mouth. It shouldn't have taken her so long to make the connection because this man shouldn't still have the ability to rob her of her faculties. She wasn't thirteen anymore. Suddenly she remembered the inquiry that had arrived by fax to her office yesterday.

"Lily Susan, will you confirm that Worldwide Weddings Unlimited intends to contract Lieutenant Colonel Girard's wedding before he begins his campaign for governor?"

Sure enough...

From Lily's vantage she saw every head swivel toward Max. There were gasps and lots of scrambling for handheld recorders to capture the breaking political news.

Lily wondered if there were laws against airing a live murder because she intended to kill Max as soon as she could get her hands on him. The only thing saving him was the press leaping all over his political announcement.

"Downey, what do you know about the candidate?"

"What's the candidate's political affiliation?"

"What makes the candidate think he stands a chance in the gubernatorial election against the incumbent?"

The balance shifted and this became Max's press conference. Not as impromptu as hers, because the man clearly had an agenda, but Lily was impressed as much by the reporters' ability to switch gears as she was by Max's self-possession.

"Lieutenant Colonel Raymond Girard is my late wife's brother," Max explained. "His second tour in Afghanistan ends next May, and he'll be retiring from military service. After he comes home, he hopes to continue serving his country as governor of this fine State of New York."

"Who's the candidate marrying?"

"Second Lieutenant Jamilyn Carmichael. She's serving in Iraq. Hence, the need for the Wedding Angel to plan the ceremony. They have leave around the holidays and want an event at my family estate that will launch him into the public."

The family estate. *Overlook.*

Just the thought tugged at Lily's heartstrings. Every wedding she'd ever fantasized about as a girl had been set on the gorgeous grounds of the estate overlooking the Hudson River.

"Are you using your business connection to the Wedding Angel to get her to coordinate the wedding?"

Abusing that connection, more accurately.

But this reporter knew local history, at least, when it was obvious many didn't. Heads swiveled around to Lily as if this was the first they'd heard about a Worldwide-Weddings-Unlimited and Downey-family connection, both personal and professional.

Lily wrested control of the conversation again.

"I expect the bride and groom will want peace at their event since they've both been living on the front lines."

"The Wedding Angel can provide peace. She's the best in the business," Max said softly, but his voice carried. She detected a hint of a challenge in his demeanor.

"I thank you all for your interest, but a response would be premature. I simply don't have any answers except to say Mr. Downey's inquiry will follow standard World-wide Wedding Unlimited precontract procedure."

She flashed a professional smile. "But I can promise you after his inquiry undergoes the review process your media outlets will be given an exclusive. Please fax or email the manager at my local office and mention this press conference. She'll make sure you know as soon as a decision about the Carmichael-Girard event is finalized."

That got a round of applause, but Lily knew there wouldn't be any news because she had veto power. And this event was vetoed already.

She couldn't handle another rush-job right now. Not so soon after planning her own hurried wedding, an event she'd whipped together during a whirlwind engagement that had gone belly-up in a public way. She'd salvaged what she could from the wreckage, but Lily didn't doubt these reporters knew all the gory details.

She'd turned the wedding of her dreams into a full-scale charity event, because she'd refused to waste a perfectly amazing party. Since the venue had been a palace on the Dalmatian Coast—a favorite getaway for her and Lucas—the organization she chose as recipient supported war orphans in the former Yugoslavia. Fortunately, the response had been impressive.

At least she'd been able to feel good about that.

But the emotional upheaval had taken its toll, and she'd come home because she needed to regroup and reenergize her depleted batteries and heal before she burned out her creativity completely. Max had no business putting her on the spot—and *on the record*—this way. If he thought this public announcement would persuade her...

She was here to plan her sister-in-law Riley's wed-ding—a tiny affair Lily could plan in her sleep.

"Thank you for the welcome reception," Lily addressed

the crowd. "I hope I've answered your questions." Too bad she couldn't answer her own. Like why she'd allowed her life to spin out of control and would she ever regain her equilibrium?

She might have the skills to fake the professional image, but inside her nerves were rattled. Why was Max trying to add more chaos to her life?

Retrieving her belongings, she turned to thank the pilot who appeared behind her then headed down the steps.

The crowd parted as she made her way toward the terminal of the private airstrip. She didn't slow down until she was inside, away from the reporters who were trailing her. Her baggage already waited on a trolley. Glancing around for assistance, she guessed her dad must be outside to pick her up since he wasn't in here.

Max entered. Tall and attractive with his glossy hair and light eyes, he looked the way he always had with those broad shoulders and long-legged strides. But what had happened to his good sense? Putting her on the spot that way. Honestly.

Even when he'd been in college, he'd kept his cool after he caught her drinking apple-blossom wine with her teenage friends in the Main Mall parking garage. He'd promised not to tell—this time. But he'd threatened to tell her parents if he ever caught her drinking again. Then he'd insisted on driving her home.

And kept his word.

He headed toward a bench, where he scooped up a trench coat. After sliding on the coat, he turned that striking gaze on her. Her heartbeat rocketed.

"Why are you here?" she asked. "Did you think that public announcement would get you what you want?"

He closed the distance between them, making her suddenly so aware of how she had to tilt her head back to meet his gaze.

"I'm here to give you a ride home." Stepping around her, he reached for the trolley. "Your father sent me."

"Why? Is he all right?"

"He's fine." Everything about him struck her as masculine, in charge.

"If he was busy, why didn't my mom come?"

The dimples flashed as he turned on the charm. "You know your mother. With the prodigal returning, she invited everyone for dinner. She's been cooking and cleaning. I offered because I wanted to talk to you about my brother-in-law's wedding."

He sounded wistful, almost as if he longed to have someone at home preparing for his return. Lily swallowed an urge to blast him for his comments at the press conference. How could she? How did one blast a man who had lost most of his family in a car accident? His wife, pregnant with their son, had been killed instantly and their young daughter had barely survived.

True, the accident had happened two years ago, but this was the first time she'd seen Max. She'd been out of the country at the time and while she would have dropped everything to make the trip home, he hadn't had a funeral service. With his daughter fighting for her life, he and his wife's family had opted for a simple memorial mass at church.

"Thank you, Max. I appreciate the lift."

"No problem."

His opinion, maybe, not hers. She'd need to arrange for a rental. Driving was the only way to get around this town. No matter what kind of wedding Riley wanted, there would be running around to pull everything together.

Good, Lily's head was back on business, and she was starting to wrap her brain around things. She walked beside Max as he wheeled the trolley toward the terminal entrance. She darted ahead to grab the door, remembering the restored Karmann Ghia he'd owned once upon a time. Hopefully whatever he drove today had a bit more room. She'd packed for a month-long trip.

Max led her to a late-model SUV parked directly in front. He clicked open the hatch to reveal a cluttered space. Bed pillows in bright pink pillowcases. A Hello Kitty blanket hanging over the backseat. A Dora the Explorer backpack. A rhinestone slipper that could have been Cinderella's.

His daughter's things.

The sight of his large, competent hands shoving aside pink blankets and frilly pillows to make room for her luggage struck Lily like a fist in the gut.

This was reality. The reality that he'd lost his wife, the woman he'd loved. Lily swallowed around the lump in her throat. She'd been running, working, running. The last time she'd been home had been for another funeral. For her funny, kindhearted, always-crusading-for-lost-causes twin brother.

Her better half, as he'd always said.

Both she and Max had lost people they'd loved and life would never be the same again.

CHAPTER TWO

"LISTEN, MAX." Lily placed a hand on his sleeve, waiting until he looked down with a gaze that suddenly felt unfamiliar. "I haven't seen you since Felicia and your son. I never had the chance to tell you how sorry I was."

His lips compressed, his expression so very resigned. He knew this drill. "You sent your regrets."

"I know. Flowers and Mass cards. You replied with a thank-you. It's not the same as telling you. Mom and Joey keep me up on how you and Madeleine are doing. I just wanted you to know."

He didn't say another word, but his chiseled jaw tightened as he packed her bags into the vehicle. It was as if he'd drawn an invisible shield around him that warned her to back off. There was something so solitary about this Max, so dramatically different than the Max of her memory.

That Max used to show up at her family's totally average split-level house for any excuse under the sun, from meals to cards to football to hanging out with her brother Joey. That Max also had a cook on staff and lived in a grand historic home overlooking the Hudson that had been in his family for generations and had boasted neighbors such as the Roosevelts and Vanderbilts.

Despite the rose-colored glasses of her teenage crush, Lily had never understood him or how he could be so enamored of her family. As wonderful as they were, they didn't exist in the same realm as the Downeys. The family business was a hardware store in the Valley, while the Downeys had so many business interests she couldn't have counted them on two hands.

The differences in him were accounted for by tragedy. That hurt. She hated seeing how life had battered around the kind, often-charming guy who had evoked loyalty and devotion so deep down inside her.

Had inspired her wildest fantasies.

Despite her annoyance with him, she wanted him to know that her expression of sorrow was more than words. But she didn't want to remind him of painful memories and changed the subject.

"Mom says Madeleine started kindergarten last month," she said. "How's that going? Does she like school?"

Lily knew she'd struck gold before Max turned over the ignition. Everything about him relaxed, and she recognized him again, could even see a hint of a dimple in his animated expression.

"She loves it. Can't wait to get out the door in the morning. She was student of the week the very first week."

"That's wonderful. You must be very proud. I hope she stays excited straight through college."

"Wouldn't that be nice?" He gave a laugh. "I suppose I'll take whatever I can get. I had no clue what to expect, and Riley was killing me with her horror stories."

Lily's sister-in-law had worked for Max since an internship at Vassar College. Max had actually been the one to send Riley on assignment to cover the concert where she'd met Mike. Riley still worked for Max, only as a managing editor now, which had more predictable hours for a widow with twins.

A widow who would soon be a bride again.

"I'm sure Madeleine is a total doll," Lily said. "Not like Camille and Jake. Twins can be a handful on a good day."

"As you would know firsthand."

"True, true." Only she and Mike would never get into trouble together again. "But I don't remember Mike giving Mom a hard time about going to school the way Jake gave Riley. Of course, I was an angel."

Max snorted.

"Seriously, it must be a boy thing. You have nothing to worry about."

Max sliced his gaze her way, clearly gauging whether or not she was teasing him.

Lily kept a straight face, determined to keep things light. For a long few moments, they sat in silence as Max drove toward the Valley. There were houses where forested hills had been. There had been road expansions. There was even a strip plaza filled with businesses around the corner from her old elementary school. "I can't believe how much this place has grown since I've been home. It hasn't been all that long."

"Four years."

"I've been a topic at the dinner table." Not a question.

Max nodded, clearly knowing better than to offer more information.

"All right, be like that. Let me ask you, though—who called me the prodigal?"

"I did." She got the sense he was picking his way through a mine field. "Seemed to fit."

"How's that?"

He raised his hands against the steering wheel, as much of a conciliatory gesture as he could make while still driving. "Not looking to weigh in with an opinion. It just seemed to work because you've been away awhile."

Lily might accept that at face value, but the deeper implications bothered her.

Was PMS or exhaustion making her touchy today? Or was it anxiety about returning home for the first time since Mike? Or was Max unsettling her because he'd blindsided her at the press conference and brought up that stupidity with the blog? Or worse still, was she annoyed with herself because she couldn't forget her crush on him?

Lily didn't know. She hadn't intended to rise to the bait, either, but…the years had only defined Max's chiseled cheekbones. And his haunted eyes had an appeal all their own. "Okay, Max. I'm sensing something here. Are you annoyed I didn't agree to contract your brother-in-law's wedding when you put me on the spot? And while we're at it let me ask if there was any point to bringing up that ridiculous blog."

He had the audacity to look surprised. "I thought the point of a press conference was to give the media something to write about. Raymond's campaign and that controversial blog will give you tons of mileage. I thought I was doing you a favor."

"I'd prefer not to give the blogger any attention."

"A platform for someone with an ax to grind?"

"Possibly. But if that's the case, I can't imagine whom."

"Emmelina seems pretty upset."

"Emmelina would love someone to blame. She trashed her career for a man who cheated on his wife and left her at the altar. But she hasn't mentioned me because she knows better. Mara'amu wasn't responsible. Had the winds been up, I would have moved the ceremony indoors."

"What happened then?"

"Ugh. A tabloid reporter trying to beat out the competition. He evaded security, tripped over his own video equipment and crashed into one of the dancers. Of course, only the resort security cameras had caught *that* on film and they wouldn't release the footage."

"You could have given a statement."

"I will not dignify this stupidity with a defense."

Max didn't look convinced, which annoyed Lily more.

"Also for the record, the point of not releasing my travel information was so the press didn't have anything to write about. I would have thought that much should be obvious to you, as you're privy to intimate details about my personal life."

Too many, it would seem.

He lingered at a traffic light after the signal turned green as he frowned at her. "Are you saying you didn't call that press conference?"

Now it was Lily's turn to frown. "Are you telling me you didn't leak my travel plans?"

"Of course not. Riley made it a point of telling me that you were keeping your arrival on the Q.T. And your mom. And dad. And my mother. Hmm...let me think. There wasn't anyone who *didn't* mention it. That's why I was so surprised when my assistant told me she got a notice with your arrival details."

Lily stared at the road ahead. "Well, that's interesting. I wonder who leaked the information. That was quite a crowd. By any chance do you still have the notice?"

"I'll ask my assistant. It was an email, I believe."

No surprises there. Wasn't as easy to cause trouble using fax and a landline. Or snail mail, either. But emails could be bounced all over the globe via satellite to effectively mask the sender. As she'd learned while trying to discover the identity of the culprit behind the All About Angel blog and got quoted privacy laws for the effort.

Now someone close enough to know her travel plans thought it was okay to leak to the press. Lovely. And she'd thought her plate was already full.

"Why would you think I'd reveal your plans?" Max asked.

"You were capitalizing on the moment, if memory serves."

He slowed to navigate a sharp turn. "Back to the point of a press conference. Assuming you'd arranged it—which I did—I thought you'd appreciate the connection between you and the exclusive about Raymond's campaign. I seized an opportunity. For both of us."

"I haven't contracted the wedding. We haven't even spoken about it."

"I didn't want to waste any time."

"You seem to have bypassed the part about choice, Max. Don't I get one?"

"In case you haven't noticed, I made it a point not to go through my mother."

"Why?"

"Because I didn't want you to feel pressured. I thought Raymond's wedding would be right up your alley. And the timing couldn't be more perfect since you'll already be in town."

"I'm here to whip up a *family* wedding."

"I know. But I need you to whip up one for me, too. I realize the time frame is somewhat of a challenge, but you're the Wedding Angel." He flashed that dashing grin, dimples and all, but Lily couldn't seem to move past a few tiny words.

Somewhat of a challenge?

She was *somewhat* speechless. It took her a moment and a few deep breaths, but she did manage to squeeze out a question purely for clarification purposes. "I thought you said Raymond and Jamilyn had leave around the holidays."

"I did."

"Christmas is barely twelve weeks away."

He shook his head. "Thanksgiving. They'll be on duty before Christmas."

Lily could only stare. Did the man think she snapped her fingers and—*poof*—a media-worthy fantasy magically appeared out of thin air? Was it possible he didn't realize there was actual work involved? Including seventeen thousand decisions about the venue, catering, costuming, licensing, guests... Hadn't he walked down the aisle once himself?

"Max, seriously. Have you lost your mind? Thanksgiving is *eight* weeks away."

"How hard can it be? You'll be planning Riley's wedding. Can't you do one more of whatever you do for her? You know, order two cakes instead of one. That sort of thing."

Condescension? Did he think she was exaggerating?

"No. No. No." Why didn't she remember Max being so dense? "Riley wants a simple affair. A wedding for the twins because I think she and Scott would be happy at the courthouse. They want tasteful, which will be challenging given the circumstances."

"I wonder why she called you then."

"That's why she called me." Lily really didn't remember Max being this obtuse. If she had, surely she wouldn't have spent so many years imagining him as the groom in all her weddings. "Scott was my brother's best friend and partner. The situation has potential for social awkwardness since they all have the same friends and this town is so small. She doesn't want to elope and leave the twins feeling less than excited about their changing family. Riley trusts me to figure out what'll make everyone happy. You, on the other hand, want me to whip up a full-scale wedding on a dime."

"I thought that's what you did."

"I create fantasies, and fantasies take time. An intimate family wedding is another beast from the extravaganza you want."

"You've got eight weeks."

This man... "I am not planning Raymond's wedding."

She didn't feel obligated to explain. Even if he wasn't being so high-handed, she had no intention of explaining that she'd come home to kick back, regroup and relax.

And while she rested, her crews would be working overtime. They needed to focus on the current contracts to ensure every *t* was crossed and every *i* dotted so there weren't any more disasters. And she'd still be working by cell phone, laptop and fax. To take on even one more project would be insane.

Perhaps there was another solution, and out of respect for the man's losses and the close connections between their families... "What if I arrange something with this office? Your mother is still my partner in that particular venture."

He shook his head decidedly. "I want *you*."

Max and everyone else. But there was some childish, forbidden and undeniably sick part of her that thrilled to hear those words. Ugh. She waved him off with a dismissive hand. "Unavailable. I'm tired. Can't you see the circles under my eyes?"

He gave her a sideways glance. "You look fantastic."

"The concealer I'm wearing is fantastic. Underneath... not so much."

"Are you fishing for compliments? I'll gladly give them, Lily Susan."

Lily Susan.

What was it about her name said in that voice that *still* dissolved her insides into jelly? Even when he was arguing with her?

She would not dignify his comment with a response. He took the last turn out of the Valley onto the road that would lead to the house where she'd grown up. She had no desire whatsoever to continue this conversation, so she whipped out her BlackBerry and logged on to Twitter.

Okay, so who leaked my travel plans? LOL I arrived safely in my hometown to find the media waiting. Unexpected but *lovely* reception. Hello again, Pleasant Valley! Blessings to all;-)

Lily depressed the send button, tweeting her followers on the status of her arrival.

What she really wanted to write was: Hell is a real place, people, not some fiery netherworld across death. It's right here on earth in a town deceptively named Pleasant Valley. I know because I'm in it.

CHAPTER THREE

WHAT WAS IT about Lily Susan that always took Max so off guard? He wasn't sure. But he was on edge. The feeling was vaguely familiar. He resisted the urge to flip on the radio and nix the possibility of further conversation when she fell silent, so obviously annoyed.

She thought he was a jerk. Maybe he was. But there was a method to his madness. *She* needed to plan Raymond's wedding—not an assistant. Because it was Lily Susan herself who garnered publicity. And his brother-in-law needed all the free publicity he could get to launch his political campaign. Max would see that it happened. Period. Besides, her own family was worried about her and wanted her to stay in town as long as possible.

While he was uncomfortable pushing himself onto Lily Susan, he wouldn't back down. She was the one Angelica who had never felt much like part of the family. To him, anyway. But he didn't have room to talk, since he wasn't technically family, either.

But long ago Max had learned that Joe and Rosie Angelica operated on a philosophy that transcended blood. Family by love, they called it. Through the years, Max had learned those ties bound tight. He'd been grateful for this family since long before he'd even understood what he was grateful for.

Love and support. Selflessness instead of selfishness. The things that counted as far as Max was concerned.

Looking for a place to park in front of the neatly kept house, Max wondered if his passenger's mood would be improved by her welcome committee. Cars filled the driveway and spilled into the cul-de-sac. No one would dare park on the lawn, lest they incur Joe's wrath.

"Wow, I thought everyone would be at work or school."

Max couldn't tell whether or not a big reception was a good thing. "You're surprised?"

"Not surprised," was all she said as he maneuvered the car against a curb.

"I'll bring your things inside," he told her.

"Thanks. No hurry."

She didn't move though, and he thought she was waiting for him to get her door. He had his own opened before noticing how still she was. In his periphery, he saw her inhale deeply.

Nerves? From a woman who could work the media and address massive crowds in her sleep? That couldn't be right. By the time he circled the car and got her door, he found Lily Susan her usual gracious, poised self.

They wove a path through the cars, her long, lean legs easily matching his pace. Max wasn't surprised by the royal welcome. This family had been waiting a long time for their youngest to come home.

He got a welcome reception himself when the screen door shot open and his daughter appeared.

She skipped down the stairs with a light step, black ponytail bobbing, excitement glowing from her.

His pulse lurched at the sight. It was a familiar reaction, the instant he came face-to-face with the fact that everything that mattered in his life was all wrapped up in his little girl. There was always a second of awe that she was real.

And alive.

"Daddy!"

Max wished that squeal of delighted glee had to do with him as much as their guest. But his daughter was caught up in the excitement of Lily Susan's homecoming.

Striding ahead, he braced himself as Madeleine leaped into his arms. Catching her against him, he twirled her around, eliciting another squeal—this one all for him. She tilted her cheek for a kiss, but her curious gaze fixed over his shoulder on the woman behind him.

"Is that her?" Madeleine asked almost reverently.

Max kissed her again to hide his smile. "It is. I'll introduce you."

Letting his daughter slide to the ground, he straightened. To his surprise, he found Lily Susan already dropping to Madeleine's height, which brought his attention to her graceful neck and feminine shoulders in a way he'd have to be dead not to notice.

But he was only dead on the inside.

Smiling warmly, she extended her hand. *"Bonjour, Mademoiselle Madeleine. Ça fait plaisir de te revoir. Nous nous sommes rencontrés quand tu étais une petite fille. Regarde-toi. Tu as grandis pour être très, très belle."*

"Merci, madame." Madeleine beamed, clearly surprised their guest spoke French. Grown up *and* beautiful—a double compliment if Max's translation was close. His French was rudimentary at best. She politely replied how pleased she was to see Lily Susan again, too, but Max knew his daughter had no memory of their previous meeting. She'd barely been two the last time Lily Susan had graced the family with her presence.

Felicia had spoken French to their daughter since birth even though her parents had moved to the States before she or Raymond had been born. Max had kept up the tutoring by bringing an au pair from France who was a relative of the Girard family.

Lily Susan had told him she'd been keeping up with his family, and he was astounded she was interested in what was happening in a place she couldn't find time to visit.

He was also astounded by the way she engaged his daughter in a chat about kindergarten and teachers and friends—in a random mix of English and French Felicia would have appreciated.

Kneeling in the leaf-strewn yard, Lily Susan listened intently to a story about the student-of-the-week breakfast reception that served cookies. Her whiskey-gold hair tumbled down her back, and her long skirt emphasized sleek legs as she wrapped her arms around her knees and nodded in all the appropriate places.

His daughter was generally reserved around strangers, but with the attention Lily Susan graciously provided, she was shedding her shell.

"You got to be on *The Morning Show* with your student-of-the-week ribbon, too? Wow. Does everyone watch *The Morning Show?*"

"Oui, madame." Madeleine beamed. "Even the fifth graders and the patrols."

Lily Susan gave a suitably impressed gasp. And he was impressed she knew what an elementary-school patrol was.

They made quite a sight. Lily Susan in all her designer-clothes glory. Madeleine, still bearing evidence of summer swimming lessons and weekends spent at the lake. She'd been nut-brown by Labor Day, compliments of Moroccan ancestors. He wondered if their son would have had his mother's skin, too.

Not the first time he'd wondered.

"Aunt Lily Susan!" More squeals as the screen door creaked open and Riley's twins burst onto the porch.

"We'll make time later to chat." Lily Susan gave Madeleine's hands a little squeeze before she stood. "I want to hear more about your appearance on *The Morning Show.*"

His daughter nodded eagerly then Lily Susan was spreading her arms wide to greet her new visitors.

"My little twinnies!"

Riley's kids weren't so little anymore. Jake and Camille were a whopping almost nine years old, as Jake was fond of reminding everyone. But they were thrilled to see their aunt, and he witnessed firsthand the results of Riley's determination to keep everyone in touch with text, email and phone calls.

Max bore a similar responsibility. Felicia's family was all Madeleine would ever have of her mother. If his in-laws hadn't been so accessible, he would have made the same effort as Riley.

He hung on to his daughter's hand while Lily Susan hugged her niece and nephew. "I can't believe how tall you've both gotten. How long has it been since I've seen you—a year?"

"Not a year, silly." Camille laughed. "We saw you this summer. Don't you remember we went on the boat ride to the Statue of Liberty?"

"How could I forget? You hid so we missed the ferry back."

Camille giggled and Lily Susan ruffled that white-blond head fondly.

"You're such a little squirrel," she said. "It just feels like forever since I've seen you."

While Lily Susan laughed and chattered cheerily, she seemed to be hanging on to the twins for dear life, unable to stop touching and kissing them. Did she see

her brother in them? Max remembered how close she and
Mike had been.

"Well, it's about damned time," a loud voice boomed
from the doorway. Joey appeared with his wife, Sarah,
behind him, and shoved open the screen door so hard the
hinges groaned. "Your father's about to disown you because he can't remember what you look like."

Actually, Joey was the one about to disown his baby
sister, as Max well knew.

"Then he must be getting senile since I saw him two
months ago," Lily Susan replied.

Angelicas poured onto the lawn calling out greetings.
That was the last Max saw of Lily Susan as the family
converged on her. He knew they would all wind up in the
kitchen, so he broke from the crowd and headed to the car
to unload the luggage.

Madeleine didn't want any part of leaving the chaos.
She stuck like glue to Camille, who stuck like glue to her
aunt. He wasn't surprised his daughter was so caught up
in the whole Wedding Angel craze. Lily Susan was the
family celebrity, and Madeleine had been listening to everyone discuss her long-awaited return. Particularly Camille, who idolized her aunt and with whom Madeleine
spent a good deal of time.

Riley's twins were the youngest of all the Angelica
cousins, so Madeleine was a welcome addition at family
gatherings as the one person who was younger. For Camille anyway, who enjoyed sharing girl things like mani-
cures and hairstyles—the types of activities mothers and
daughters shared, but daddies were uncomfortable with,
no matter how hard they tried.

And try though Max might, the nuances of shimmery
nail polish escaped him.

He'd barely reached the car when he realized that Scott had caught up with him.

"Need a hand?" he asked.

Max nodded. "Anyone but Lily Susan, and I'd think she was moving in for good."

Scott eyed the hatch and backseat stacked with suitcases and nodded. "Sure looks like it."

Max liked Scott Emerson. He was another honorary Angelica family member. He'd been Mike's partner on the vice squad before Mike had met Riley. Scott was now the chief of detectives, and if Max's sources were correct—which they usually were—Scott was being groomed to become Poughkeepsie's chief of police.

Once he married Riley, he wouldn't be an honorary member of the Angelicas anymore. He'd be the real deal.

Between them, they managed the luggage with one trip and headed inside by way of the garage. They couldn't escape the chaos, which had started trickling in by the time they'd stowed the bags in Lily Susan's old bedroom upstairs. Max got trapped on the staircase behind Scott, unable to make his way into the hallway through the crowd burrowing to get in from the cold.

An expectant hush fell over the noisy family when Lily Susan approached the stairs. While she'd known of the relationship developing between Scott and Riley for a long time and had agreed to plan the wedding, Lily Susan hadn't actually seen Scott in person since the engagement.

"Finally, here's the groom. I wondered where you were." She stopped the flow of traffic and smiled at him, obliging him to step off the stairs for a hug.

Max heard her whisper, "Couldn't ask for anyone better to be dad to my little twinnies."

Her gracious acceptance smoothed over a tough moment, and the effect was visible. Scott gave her a hug that practically lifted her off the ground. "Welcome home, Lily Susan. Thanks for making the trip."

"Wouldn't miss your wedding for the world." When she was on her feet again, she winked at him. "Even if I didn't need to plan the whole thing."

With a laugh he moved to let traffic pass, and Max caught sight of Riley and her suspiciously misty gaze.

Bravo for Lily Susan. She might have been away from the family for a while, but distance didn't mean she couldn't come through for the people who loved her when it counted.

And that was a very Angelica trait.

CHAPTER FOUR

MAX CAUGHT UP with his daughter again, and they made their way through the kitchen to the adjoining dining room, where so many chairs had been jammed around the table people would be practically sitting on top of each other. Sturdy card tables had been added on both ends to eliminate the need to separate adults and kids. This made Madeleine happy, but there were so many place settings another fork couldn't be set between them. He wondered where Rosie intended to put the food.

"Come on, come on. Find a seat." Joe herded everyone into the dining room impatiently. "Lily Susan, you sit there."

Max watched Lily Susan head to her honorary place at the center of the table, knowing he didn't stand a chance at getting close. The best he could do was grab a spot across from her, where he had a decent view.

He was surprised by how much he wanted a view. Lily Susan had changed into casual sportswear, the fabric clinging to her every lean curve.

Thankfully the chaos distracted him from thoughts that were traveling in unexpected directions. Everyone knew the drill and was soon crammed elbow-to-elbow. Joey and his wife Sarah and their three kids. Caroline and her husband Alex and their three kids. Riley and Scott and the twins. Only Joe didn't sit. He was the pulse of the family, with his bald head and hearty laughter—the one who roused everyone into action, the one they all went to for advice or opinions.

And if Joe was the pulse, then Rosie was the heart. She set the tone with her hugs. When she was happy, her nicknames for everyone were happy. Her husband was Joe and her son Joey. When she wasn't, though, those nicknames were warnings. Joe and Joey became Old Man and Little Boy or Fat Joe and Healthy Joe when she was on a tear about someone's eating habits.

Still, Rosie managed to keep everyone close with her nurturing kindnesses. A thousand kindnesses.

Max didn't know what he would have done without her through Madeleine's recovery during the long months after the accident. And he didn't understand how Lily Susan could have spent so much time away from this warm and gregarious group.

"Close your eyes, honey-bunch," Joe commanded Lily Susan in his booming voice. "Jake, make sure she doesn't peek."

Jake, who had claimed the spot to his aunt's right, crawled to his knees in the chair, stretching his hands over her face. She laughed good-naturedly, and Joe made a production of going to the refrigerator then returning to the table. He plunked down a glass jar in the middle of her plate.

"Good job, kiddo. Let her look."

Jake sprang back, and Lily Susan glanced down. Her lush lips parted then broke into a smile. A real smile. Not the kind she'd been giving Max. Instead of warm and happy, she gave him cool and professional. He wondered why he noticed that she seemed to save her warmth for children and preserved vegetables.

"Aunt Nellie's pickled beets?" She laughed. "Daddy, you remembered."

"Of course I remembered. They're your favorite." Joe handed her a fork. "You don't even have to share."

There was no missing how his expression blurred around the edges when he dropped a kiss onto the top of his youngest daughter's head. Lily Susan's eyes fluttered shut for the briefest moment, a rare sign of emotion for a woman so skilled at keeping up appearances.

Taking his seat at the head of the table, Joe said, "Let's eat."

The meal began with a blessing then conversations erupted randomly as kids vied with adults to steal Lily Susan's attention with stories of what was happening in Pleasant Valley. There was a lot to relate. Phone calls could never take the place of Sunday dinners for filling in the details.

Lily Susan fostered the conversations with her questions, asking far more than she shared. But there was one subject that was noticeably avoided by everyone: her broken engagement.

No one asked, and she didn't offer. Not a word about how she was doing although every adult asked leading questions. Lily Susan skillfully deflected them all. So he wasn't the only one who got the professional treatment. She was closed with the people who cared so much about her.

And why did that thought make him feel better?

Why was he so aware of her?

She was a beautiful woman, no question. Photos of her crossed his desk all the time, but Max had to admit that no photo came close to doing justice to the real woman. She was a media darling for good reason with a sweet, heart-shaped face. Her Italian heritage lent her an interesting blend of earthiness and wholesomeness with her light olive skin, whiskey-gold hair and caramel-colored eyes.

And that mouth of hers played so well to the camera, whether she was talking, laughing, smiling, kissing…

He remembered one photo in particular. The paparazzi had snapped the shot after she'd announced her engagement. She and her fiancé had been celebrating with friends on a yacht in the French Riviera, their heads close as they kissed.

Max wasn't sure why he remembered. Maybe because they had seemed so different from the Angelica family he knew. They seemed matched to each other. Both ambitious. Both part of the jet set. Both tanned in their Mediterranean near-nudity, sipping champagne on a yacht, creating the illusion of fantasy romance.

The picture had looked perfect. Apparently the perfection *had* been an illusion since the ex-fiancé had proven himself a world-class deadbeat. The man hadn't troubled himself to come here to meet his fiancée's family—Joe and Rosie had been forced to travel into the city. That said something. As far as Max was concerned that something wasn't good breeding.

To this day, Joey had never met him.

"A matter of principle," he'd told Max. "If the guy wants the family seal of approval, he'll have to make an effort. Not that family seems important to my sister anymore."

Max understood how Joey felt. But now, watching Lily Susan, he had to wonder why she hadn't brought the man home.

"How will Raymond's wedding impact your plans?" Joey asked her. "Are you going to stay in town or commute from the city?"

Lily Susan shot Max a look that seared a path across the table, but she answered her brother diplomatically. "We haven't quite gotten there yet. Max's inquiry arrived in my office yesterday and I haven't had a chance to figure things out."

"What's to figure?" Joe asked. "You're in town."

"Daddy, my calendar's booked. We schedule a year to eighteen months in advance."

"You've got a lot of offices, honey-bunch. You can't rearrange a few things and make some room? Max needs your help."

That was that as far as Joe was concerned.

The entire table quieted to listen to the exchange, and Lily Susan was suddenly on the spot. Max dodged another glare and leaned back to enjoy the show.

"I understand," she said in a conciliatory tone. "But I'm afraid it's not so simple. A lot of offices means I've got people in four countries at different stages of event planning."

Max recognized the it's-out-of-my-hands approach and knew she intended to turn him down. He wished her luck with that.

"You've been planning weddings since before you could walk." Joey didn't even bother with an attempt at humor. "I thought you were supposed to be good. One little wedding shouldn't be that big a deal."

"In case it slipped your notice, Joey, I'm already planning one little wedding. That's the reason I'm here."

"How in hell could I *not* notice?" he scoffed. "Weddings and funerals. You don't bother coming home for anything else."

There was a collective gasp, and Joe growled at his oldest son. Lily Susan didn't visibly react—she was too skilled to let emotion bleed through her lovely veneer—but Rosie stepped into the breach with evasive maneuvers as she returned from the kitchen, where she'd been refilling a gravy boat with sauce for the manicotti.

"Lily Susan, if you help Max with the wedding, you'll have all of us to assist. I'm sure everyone would look forward to spending some time with you. Isn't that right?"

Nods and enthusiastic consents all around.

"I appreciate that, but everyone has a life. And the time constraints will make the planning a challenge, not to mention that the couple isn't here. That's going to complicate things further. There'll be a zillion decisions and interviews and fittings—"

"I thought you specialized in destination weddings." Joey wasn't helping the cause with his hostility. "At least that's what your website says."

Lily Susan frowned. "Destination for *the wedding,* Joey. I consult with the couple in person."

He apparently didn't have an answer for that, and Sarah, who was positively scowling, must have kicked him because he winced then glared at her.

Lily Susan seized her chance with both hands. "Please let me explain. There will be decisions that need to be made about every tiny detail before I can *arrange* anything. If the bride and groom aren't available, then I have nothing to work with."

"You've got Max." Joe waved a hand Max's way. "Raymond and his fiancée asked him to take care of those sorts of things. Isn't that right?"

"It is."

Lily Susan fixed her gaze on him, an eyebrow arched. "Jamilyn asked you to try on her wedding dress so the seamstress can fit it, did she?"

At the mention of Max trying on a wedding dress, Jake howled with laughter and got the older cousins going.

"I want to see that," Caroline's son Brian said. "Bring a camera."

"Make it your profile pic on Facebook," Joey's daughter suggested.

"Daddy lets me polish his nails," Madeleine informed the table proudly.

"Pop Scott, you going to let Camille paint your nails?" Jake snickered. "That's what good stepdads do."

"Oh, yeah," Camille chimed in. "Luscious lilac will go perfect with your dress uniform."

Riley rolled her eyes, but Scott shot a look at his soon-to-be stepchildren and said, "Thank you, Max."

"No problem." He ruffled Madeleine's silky hair.

Lily Susan grinned at her niece. "Camille, we'll discuss Pop Scott's polish color once he decides whether he's wearing his dress blues or a tux. Or his chaps and cowboy hat. I don't have a clue. *Yet*." She spread her hand in entreaty, her expression transforming as she shot Max another glare. "This is exactly what I'm talking about. More decisions come up with the fittings and menu tastings and everything else that makes up the sort of high-profile event Max wants. We're talking about a wedding at Overlook."

Rosie set the gravy boat in front of her daughter. "You've always wanted to set a real wedding there, ever since you were a little girl. This sounds like the opportunity of a lifetime."

"That's true, but not if I have to divert my attention from Riley and Scott. I won't sacrifice their special day."

Lily Susan thought fast on her feet. She kept her cool, sounded completely reasonable with her arguments. Max also noticed that she hadn't yet mentioned her vacation or her need to rest. In a way, he almost wished he could give her the time she wanted. Then he'd have time to figure out why he was suddenly thinking of ways he might help her relax.

But his interests weren't the issue here. His brother-in-law needed a wedding and Lily Susan was the perfect person to plan one. Not only did she have expertise, but she'd also guarantee press—an essential element to launch a political campaign.

Joe shot Max a commiserating look. They'd known this wasn't going to be an easy sell. "Of course you can't sacrifice Riley and Scott's wedding, honey-bunch. But you've got nearly four weeks to plan theirs and you seem okay with that. Why can't you hang around a few extra weeks to plan Raymond's?"

Lily Susan finally put two and two together. She'd been set up and knew it.

"Okay, people. Listen to me." Her tone was all about corralling crowds to get things done. "I get that I haven't been home in a while. I'm sorry. I won't make excuses, but I will promise to make more time from now on. I hope you'll take me at my word. I want to help out Max. Truly, I do. But you're asking the impossible. The difference in work between planning an intimate family wedding for sixty guests and a high-profile, five-hundred-plus guest list is staggering. I won't take on an event I can't do well. And when I offered to look into my local office, Max didn't like my suggestion."

Max shook his head. "I want the Wedding Angel."

He didn't say another word because he recognized a few things at that moment. First was that Lily Susan didn't like her family pressuring her on his behalf. She also didn't have a clue about how worried they all were about her. About why she was distancing herself. About how she was handling a very public breakup a mere month before she would have tied the knot.

Max also didn't think she realized how determined her family was. Now that they'd gotten her home, they intended to do whatever it took to keep her here for as long as possible.

"Max, this wedding needs professional and careful attention. *Not* a rush job." She eyed him stoically. "You need to trust me on this. The press will be all over it."

"That's exactly why we need you."

She made a frustrated noise. "What happened to visiting, as in spending my time catching up and not working?" She dropped her face into her hands.

No one said a word.

Lily Susan didn't look up.

The silence lengthened.

Jake was the first to give in. He rubbed the back of her neck consolingly. "It's okay, Aunt Lily Susan."

Joe caved next. "Honey-bunch, will you promise to give it some thought before you say no? This is important. And if you stay longer, we'll have time for that visiting you're wanting."

She lifted her head and ruffled her nephew's hair, her poise firmly in place. "If I promise to think about it, you've got to promise to accept my answer whether you like it or not."

"Deal." Joe must have decided he'd pushed enough. For now.

They'd reached a truce. Max noticed how relieved she looked—it wasn't obvious but it was there if he looked closely. And he didn't mind looking.

Rosie jumped in to salvage the meal. "I'm sure Lily Susan will do whatever she can to help. Now she just got here, so let's give her a chance to settle in."

"Well, let's say you decide to stay." Joe speared another sausage on the end of his fork. "Hypothetically, of course—"

"Daddy!"

"Old man!"

Caroline switched into protective big-sister mode and elbowed Joe. "Come on, Daddy. Cut Lily Susan a break. She's the baby, remember. She's not used to getting pushed around the way you push around the rest of us." She winked at her sister. "And now that you're finally here, you can't stay with Mom and Dad the whole time. You've got to spend time with me. When was the last time we had a girls' night?"

"Or a slumber party," Riley added. "The kids can stay up late and we can watch Disney movies and eat popcorn—"

"And drink cocoa!" Jake added. "With the big marshmallows."

"It'll be like playing musical Aunt Lily Susan," Camille chimed in, and Riley laughed.

Max grinned, too. He hoped they all had lots of extra space for all her suitcases. Lily Susan didn't travel light.

Suddenly Madeleine was pulling on his sleeve. "Daddy, I want to play musical Madame Lily Susan, too. She can sleep with me in my princess castle."

And the conversation split off into smaller ones again.

Lily Susan exhaled a dramatic sigh but kept her mouth shut, clearly refusing to add any fuel to the fire since she was off the hook for the moment. But Max watched her, marveling at how effectively she was able to maintain her poise and reserve. Every one of the Angelicas was grounded and down-to-earth in their own unique way, and all of them were so very open. Not Lily Susan.

His cell phone vibrated at his waist. He reached for it, hoping there wasn't some emergency at the office that would drag him away, but Madeleine got there ahead of him, her tiny fingers slipping the phone from its case easily.

She glanced at the display. "It's Goddess."

"Hop up and take the call into the kitchen."

Madeleine slid from the chair, whispering into the receiver so loudly the entire table could hear, "Hi, Goddess. It's me. I have to whisper till I get away from the dinner table."

"Goddess?" Lily Susan glanced his way, amusement transforming her expression, making her seem relaxed and beautiful. "Your mother?"

Who else's mother refused to let her granddaughter call her by any name that made her sound old? "She's probably checking to see if you made it in safely."

"She knew you were coming to get me?"

He nodded, not wanting to go into the details about how much he'd actually told his mother...and then it hit him. Max suddenly knew exactly what it was about Lily Susan that always took him off guard.

She reminded him more of his family than her own.

CHAPTER FIVE

"MADAME LILY SUSAN," Madeleine said. "Goddess wants to talk to you."

"Merci." Smiling at the little girl, Lily grabbed the phone and dashed to the back porch for privacy.

"Thank you, Ginger," she whispered into the receiver.

Max's mother certainly knew how to make an entrance, even on a telephone. Not a surprise. Her last name was Downey. Came with the territory. Even Max, who enjoyed hanging out with Joey with a cold beer after a day bow hunting, was nothing if not socially adept. And always had been. She could remember when Joey had first brought Max home after a baseball game. He'd walked into the kitchen, handsome in his dirty uniform, thrust out his hand to Joe and introduced himself.

"Nice to meet you, sir," he'd said. "I'm Max Downey."

He'd seemed the epitome of everything a charming boy should be—everything her big brother wasn't—and Lily had formed her opinion of what her perfect groom would look like in that instant.

She'd grown up since then, regardless of the way her pulse raced when Max looked at her now.

Slipping through the door, Lily closed it behind her, the chatter of dinner-table conversation muted enough so she could hear. Taking a deep breath, Lily let the calm overtake her. She loved her family, but it didn't take long for them to make her vibrate with the noise and the demands.

Ginger's timing was impeccable because Lily could use a few minutes to catch her breath and regroup. Although she should have known Ginger wouldn't wait until Lily visited their office tomorrow. No, she would want top billing now that her long-time business partner had returned.

"Welcome home, my dear," said the cultured voice on the other end of the line. "The natives restless?"

"Please remind me never again to let so much time pass between visits."

"It has been a while."

"I know." Lily stopped in front of the picture window and stared out at the yard. The old swing was still there, hanging from a sturdy branch of the oak tree. Her dad had carved and hinged that swing himself. He'd varnished the wood with some cutting-edge product he'd gotten in the hardware store so it would last forever.

Lily remembered swinging on it, faster and higher, as if she could launch herself over the treetops and out of her little world into the great wide somewhere else.

"I have no excuse," she admitted. "Except there's been so much going on with work."

"And your fiancé. Let's not forget him. No matter what poor choices he made at the end of your relationship, you've been involved in a sweeping romance for quite some time."

Thank you for the reminder, Ginger!

But even Lucas had been about work in a lot of ways. Lily sometimes thought they wouldn't have been together so long if not for the way their business interests meshed. The wedding world had given them so much common ground. Same crazy schedules. Same business acquaintances. Same friends. They supported each other, liked each other, loved each other even. It had been so easy to be together.

But she couldn't deny that their relationship had been centered more on business than romance no matter what the press made of it. They'd been comfortable, but lacking in some areas. "I really can't believe how much time has passed."

"You're a busy woman with lots of irons in the fire."

"True. But no one's cutting me any slack."

"Well, try to sympathize with where they're coming from, my dear. I can't imagine how I'd feel if one of the boys stayed away so long. At least when they were off at college, they showed up around the holidays for gifts."

Ginger's boys were now all grown men. Max was her eldest, the heir to the Downey dynasty, so to speak. Her middle son was engaged to a perfectly suitable girl, although no wedding date had been set as of yet. And the youngest who was Ginger's favorite—although she would never admit that aloud—was also following his own life path.

"If Mara wasn't so capable, I'd have to visit our office more often," Lily said to move the conversation along.

"I'm sure she'll be relieved to hear it. But she has a lot of help, you know. Some very exceptional help, I might add."

"I've heard. So why have you been spending so much time in the office?"

"When I saw the numbers on your renovation budget, I shivered to think about the damage Mara could do with such an obscene amount of money to spend. I felt the renovation budget needed competent supervision."

Mara would have been quite capable of handling the renovations, Lily had no doubt, but Ginger had wanted to be involved. And whenever Ginger became involved, she wound up in charge. "I had no choice, Ginger. You know that. Not after the historical society got ahold of the area."

"I do. But I also know you wouldn't make the time to involve yourself, and Mara needed some guidance." She gave a teasing laugh to take the edge from a statement that sounded more like an accusation. "You'll be amazed when you see the place. Photos simply don't do it justice."

It seemed Lily could add another name to the list of people who were feeling ignored.

She could hear laughter through the doors—her family having a good time while she was working.

What else was new?

"Are you still coming into the office tomorrow?" Ginger asked. "I want to be there. I know you'll want to get moving on Raymond's wedding, and Mara's in the middle of the Eversham/Raichle event. Good thing I've been hanging around so much. You're going to need my help."

Lily blinked. "Max told you I'm definitely planning Raymond's wedding?"

"Of course, dear. Why do you sound so surprised? I wasn't. I knew the second he told me about launching Raymond's political career that you'd come up with something brilliant so you could get new photos to add to your website."

She referred, of course, to Worldwide Weddings Unlimited's website. Lily's public relations firm had come up with the idea. They'd taken copies of the childhood photos of Lily with her fairy-inspired woodland weddings, windswept nautical nuptials beside the river and historically themed bridal parties in the church hall to brand the business. Living proof that Lily was the one and only Wedding Angel and always had been.

"I have to tell you, Ginger, I'm concerned that now isn't the best time to attempt a breakneck wedding." Lily planted the seed, hoping beyond hope it would take root. "The press I've been generating lately might not be the best way to launch anyone's career."

There was a beat of silence. Enough time to allow Lily to hope that she might finally get someone in her corner.

"Don't worry too much about your detractors," Ginger said. "That's the nature of the beast. You know that. And you're used to receiving glowing reviews. You've been fortunate. Consider this a challenge to be brilliant and prove them all wrong. Besides, who else would you let plan a wedding at Overlook?"

Every fiber of Lily's being rebelled at being pushed. She needed a rest. Her creativity was suffering. Her mental health, too. She already wanted to escape her family, and now felt the same about Ginger, which told her how close to the edge she was. She needed this vacation like she needed to breathe clean air, like she needed to find her footing again.

But this was *Ginger*.

Ginger, who had supported Lily when no one else in the world believed in her, let alone been willing to plunk down good money to let a young girl barely out of high school start a business. Max's father ran the bank where she'd applied for the personal loan to get started. He'd called her into his office, praised her aspirations then turned her down cold.

Ginger had reveled in the chance to work in business as a shareholder, to prove to her family she could do something more than charity work. Not only had she provided the starter cash for Worldwide Weddings Unlimited, but she'd also gone head-to-head with Lily's parents, who had been afraid this business would distract Lily from finishing college.

How could she possibly deny Ginger an opportunity to assist planning a family wedding at Overlook?

And Max had known. Stupid man.

No *smart* man. He'd loaded the bases against her.

Staring into the backyard, Lily wondered if the frayed rope swing was strong enough to bear her weight now. "I would never let anyone else plan a wedding at Overlook."

She was exhausted already. She couldn't possibly get any more tired, could she?

CHAPTER SIX

All About Angel—October 5
The Luck of the Devil

Did the Wedding Angel sell her soul to the devil? Or is she so desperate to get a few nondisastrous events under her belt that she's calling in favors to contract new business?

That's the question readers are asking today.

What other explanation could there be for this breaking news that the Wedding Angel will plan the Carmichael/Girard wedding?

While the names of the bride and groom may not be readily recognizable, their connection to the well-known Downey family may ring some bells.

Raymond Girard is none other than the brother-in-law of Maxim Downey, newspaper magnate and heir to the multigenerational dynasty.

So how did the Wedding Angel—whose tattered reputation has her scurrying into the backwater of her hometown to lick her wounds—manage to contract an event that is sure to garner a vast amount of media attention?

The luck of the devil?

Or, if readers don't have a religious bent there's the much more worldly explanation.

The Wedding Angel is calling in favors.

Let's ask ourselves: who in their right mind would pay seriously good money to invite chaos and mayhem to their special event? People currently under contract must be asking themselves if there's some sort of curse dogging their wedding planner.

And what disaster will strike next?

Of course these unfortunate victims have already paid huge sums to engage her services and don't have much choice but to hold their collective breath and hope her luck isn't devolving into something of monumental proportions.

So the Wedding Angel muscles her way into a new contract that will—let's hope!—clean up her muddy reputation, and she manipulates everyone she knows in the process. Who else but family and close friends would court disaster (and risk political suicide at the all-important start of a career) by allowing the Wedding Angel to plan an event?

Who else, indeed?

Visit the Wedding Angel's photo gallery on her website to see proof of how far back her connection to the Downey family and Overlook goes.

Today's poll: Will the Wedding Angel pull off her own *Miracle on the Hudson* or will she crash and burn? Cast your vote.

THE BLACKBERRY VIBRATED on Lily's pillow. Her eyes shot open wide and she took in the dark bedroom to orient herself.

Riley's wedding. Pleasant Valley. Her parents' house.

Weird how she'd grown up in this bedroom but no longer thought of it as home. Then again maybe not so weird because a lifetime had passed since she'd lived here. She was on the road so much even *her* place didn't feel much like home. Blinking away the remnants of sleep, she reached for the phone and glanced at the display. Not her alarm but a text message.

What is going on with the Carmichael/Girard wedding? Anything I need to know?

The message was from her local office manager, Mara, who would—naturally—be in the office before the sun came up. Which was precisely why Lily had promoted Mara from the position of Manhattan assistant to handle this office.

Mara Tepper had been with Worldwide Weddings Unlimited ever since Lily had contracted her as temporary help for the Bristow/Sonnenburg wedding in the Hamptons nearly five years ago. With half the Democratic National Party in attendance, she'd had to call in two crews from the field, as well as hire local labor.

When several of Lily's crew became sick with an unfortunate case of food poisoning barely thirty-six hours before the event, she discovered Mara knew her way around weddings. Within a year she'd become an assistant in the Manhattan office. A few years after that she was running this branch in Poughkeepsie.

Lily didn't bother texting a reply, but instead depressed the speed dial. The first ring had barely ended before the call connected.

"I thought that inquiry was on top of the queue for the next proposal review," Mara said.

Lily sighed. "It was. Now it's a go."

"Um, yeah. Got that part. Ginger's been talking about the wedding nonstop. She seems to think you've already agreed, and I didn't have the heart to break it to her. The part I don't get is why I had to read that you'd accepted the job online."

Lily usually awoke with a clear head. Whether she was

a morning person or because she lived in a constant state of semianxiety, she wasn't sure, but this morning she must not have been thinking as clearly as usual. "What are you talking about? I simply…well, not agreed per se, but sort of got maneuvered and guilted into saying yes."

"Lily, what are you doing? You need a vacation."

"It'll have to wait."

"Even so, how on earth can you possibly squeeze in another event?"

"We'll manage."

"This is not doable. You've got a lot on your plate right now. We're forty-eight hours out in Brussels. Three weeks in Los Angeles. Six in Geneva and Aruba." Mara paused to exhale an exasperated breath. "You've got four more events in production right behind those and that lineup doesn't include my office, which you well know operates like the redheaded stepchild."

A rather witty comment as Mara was a tried-and-true redhead—freckles and all. But the pressure Lily suddenly felt precluded humor.

"I know. And I refused. Everyone ganged up on me. It would have taken the Jets' defensive line to stop them." The muscle under her left eye twitched. "But what do you mean you read about it on the internet? Where?"

"The All About Angel blog."

How could a day go south so fast? "You. Are. Kidding. Me."

"*Not* kidding. Log on and read it for yourself if you must, but that would be an unpleasant way to start the morning. And you've got unpleasantries that takes precedence, I'm afraid. There are some unhappy media outlets at the moment. You promised an exclusive. I followed up last night by assuring they'd get one."

"Oh, no."

"Oh, yes. Several have already read the bogus blogger and word's getting around fast, apparently. My inbox was practically smoking when I logged on this morning."

Lily rubbed at the twitching muscle. "Let me check something and call you back."

She had no clue what Max's typical morning schedule might look like beyond knowing he had to get Madeleine off to school. If it was a little early for him...well, he could lose some sleep. She certainly would because of this big wedding he'd dropped in her lap.

Scrolling through the contacts on her phone, she found his number.

He answered quickly. "Lily Susan." His voice soft and gravelly, a morning voice.

"Good morning, Max. I've got a question for you."

"Shoot."

"After you left here, did you speak with your mother last night about your brother-in-law's wedding?"

"No. I didn't actually see her last night. She and my father had some sort of engagement that kept them out late. How come?"

Lily frowned. That wasn't what she'd expected at all. But she couldn't imagine why he'd lie when he'd been so blunt with his opinions.

The prodigal, indeed.

"The All About Angel blogger somehow knows I've confirmed for your wedding."

"You thought I jumped on the exclusive?" He sounded offended.

"That seemed the most likely way for the news to get out. I mean, your mother thought I'd already agreed. I wonder where she could have gotten that idea?"

The cad didn't even bother defending himself. "Did you agree?"

She wanted to say no, simply because he was irking her. "I agreed."

"I thank you, then." That voice rippled through all her still-sleepy places without permission. "I know you wanted to relax on this trip, and you will. Like your mom said yesterday, you'll have help. You have my word that I'll pitch in any way I can."

"Oh, you will, and I'll need help. Lots and lots of it. Be forewarned."

"Not a problem." There was a chuckle in there. "And for the record, I would not jump on an exclusive, even if I had spoken with my mother last night. But I didn't know you'd agreed. I can prove it—"

"You don't have to prove anything, Max. I don't think you're a liar for the record. Merely pushy. And I can't figure out what's going on. Two days in a row, I've got personal information going public without my knowledge or consent."

"That is disturbing. Any ideas?"

"No clue. I didn't tell anyone." Because she was still in denial over being outmaneuvered so handily. She'd wanted to savor the first night of her vacation in peace. "My assistant in Manhattan doesn't have a clue. The last he heard, we'd put the inquiry on top of the pile for the next review meeting. And I didn't even talk to my office manager here after I confirmed with your mother."

"Could the blogger be speculating? You've said yourself that their information isn't accurate."

"But how would the blogger even know about the wedding? Unless he or she was at the airport yesterday when you announced— Damn it." She practically growled. "It's in the news. The press might not know whether or not I was planning the wedding, but they knew I was considering it."

There was silence for so long that suddenly Lily knew without a shred of doubt where she'd find the first headline.

"You didn't." Not a question.

"Well, it is news." He didn't sound in the least bit repentant. "*Big* news."

"Max, you knew I was trying to lay low—"

"Excuse me, got to run. I hear Madeleine."

Before the call disconnected, she could hear his throaty laughter.

Argh!

Her feet hit the floor and slid right into the slippers perched beside the bed. She snatched her robe off the poster and thrust her arms into the sleeves while heading out the door. With the bulk of her life spent traveling, her wardrobe was public ready. Hotels. Rentals. Recreational vehicles. Whatever. She'd long ago established routines to make temporary housing comfortable, which meant being always prepared to meet people.

The shadowy house in the quiet predawn felt vaguely familiar as she descended the stairs with the phone cradled against her ear. Another lifetime. She bypassed the front door because the telltale clinking of china let her know someone was awake. She found her dad at the kitchen table.

No surprises here. He'd always been an early riser, preferring a leisurely awakening over coffee and the newspaper before heading to the hardware store. Her mother had probably set up the coffeepot last night before she went to bed, so the brew would be ready by the time he'd gotten the paper from the yard and settled at the table. A once-familiar routine.

"You made the front page," he informed her without glancing away from the sports section.

How he knew it was her was another question. Lily had long ago accepted Dad had a sixth sense when it came to his kids. Her and Mike, anyway. They were later-in-life blessings, as her mother always called them, which meant her dad had gotten a head start with parenting her siblings. He'd been tough to put one over on.

"I knew it," she said when he handed her a section of the paper. *Only in Pleasant Valley would I be front page news. In the civilized world, I'm relegated to local and society pages, and that's fine by me.*

She reassembled the mess her dad had made of the newspaper enough to find the front page. The headline read:

Extreme Romance Hits Hudson Valley

She scanned the article. Title aside, which made World-wide Weddings Unlimited sound like the worst sort of reality show, the piece was well-written and slanted to stake claim to her success. Max had provided the details of her arrival and established her roots in the area from her birth at St. Francis Hospital through graduation from Vassar College. He plugged the hardware store, too.

But his account of the Carmichael/Girard wedding was factual—currently under inquiry. And while he detailed his brother-in-law's intention to campaign for governor, Max was very clear on the fact the wedding hadn't been contracted yet.

She couldn't fault him anywhere.

And she wanted to, so badly.

Why was he under her skin so completely? Because he was bullying her? Must be. Tossing the section on her dad's pile, she headed toward the coffeepot while dialing Mara again.

"I had a thought," Mara said. "Could the blogger be monitoring the wire services? If so, he or she might have read what happened when you got off the plane yesterday."

"That was my thought. We need to see what time the entry posted." Grabbing a mug from the drain board, she poured coffee then headed to the enclosed porch so she could talk without disturbing her dad.

"You know what bothers me, Mara? The way the legit media is monitoring that nobody blog. That's worrisome."

"Agreed, but don't be too surprised. It's dog-eat-dog out there. Print media is fighting to survive in the digital age. They're monitoring everything to get a jump on everyone else."

"*Tabloid* reporters, maybe."

A chuckle on the other end. "You wish. If you didn't want to risk a leak, then you should have kept your arrival quiet like you said you were going to."

"I did."

There was a beat of silence. "Oh, my apologies. I assumed you changed your mind and didn't see fit to notify me."

Lily was already tired of assumptions and the sun wasn't even up yet. "Why would you think that? If I didn't tell you, how would you keep me organized on this trip?"

"Like you need my help with that. You're a machine, and you know it. I'm just making it possible for you to take on more work than humanly possible when you're already superhumanly tired." Mara gave a short laugh. "Any clue who sprung the leak? You told everyone to keep their mouths shut. I can't imagine anyone deliberately… Max didn't say anything, did he? Is this a strong-arm tactic?"

"I thought so at first, too, but he received an email about my arrival. I don't think he'd lie."

"This has gone beyond the mere celebrity stalker with

nothing better to do than rant online," Mara said. "I'm getting a sense this blogger has a bitch to square with you. What about your ex? Or his new girlfriend?"

"I can't imagine he'd stoop that low." At least, she hoped not. Could she honestly have missed that the man was *that* depraved? "And Lucas doesn't have a new girlfriend from what I understand. He dropped the fling as soon as he found out she was the one to give the story to the press. He doesn't want the bad publicity any more than I do. His company has taken an even worse hit. So what possible bitch could the ex-fling have to square with me? I'm not the morally bankrupt gold digger, remember?"

"You make her look bad."

"I didn't say one word." Lily rested her forehead against the chilled glass. "All I've said is no comment."

"Of course. You've been brilliant. That's why she looks so bad. Try to come at it from her point of view. She makes a bid for the big leagues by getting involved with your fiancé. She tips off the paparazzi, so they're caught and she's suddenly all over the news. You dump the jerk and call off the wedding. The jerk freaks with the media explosion and dumps the fling. The whole situation is Emmelina in reverse. Look at what that fiasco has done for Drew Hatcher's ex-wife. She jumped from television to movies and landed a fifteen-million-dollar deal."

Just what Lily wanted to do—go from the media's favorite wedding planner to their favorite victim. "Shoot. Me. Now."

"Oh, come on, now. If Martha can weather jail, you can weather a breakup and some bad press." Mara was nothing if not pragmatic. "Now what do you want me to do about the exclusive?"

"Give it to them. Tell them not to put so much stock in worthless internet speculation." She heaved a sigh. "Tell them I reviewed the inquiry last night. It's official if they want to go to print. I'll be hammering out the details today and will make them available by their first deadline. If they break the news online, all I can tell them now is the function will be at Overlook around Thanksgiving and will launch Raymond Girard's political career. Max's article will prove I didn't give the jump to anyone."

She might have to thank him instead of blame him for keeping her in the news. The front page? Honestly.

"Got it," Mara said. "When will you get the details to me?"

"As soon as I track down Max." Which meant she wouldn't be doing much work on Riley's wedding today. Wonderful. And she had a grand total of three and a half weeks to plan that one.

Lily sipped her coffee and stared as the sunrise slowly lit the swing and the trees. How did she wind up back here again?

"How in the world am I going to pull this off?" A rhetorical question that echoed dully in the predawn quiet. "I'm going to need a miracle."

"You're the angel. I don't think a miracle will be a problem."

Lily found herself smiling. "I'll be by later so I can start delegating. Will you be around? What do you have on your plate with the Eversham/Raichle event today?"

"I'm in the office, so come at your convenience."

"Great. See you then." Lily disconnected then set the cup on the windowsill. With the smile still on her face, she tweeted:

I don't believe in luck. I believe in blessings, common sense, a strong work ethic and surrounding myself with wonderful, competent people—my life is filled with them.

That was as much of a rebuttal as her followers would get today, and Mara would know how much she was appreciated.

CHAPTER SEVEN

MAX SQUINTED at the computer monitor. Leaning in closer to the display, he scanned the dummy Riley had sent detailing the proposed layout of copy and photos for tomorrow's edition. Of course it was still early in the day yet, so the layout was bound to change as reporters returned from the field and news broke over the wire services. But Riley was never one to save things until the last minute, and that lent a level of calm to the newsroom that Max enjoyed a great deal.

Promoting her to managing editor had been a smart move, as he'd known it would be. They'd been friends since Riley had interned at the *Herald* as an undergrad at Vassar. He knew her work. Knew the friend she was. Life had dealt both of them hard blows with death and grief, and that had made their friendship even stronger.

He'd met resistance from his family over Riley's lack of actual experience, of course, but she knew her way around the newsroom and Max knew Riley. She learned on her feet and was the best person for the job.

He'd won that skirmish. Largely because his grandfather had supported the decision. He may have retired from the *Herald*, but he hadn't stepped down from his role of family patriarch yet.

An electronic screech cut through the quiet, and Max reached for the intercom. He didn't get a chance to say a word before his assistant's voice said, "Code 125."

His mother swept into his office the way she always did—as if she owned the place. She did, so her refusal to knock wasn't personal. And she wasn't the only one with that sense of entitlement, either. Various Downey family members could be counted on to show up unannounced at any time of the day or night, which was a job hazard of working in any of the family businesses. His clever assistant had come up with a series of codes to give Max a heads-up on who was about to barge into his office.

"What a nice surprise, Mom. What brings you by today?" he asked, although he suspected he already knew the answer.

She was carrying a copy of today's edition.

"Hello, Maxim." She didn't say another word. Dropping her purse into a chair, she cocked a hip against his desk and peered down at him.

His mother had always been an attractive woman. Quite beautiful even with the black hair and green eyes she'd passed along to him. She was tall and willowy with the benefit of a fleet of capable cosmetic surgeons who kept age at bay. Not that she was elderly by any stretch. She hadn't yet reached her mid-sixties and wore that stylish, timeless aura privilege and breeding could buy.

He waited while she shook open the paper to display the headline above the fold.

Extreme Romance Hits Hudson Valley

"Catchy headline. Bet there isn't a paper left in a box anywhere in this town." She smiled, clearly pleased.

"Here's hoping."

"You did a fine job with the article, Maxim. Informative and tasteful."

"I'm glad you approve."

Mission accomplished, then. He'd known when he'd written the piece a lot of folks would be paying close attention. His mother included, as it concerned her favorite pet project.

Worldwide Weddings Unlimited.

"I do." She set down the paper. "And that's why I'm here. Now that Lily's in town, we need to make some decisions regarding Raymond's wedding. I'm on my way into the office to meet with her. I thought you might want to weigh in."

Very nice of her to consider him since he was, of course, hosting the event. But here was something else Max knew wasn't personal. Any event involving Overlook and Worldwide Weddings Unlimited would create a pot his mother simply wouldn't be able to resist stirring. Overlook was her home, too, and as the reigning matriarch, all things social were her exclusive domain. That unspoken rule had been set in stone for more generations than Max had been around.

But he sometimes thought they'd all be better off if they put his mother to work at any one of their business interests since his mother's charitable endeavors and social calendar obviously weren't fulfilling her. She was a smart woman. Unfortunately, he couldn't see her catering to VIP clients at the bank. *Dictating* more described her personal style.

"Raymond and Jamilyn have given me a general idea of what they're looking for," he said. "Shouldn't be too hard to figure things out. They'll be calling whenever they're able, and they're both accessible by email when they can't make a phone call."

"Maxim, that's all well and good, but this is going to be a grand affair. Raymond's future career is on the line here, and you've already given the media a heads-up. Add Lily's involvement and this wedding simply must live up to its press. I'm afraid the planning won't be quite as simple as you're making it out to be."

"So I've heard." From a very beautiful wedding planner in no uncertain terms.

She leaned forward and patted his cheek, her fond smile making him brace himself before she uttered her next words. "Leave everything to me. Lily's here and we've got Mara and the office at our disposal. We'll run everything by you if you're worried. We all know how busy you are."

"I'm not worried, Mother." A lie if ever there was one, but here was a place where all of Lily Susan's arguments came in handy. "I don't want us to get ahead of ourselves, though. Lily Susan only heard about the wedding the day before yesterday. She has another wedding to plan first."

His mother waved him off with an impeccably manicured hand. "She can plan more than one wedding at a time. That's her job."

Given Lily Susan's history, the assumption was a reasonable one. But his mother didn't know how exhausted Lily Susan was, although saying so might violate what she'd told him in confidence. "I'm only pointing out that we've sprung this on her, and it won't serve anyone's purpose if we don't give her a chance to figure out her own schedule."

His mother frowned. "She needs to move on this. There's isn't much time."

"Give her some room, please."

"Honestly, Maxim. I gave the girl her start in business, and she's still my partner. We enjoy working together. It's going to be fun."

Fun? The only fun that Max could see in the entire equation was the time he could spend with Lily Susan.

But he'd barely admitted that to himself—and certainly wasn't ready to say a word to his mother.

Lily Susan intrigued him more than he'd expected. Her cool, polished exterior contrasted with the warmth she'd shown with his daughter. And the challenge in her eyes fascinated him. Especially her strength and the vulnerability he sensed she was hiding. Oh, yeah, the woman fascinated him.

He was having life signs where he'd least expected them. Figured that he'd start to emerge from his shell for a woman who in no way meshed with any aspect of his life.

Max leaned back in his chair and considered his reply. He needed to redirect before his mother thought she had permission to assume control. His mother understood money.

"Please keep in mind that while *I*—" emphasis on the singular "—may be hosting this event, Raymond and Jamilyn are paying for it, so I'm accountable for every dime. I have no choice but to be involved with the decision making otherwise I won't be able to adhere to their budget."

Rising quickly, he kissed her cheek. "But I do appreciate your connections and your help. You know that."

Her expression said she recognized the dismissal for exactly what it was. There was nothing left to say as far as Max was concerned. Of course, he didn't think for one second his mother would back off of the planning even if she didn't have carte blanche to assume control.

"Kiss Madeleine for me." She sounded cool as she retrieved her purse and copy of the paper. "Please let her know we're scheduled at the spa Friday afternoon for our nails. Brigham will pick her up after school."

"I'll tell her."

She didn't say another word as she strode out the door, unhappy. Max rubbed his temples, determined to come up with the next move before he had a train wreck on his hands.

But at least his mother hadn't taken out her displeasure on his daughter. That was definitely something. Madeleine always enjoyed outings with Goddess, usually involving grooming or shopping expeditions. His mother wasn't exactly an involved grandparent—nothing along the lines of the hands-on Rosie—but as his daughter and mother were both female and kindred souls in a family with a lot of men, he encouraged his mother whenever she reached out.

Max didn't want to strain their relationship, either, but he refused to allow his mother to ruin his plans. He had to tread carefully because Lily Susan was comfortable working with his mother.

He had no intention of stepping aside. His mother and Lily Susan had no choice but to deal with him.

CHAPTER EIGHT

LILY DROVE DOWN Main Street with the noon traffic in her dad's Cadillac, which she'd commandeered as her own until arranging for a rental. Downtown Poughkeepsie had come a long way since the days when she and her friends used to sneak into town to hang out at the Main Mall and ogle boys. The pedestrian mall had been built to preserve the nineteenth-century commercial buildings that lined the town's main street. While it had been a noble endeavor, the inception of suburban shopping centers had degenerated Main Mall into a seamy place that had fascinated teens from the rural hamlet of Pleasant Valley.

Main Mall had met its official demise only a few years before Lily's last visit home. The street had since been reopened and all those commercial buildings were now on the historic register.

Her own building had undergone a similar transformation, and as she turned onto a side street and found a parking space, she remembered how this row of Victorian town houses hadn't looked nearly so well-preserved a decade ago. But to the twenty-year-old college student with very big dreams, the three-story town house, with its mansard roof and dormer windows, had been the epitome of worldliness and charm.

As the property had needed considerable work and everyone had believed the demise of the Main Mall inevitable, she'd purchased it for a song. Then, with the help of her father, brothers and friends, she'd undertaken the renovations of the interior and exterior herself.

Not much of that quirky, hand-renovated memory remained in this latest upgrade. While always a part of the **Mill Street-North Clover Historic District**, this row of town houses had only recently been listed on the register. Only the wrought-iron nameplate beside the door indicating the name of the business looked familiar.

That nameplate was the reworked original—the very one her dad had given her as a shop-warming gift so long ago. As he proudly displayed the first dollar bill he'd ever earned above the cash register, he'd given Lily that nameplate to display.

The suggestion had actually been Ginger's, who always had plenty of suggestions and was never shy about sharing them. Many were sheer brilliance.

"You want to establish yourself as a professional consultant from inception. You do that by tasteful subtlety," she'd explained when they'd first viewed this location as a potential office.

Ginger's reasoning had proven as good as her word, and now when Lily was far more experienced, she recognized that no strip plaza could have ever laid the groundwork for Worldwide Weddings Unlimited in the same way this Victorian town house had.

She'd emulated that same sense of style with each operational expansion. Her offices in Manhattan, Los Angeles, Paris and Beijing all exhibited similar cultural appeal. And on each, no other signage was necessary beyond a replica of that tasteful nameplate.

"Welcome home, Lily." Ginger appeared in the doorway. "Are you not amazed? I'll bet you barely recognize the place."

"You have outdone yourself." Lily crossed the street

and hastened up the brick steps, running a hand along the new wrought-iron railing. "Definitely better than the photos."

While kissing Ginger's cheek in greeting, Lily suppressed a twinge of guilt that she hadn't had the time or inclination to make a personal appearance during the renovation process.

"A year from start to finish," Ginger said proudly. "The attorney on the opposite corner began four months before we did and still hasn't wrapped up yet."

"You have worked a miracle."

"You'll definitely think so when you see inside."

"I already do. The trim looks remarkable." She shielded her eyes from the autumn sun. "I fell in love with all that gingerbread trim. I actually think it's what convinced me this was the perfect place. So who owns the house next to the attorney now?"

"Another musician. She kept the place a studio and is doing extremely well by the looks of it. And she's a young woman, too. Obviously motivated. Reminds me a lot of you."

Lily smiled. "I took piano lessons from Mrs. Carr, the previous owner, when I was younger. Bless her heart. She was so patient with me."

"You didn't play well, dear?"

"I played very well. Just not what Mrs. Carr wanted me to play. I loved classical and ragtime—anything above my level that presented a challenge. I couldn't be bothered with the scales or the theory."

"No surprises there. You've always been impatient."

"Me?"

Ginger didn't reply. She didn't have to—her expression said it all. But she beamed as she swung open the door. "Ta da!"

Lily knew the details of the interior, had authorized every purchase after reviewing photos and prices and sketches of proposed layouts. But the reality of the lavish colors and fabrics and patterns, the way the gossip bench and chairs and side tables transformed the foyer into a cozy entry, made her smile. The atmosphere couldn't have been more Worldwide Weddings Unlimited if she'd wielded the hammer and nails herself.

She had no words, only an excitement that took her by surprise. The hug she gave Ginger seemed to take her the same way. But she was clearly pleased. "I knew you'd love it."

"It couldn't be more perfect."

"Just wait." Ginger motioned around them with a sweeping gesture, and Lily actually giggled as they began a grand tour.

In addition to the foyer, there were two offices and a viewing room on the first floor. There was a kitchen in the back, too, but that had never seen much use beyond providing light refreshments for clients. A cup of espresso or herbal tea. A glass of wine. Cheese and crackers or a fruit-and-veggie tray for fittings that ran into the night.

The second floor at the top of the sweeping staircase had changed little.

"Not much to do in here," Ginger said. "The lighting has been upgraded, of course."

Lily had originally done extensive work by knocking out every wall down to the support beams to transform the entire floor into a workroom. With mirrored walls and tall windows and support beams transformed into decorative columns, the workroom had always reminded her of a dance studio. Bright and airy and absolutely perfect to view wedding parties in full regalia or test runners and trains for all-important walks down the aisle.

"They did a nice job bringing the floor back," Lily said. "I'm so glad we didn't have to replace the original."

"I was, as well. Allowed me to put the money to good use elsewhere."

The third floor—an odd-shaped attic behind dormer windows—was still used for storage. Ginger had upgraded with custom-built shelving, drawers and cabinets to store everything from office supplies to wedding arches.

But once upon a time Lily had commandeered a corner of this attic for herself. She'd fitted one of the window boxes with cushions, so she could sit and stare out at the lights twinkling on the Hudson River at night, and a bed where she could nap when studies or work kept her too late to make the drive home.

Her corner was no more. And for some reason that tugged at Lily a bit, even though she had offices as elegantly furnished in much more exciting cities. Nowadays, she seemed only to breeze through those offices on her way through whatever part of the world she was currently working.

Once upon a time, however, this had been her place. She'd worked her heart and soul out in this town house. Had greeted her first clients in the foyer. Had dragged herself up to this attic to catch a few hours of sleep when she was so wiped out she couldn't keep her eyes open another second.

This town house had memories.

"You missed all the excitement," said Mara. "And the headaches."

Lily shook off her reverie and smiled automatically at the woman who appeared in the doorway, making an entrance in her tailored pencil skirt and filmy blouse, straight red hair falling over her shoulders and down her back.

"No question about that," Lily agreed. "Thank you for all your effort. Ginger has said it was a joint venture."

Mara smiled. "Then she's being generous. I've been busy with our events. She's been doing the actual renovation work."

"It's simply lovely. You both worked a miracle."

"Now aren't you pleased we didn't sell this office?" Ginger asked, satisfied smile in place.

Lily gave a laugh. There was only one way to answer that question, but there was actually more to the decision, as Ginger well knew.

As business had expanded, the need for offices in central locations had become essential. Professionally it hadn't made sense to keep this place, but Ginger had resisted selling her shares of this original venture, even though she wasn't interested in being a stakeholder in the expansion.

She'd never been ugly about it, of course, but she'd always played the guilt card. So Lily had allowed herself to be manipulated because she understood Ginger's desire to remain quasi-involved. But Lily also refused to become passive-aggressive about running a location she no longer had time for, so she'd long ago limited the scope of this operation, largely as a form of damage control, since the office still bore her name and Poughkeepsie wasn't a regular stop in her hectic schedule.

The redheaded stepchild, indeed.

"There are so many memories here," she said wistfully. "And this branch of Worldwide Weddings Unlimited is still making brides' dreams come true. What could be better?"

Diplomacy as its finest—even Ginger seemed appeased. She continued the tour, pointing out various improvements as they made their way downstairs to the working office, as Lily had always thought of it. Clients weren't shown this space, but it's where most of the work was accomplished.

"I didn't intend to interfere with your schedule since you're in production in Rhinebeck," Lily told Mara. "But with a full-scale event at Thanksgiving, I'm going to need your help."

Mara spun her chair from the desk and removed a file from a drawer in the credenza. Without a word she flipped it open to reveal sketches and notes in Ginger's familiar handwriting.

"The instant Max mentioned the time frame, I knew we didn't have a moment to lose," Ginger said.

"Looks like we've got a jump on things then," Lily said, flipping through the pages. She recognized the grounds at Overlook and potential arrangements for the flow of traffic inside. At first glance there were a few good possibilities.

Why had Lily ever wasted the energy trying to circumvent the inevitable? She'd never had a choice about this wedding.

"I've got to nail down some of the details today. I promised the press an exclusive before business close," Lily said matter-of-factly. Then it occurred to her that she hadn't seen Mara's assistant anywhere. "Mara, where's Denise?"

"She's on bed rest until the baby comes. But no worries. We'll get everything done. I've been keeping up with the paperwork. Denise transcribes from home when I need her."

"When did this take place?" They couldn't manage

without an office assistant. "I don't remember seeing anything about Denise going on leave."

"No?" Mara frowned. "That's strange. It's been nearly a month, Lily, and she's not due for another few weeks yet. I was sure I sent an email."

Lily shook her head.

"Not sure what happened there. I'll take a peek at my email and see if I can find the original message. Thought it was strange when I didn't hear anything about it from you." Mara shrugged. "Things have been hectic. Thank goodness for Ginger helping out. Not sure what I'd have done without her."

They should have brought in a temp—it wasn't rocket science. But Lily let it go. She'd touch base with human resources to check on the details. At the moment, she was more concerned in what was bothering her about this new development. She couldn't put her finger on it. And with two weddings that should be in production, Lily didn't have time to figure it out.

"Let's start with the contracts then," she said. "If you'll get me the standard workup, I'll track down Max so we can decide on these sketches. Has Max seen these yet, Ginger?"

Ginger waited until Mara left the room before saying, "Not yet, dear. I thought you'd prefer presenting."

Lily didn't flinch. She'd known this was coming, known this situation wouldn't be simple. But she wasn't playing games here. Dialing Max's number, she waited for the call to connect.

He finally picked up. "Hello, Worldwide Weddings Unlimited."

"Hello, Worldwide Weddings Unlimited's newest client. You want a wedding so I need your undivided attention for an hour. Preferably ASAP. We have to hash through some details so I can provide an exclusive to your competition before business close." Which would teach him to sandbag her at press conferences. "How soon can you be at the office?"

Before he had a chance to reply, the chimes from the front doorbell rang gaily throughout the office.

"Shall I?" Ginger asked.

Lily shook her head as she was already closest to the office door. "Hang on a sec, Max," she said into the phone while making her way through the foyer.

"No problem."

Cradling the phone against her ear, she pulled open the door then let out a gasp at the unexpected sight.

Max in all his tall, dark and business-suited glory, holding a cell phone to his ear. His green eyes glinted with childish mischief but there was nothing childish about the set of his wide shoulders that tapered to a flat stomach.

"This ASAP enough for you?" he deadpanned, still speaking into the receiver.

Lily rolled her eyes and disconnected the call. She stepped aside and waved him in. "I hope you'll be equally accommodating through all the planning."

"I can be accommodating. Very accommodating." His voice was low and husky, and sent a shimmy of heat down her spine. But she ignored his teasing. Max was good at that. And as her older brother's best friend, he'd enjoyed pushing her buttons for years. But she wasn't rising to this bait.

"Behave," she admonished. "Come into the office. Your mother's here."

He didn't say anything, but Lily couldn't help noticing his playful expression faded. She had no idea what was up between Ginger and Max. But she didn't need more complications.

As if life wasn't already convoluted.

"Please make yourself comfortable," she said, as she settled Max into the client office. "I'll be right back."

She found Mara in the staff office.

"Contracts," she said, handing Lily a thick folder.

Lily scooped the file of sketches off the desk and glanced at Ginger. "Coming?"

Ginger smoothed an imaginary speck of lint off her pants and yawned delicately. "You run along, dear. You don't need me for those sorts of details."

Lily returned to find Max had done exactly as she'd suggested—made himself comfortable. He'd removed his suit jacket and it now lay across the settee. He wore a soft green shirt that brought out the intensity of his eyes. He'd rolled up his cuffs. His appearance was one of lean, catlike elegance.

He'd settled in a chair in front of the desk and set up a notebook computer with a remote wireless attachment, and she could make out Skype on the screen.

"Bride or groom?" she asked.

His long fingers tapped the keys. "Both if we need them."

"Wonderful." Lily took a deep breath to dispel her mood because she was already feeling annoyed and pressured and bullied, which was not the place to begin. "Let's talk wedding."

Sinking into the chair behind the desk, she faced Max and noticed the way the sun from the window silhouetted him until he sort of glowed around the edges. He might know nothing about weddings, but one wouldn't know it from his calm demeanor. Since he'd strolled in, he dominated the space around him.

Damn. He looked yummy. From the soft crinkles around his eyes, to his full lips and square jaw, he was all male. She thought she could detect a hint of his cologne, a smell that was all uniquely masculine and *him*.

Poising her pen over her own notepad, she jotted: *I am thirty-two, not thirteen, and I do not have time for distractions right now. Not one measly second.*

CHAPTER NINE

MAX SAT in Lily Susan's office, explaining the vision for someone else's wedding, in broad strokes, as Lily Susan termed it. She hadn't started asking questions yet, but Max knew one thing already—he hadn't been this involved in his own wedding.

But, he reminded himself, he was involved for a good cause. And he would use this time to get to know Lily Susan. He wanted to know what made her tick. Was she as romantic at heart as her career would suggest? She'd been younger than he and Joey so Max had never paid much attention to her.

No, back then she'd simply been the girl twin, one of the two reasons Joey would occasionally miss ball games or fishing trips or other activities. The other reason had been her twin brother Mike. They'd been too young to leave unsupervised at home, so whenever required, Joey would have to take his turn being home to babysit. It wasn't fair that the task always fell to Caroline because she was a girl. Rosie and Joe were all about fair.

But life didn't play fair. He'd been dead inside for so long and had been okay with it. Now, around Lily Susan, he suddenly remembered he was a man. Of course, Max was a father, too. A father *first,* in fact. That was his choice. Lily Susan lived a life diametrically opposed to everything he wanted for himself and Madeleine. Lily Susan's main priority appeared to be her career. Her own family didn't factor high on her list from what Max had seen. And he couldn't imagine she'd been looking for any kind of family life by marrying Lucas Olivier.

So what was the appeal? Why was he so affected by the way she gazed at him from under her lashes? True, she was exquisite, with her heart-shaped face and that cool poise as she listened to him share what he knew. Jamilyn hated seafood. Raymond wanted a small wedding party because he only had a few close friends.

She scrawled notes on a pad, her slender fingers moving gracefully across the page, her lips pursed thoughtfully. She had a mouth made for kissing. Why should he be so surprised that he would think about kissing her?

Still, Lily Susan?

Maybe he shouldn't be so surprised. Lily Susan wasn't a stranger. He'd known her most of his life. He simply hadn't realized how beautiful she'd grown to be because he hadn't been looking at her as anything but Joey's little sister.

Not anymore. The beautiful woman sitting across from him was impacting him on so many levels.

All his life he'd struggled to keep grounded, keep balanced between his family obligations and everything else he considered to be important. Even before he'd learned the hard way how very short life could be, how precious each moment was, he'd struggled to keep his life—and Madeleine's—*real*.

Lily Susan was the opposite of real. She lived in a fantasy world that was possibly more disconnected than his own family, and that was saying a lot.

He didn't see how his feelings could lead anywhere except to a dead end.

"Tell me about Raymond," she said.

"My brother-in-law is a career military officer." Max was impressed by how normal he sounded. "He cares enough about this country to make protecting it his life."

"How many of the groomsmen will be in uniform?"

Max nodded. "All of them. Marines. Except the best man—my other brother-in-law. He's air force."

"How many siblings are there in Felicia's family?"

"Five. Two brothers and three sisters. She was the baby, like you."

"Then you should know that we family babies aren't so easily bullied. We toughen up fast. We have to."

Felicia had definitely been one to hold her own in any situation. "No arguments there. But what if I'm not looking to bully?"

The statement implied a question: What was he looking to do then? Not even Max was sure.

She seemed to arm herself with professional detachment. "So, this is Raymond's first marriage?"

"It is. He's always been focused on his career. My in-laws had almost given up hope that he'd ever settle down and make a life for himself. I can't say it's shocking that he wants to continue to serve in some capacity after his retirement. He'll make a good governor."

"And this wedding is going to show that to the world."

Max nodded. "A normal society wedding. Nothing trendy, just a traditional romantic wedding. I know it's not *your* typical fare, but it will be supersize and high-profile so you're the best person for the job."

Lily Susan kept her gaze fixed on her notebook. "Contrary to popular belief, I do plan my fair share of normal society weddings. I happen to like traditional romantic."

Had that been the sort of wedding she'd planned for herself? At heart was she still a small-town girl? "I meant the destination part, actually. I'm sorry if you feel I've dumped everything in your lap—"

His gaze dropped to where she played with her open collar. A flush on her cheeks suggested she'd noticed. Was she flustered? That surprised him. She was such a beautiful woman. Surely she was used to men openly admiring her.

"Max, you have dumped everything in my lap," she said matter-of-factly. "You're asking me to accomplish eighteen months of work in eight weeks."

"Only out of necessity and only for a good cause." Several good causes, actually. Especially the one that made it necessary for them to work closely together. To get to know each other as adults. Max wasn't going to analyze the feeling too closely. He wasn't going to talk himself out of a woman whose priorities and lifestyle weren't his own. Not now. Not yet. Not when he hadn't felt this alive in so long. Not when her slim fingers and neat French manicure made him think of how her hands might feel running through his hair. Or down his back.

She leaned forward with a secretive expression that drew him forward to meet her. So close he could smell her perfume—a delicate and floral scent. Probably French and expensive. Intriguing.

"It's damage control," she whispered conspiratorially. "I've already figured out that part. You need me to keep your mother in check."

Their gazes met, and from this vantage her deep gold eyes—eyes that should have been so familiar—were somehow transformed into smoldering, molten eyes.

Oh, yeah. Let her keep believing that. He wasn't going to admit that he wanted her all to himself.

Max swallowed a grin and attempted to look guilty.

"Don't act surprised and don't even bother denying it."

She gave a light shake of her head and sent waves of hair tumbling around her shoulders. "Your mother's playing the same game. She wants to be involved and expects me to run interference with you."

"You'll have to choose sides then because we're not like your family. Downeys like clearly delineated loyalties."

She rolled her eyes. "We're planning a wedding not a war."

"I know, but once I chose to involve my family, the planning was bound to become a battlefield."

She toyed with the pen and considered him. "I wonder why you chose to involve your family, then."

He shrugged. "Same reason I involved you. You're the best person to coordinate the wedding. Overlook is the best venue. Since my family lives there, I did have to mention it to avoid scheduling conflicts."

She gave a huff that seemed to say she didn't have time for any of this. Or maybe she didn't want to make time for him. Luckily for him, she no longer had a choice.

"For the record, I'm not choosing sides. I'm a professional you're hiring to plan an event. Period. Now I need numbers. I can come up with all the brilliant ideas I want, but the budget will dictate what I put in the proposal, which I have one night to produce, thank you."

"I have numbers." Max pulled up the file with the pertinent information. "And a guest list and addresses and everything Raymond and Jamilyn thought you'd need."

Not only was there a total budget, but there were also suggestions about how they'd like to see their money allocated. Jamilyn wouldn't spend ten thousand dollars on a designer dress when she could direct the cash to feeding her guests.

He turned the notebook computer to face Lily Susan

then waited while she scanned the information. He'd thought the number reasonable, particularly as they weren't going to have to rent a venue. Precisely one of the reasons Max had offered Overlook. But her silence gave him pause. "If that's not enough to cover what you need, give me an idea of how short we'll be, and I'll see if I can make up the difference. I want this to be a special event."

"Because of Raymond's political career?"

Max nodded. "That certainly factors, but even more important is the start of their marriage."

A tiny frown furrowed Lily Susan's brow. "I'm sensing more than that. Anything you can tell me will be helpful."

"Part of your process for coming up with brilliance?"

"Absolutely. Part of my expertise is translating visions. Most of the time my couples aren't really sure what they're looking for. Sometimes they think they know, but it turns out what they're saying and thinking are two different things. It's up to me to translate. I'm at a distinct disadvantage here without the couple, so I'm forced to take you at your word, which impedes my process. Please tell me what you can."

Okay, far be it for Max to *impede her process*. "You'll keep it between us?"

"Of course."

"Felicia's death jolted Raymond into realizing how little time any of us have, enough to take a chance on living his life to the fullest. He fell in love with Jamilyn and doesn't want to waste a second."

"So, the theme of their life together is new beginnings on several levels."

Max nodded. He admired his brother-in-law tremendously for taking this chance. Max wondered if he'd find the strength to do the same. He'd held onto his own past for a long time.

Lily Susan frowned at the guest list. "Most of the bride's family will be traveling in from Maryland and Ohio."

"Is that a problem?"

"It's definitely not optimal. Not only don't I have a bride to work with, but her wedding party won't be accessible, either." She was pensive as she jotted more notes on her pad. "Final fittings are going to be an issue. Jamilyn mentions here that most of the guests are aware of the difficulties, though. It might make sense to incorporate Thanksgiving festivities since everyone will be traveling. Just a thought."

"A good one. I can't imagine anyone will be thrilled about flying during the busiest travel week of the year."

"True. I think we can pull something together while keeping to the budget, though. Jamilyn seems practical about the money. But that's not really the issue. It's the time frame. Cutting corners takes work and we'll be paying top dollar to have things shipped priority, rushing alterations and things like that. There's just no way around it. Such a waste of our resources."

"It was either Thanksgiving or wait until next year. Raymond retires from the service in May, but Jamilyn won't be back in the States until August."

"Will they even have time for a honeymoon?"

"Of sorts. They deploy to Germany right after the wedding but they won't ship out to their respective duties until closer to Christmas."

"That's something at least. Let me know if they want to plan a getaway while they're there. I work with some excellent travel consultants."

"Thanks. That's generous." Max meant it. "They're

excited to start their life together. And please remember what I said about helping to pad the budget. If it comes down to a choice, give me a chance to kick in."

"Oh, I will." She managed to make that sound like a threat. One that made him smile. Turning the computer display to face him again, she said, "Would you mind forwarding that file to me? I'll need to refer to it tonight. And you can disconnect from Skype, too, by the way. We won't need Raymond or Jamilyn until tomorrow."

"Disconnecting. So how will this work? Would you mind running through the process with me, so I know what to expect?" So he wouldn't *impede.* So he could find out exactly how much alone time they would have together. He imagined intimate dinners. Testing the menus. And the champagne. And in the center of every idea was Lily Susan.

She folded slender hands together, all business. "We'll start with the proposal. I'll work up my ideas tonight and expect you to be available to view them tomorrow." She eyed him steadily. "You will be available, correct?"

"I'm at your disposal 24/7."

She acted as though she hadn't caught his innuendo, but then her lips twitched into a smile. "I really can't emphasize enough how every second will count."

"I like a woman who can make every second count."

"Max! What is wrong with you? The decision making will start tomorrow, so please be ready."

"I'll be ready…for anything," he said softly.

"Oh, please. You are so not funny." She glared. "Once we come up with some preliminary ideas, I'll want Jamilyn and Raymond to confirm before I proceed making arrangements."

"Not a problem."

"Oh, wait." She leaped out of the chair in a smooth

move that drew his attention to the way her tailored blouse and skirt managed to cling to her every curve. "There is a decision we can make today. Let me grab that book." She glided out of the room on wedge heels with the hem of her skirt swinging around trim ankles.

Max watched her go, typing a few notes on another file. She wasn't taking his innuendos and teasing seriously, which was probably a good thing. At least until he figured out how he was going to handle his newfound interest.

Lily Susan breezed in, toting some sort of display book that was so huge, he was on his feet, taking it from her. He felt as if an electrical current shocked him when their fingers brushed together, a not-so-innocent innocent touch that made him hyperaware of her.

Still, she didn't seem to notice him in any special way. But as she jerked away, perhaps a little too fast, he thought maybe he was mistaken.

Setting the book on the desk, he sank into the chair, warning himself to get a grip. Especially when Lily Susan leaned over him and he got another whiff of her delicate scent.

"I much prefer to individualize all the correspondence to the event," she explained while flipping pages. "But there's no time. Better we take what we can get and not waste a second."

Max tried to catch a glimpse of what was inside the book, but got distracted when she tucked a stray lock of whiskey-gold hair behind her ear.

"What are they?"

"Save-the-dates. They needed to go out like eight months ago for our A-list guests. Two months ago for everyone else."

He could see her scowl in profile, even beneath the fall of silky hair that kept slipping from behind her ear.

"Should we even bother?"

"If you'd like guests to attend this function, then it's probably a good idea."

He didn't get a chance to reply before she turned a page then flipped back again. "Okay, here we go. One of these will do. We have to decide which one." She straightened and gestured to the book. "Traditional and elegant. Generic, but tasteful."

He glanced at a display of cards in a variety of designs. Max's head spun with choices, the perfect distraction. Vellum, gilt-edged, layered, raised printing or pressed. He narrowed his choices down to two.

"Either will work," she said. "This one's a classic. The other makes more of a statement. Are the bride and groom the statement kind of people?"

Max considered that. If Raymond wanted to give the incumbent governor a run for his money, he should establish himself as someone willing to take chances. That might as well start with save-the-dates. "Yes."

"Okay, that's a place to start," Lily Susan said. "Would you like a suggestion?"

"I would." Keeping his cool wasn't so easy when he inhaled her scent with every breath he took, he discovered. Being too close made his thoughts drift into dangerous places.

Of course, to taunt him, she didn't go far. She half sat on the edge of the desk, so he was forced to look up to met her gaze, which meant that what should have been an unnoticeable action seemed to move in slow motion as he dragged his gaze along the lean lines of her body.

"Then why don't we bring in your mother? That'll go a long way toward fostering goodwill between the camps."

Even distracted by his sharp awareness of her, Max recognized the merit of that idea. "Agreed."

Bringing in his mother should act like a nice dose of cooling reality. He hoped.

She leaned across the desk—another smooth motion he couldn't help but notice—and depressed the intercom. "My dear Ginger, we're in the client office and we need your input. Would you mind terribly?"

His mother would eat this up. Sure enough, her familiar voice trilled over the speaker. "On my way."

She appeared in the doorway a few seconds later. "What can I do for you?"

Lily Susan motioned to the sample book. "These save-the-dates simply must get out tomorrow, which means we've got to nail the timing and sequence of wedding events."

His mother nodded. "When is the wedding ceremony?"

Lily Susan shrugged. "Jamilyn and Raymond aren't set on a particular time of day. It's Thanksgiving, so they want to spend time with family and friends. You've been working on schematics for traffic flow through Overlook, so what do you think?"

Max supposed he shouldn't be surprised his mother had already been at work on the wedding—whatever traffic flow was. Were they talking about where the guests would park?

Ginger sat behind the desk and Lily Susan slid the notepad toward her to review.

"Max, would you mind letting your mother see that file?"

He toggled windows and turned the display toward her as his mother slid on a pair of designer bifocals.

"Brunch or teatime, do you think?" Lily Susan asked.

"Any idea what you'll do with them the night before?"

"None whatsoever. They don't arrive in the States until two days before Thanksgiving. There will barely be time for fittings and a rehearsal let alone any sort of social gathering."

"You'll come up with something brilliant, dear. You always do." His mother gave a confident smile. "I believe teatime would work best, then. Schedule it early if you must. Say two in the afternoon. Unconventional, perhaps, but appropriate. The guests won't complain about enjoying a leisurely morning and you'll have time to tie up loose ends without stressing the bride, or yourself, with last-minute details."

"You're right. Max says we're looking for traditional romantic, and I believe I'm seeing afternoon melting into sunset and a very formal affair at night. Can't you see Overlook all dolled up with candles and silver?"

"I can. And if we time things properly, we might even take advantage of the long hall. It wouldn't be practical for a dinner, but it would be perfect for a cocktail party before sunset. Who knows, we might even get lucky with the weather. If the temperature doesn't drop unseasonably, Raymond and Jamilyn might take photos on the grounds. The guests can watch the photo shoot from the long hall and enjoy the sunset over the river. That might be a nice way to include them."

"You go, Ginger." Lily Susan looked so beautiful with her eyes sparkling with pleasure. "That's brilliant. Not only will the guests feel included, but it'll also buy us more time for photos before everyone gets antsy for dinner. We can work with the weather, too. We'll winterize Jamilyn's gown."

"Oh, I like that. So will the photographer. Jamilyn's so beautiful. I can't imagine she won't enjoy getting more than the usual shots in her finery."

Max watched as Lily Susan and his mother touched manicured fingers in the air in sort of a ladylike high five.

He sat on the periphery, content to let them conduct business—they were two women clearly on the same page. Watching them together seemed to confirm his observations from the previous day.

Lily Susan *did* remind him more of his family than her own, which in no way explained why he was so interested in her.

CHAPTER TEN

"WILL YOU PLEASE find out how much Denise is willing and able to do?" Lily asked Mara, who stood in the doorway of the greeting office. "I need to know if I have to bring in a temp assistant."

Mara nodded. "I'll give her a call right now. I'm sure she'll be glad to do as much as possible."

How much Denise was willing to do might be different than how much she was capable of doing. Lily didn't point that out.

"Thanks," she said. "I'm heading to Pleasant Valley to work on my sister-in-law's event. Call my cell when you know something. I probably won't come back here tonight."

"I'll take care of it, Lily. No problem."

"Okay. We're good to go, then. You're going to deal with the local vendors and keep in touch with me about who has the date free. You'll start with the A-list."

"And keep my fingers crossed that we luck out since the wedding is on a day most people are home with their families."

Lily hoped the vendors wouldn't feel the same way. "I think we stand a chance, don't you? I have a good feeling."

Mara raised two sets of crossed fingers.

"And Ginger's on top of Overlook. She'll inspect the house and the grounds and make arrangements to have the cleaning and any work that may need to be done. So as soon as you lock down the vendors, I'll schedule to meet them at Overlook to finalize details."

"Don't forget Ginger has the florist already."

"Nope. That's one thing off your list. Sure you're not overloaded with the Eversham/Raichle event?"

Mara grimaced. "Has it been that long since we've worked an event together? You pulled me out of Manhattan to deal with this backwater. I can handle Rhinebeck and Overlook. I promise."

"I know." There was no arguing the backwater part. "It'll be fun working together again. I know I see you every few weeks at the inquiry meetings, but it's not quite the same."

Leaving the office, she hopped in the Cadillac and headed to the Valley. She'd gotten a start on the big wedding, as she'd come to think of it. Hard to personalize an affair for a couple she'd never met. At the moment, Jamilyn and Raymond were still simply two individuals in uniforms.

But she'd begun the process and felt a little better. She'd sent an email to Publicity to make any style changes before forwarding the press release to the media outlets that had been promised the exclusive. And there were still three hours before the close of the business day. So she was technically ahead of schedule.

Taking a deep breath, she maneuvered through downtown traffic. Getting organized was critical right now. That was the only way she'd be able to delegate effectively, and since she was off to a decent start, she could switch gears on this drive so she could give her attention to Riley's event.

The little wedding.

The thought made her smile, and it felt good. So good.

How long had it been since work had inspired her, hadn't felt like a burden?

She waved at the hardware store as she cruised past. "Hi, Daddy."

She waved at her old elementary school, which was now educating the next generation of Angelicas. "Hi, twinnies."

Then turned onto Traver Road.

As Lily drove this once-familiar stretch with its twisting curves and forested hills, her pulse ramped up.

She hadn't seen the place since Mike...

"I found it, Lily Susan," her brother had told her, after showing up unexpectedly at her office one day.

"Found what?" she asked, unsure whether to usher him in since he was in his uniform and obviously still on duty.

"Our dream place." Of course, the dream place was actually more his dream place than that of the girl he'd recently married, but Riley seemed willing to go with it.

That smile. It stretched across his face as he hugged Lily so hard she puffed out a breath. "I'm going to put in a bid today."

"Has Riley even seen it yet?"

He glanced at her with a disbelieving grimace. "I'll take her to see it later. It's exactly what we've been looking for. Trust me. Twenty-five acres right in Pleasant Valley. The farmhouse is over a hundred years old. The barn looks like it is, too, so that'll need to be upgraded. Or leveled. Don't know which until I get inside. It has a pond and a creek."

Lily understood the significance. She would have known what those words meant without the accompanying excitement that had her brother barely able to stand still. Even without the pleased disbelief in his voice.

Mike's dream had always been a farm with enough

land for horses and some sort of water—a pond, a stream, a creek, a river. Didn't matter which as long as he could trail ride and water his horses.

"Okay, so you found it." She could feel the air around them crackle with possibilities. "Where is it?"

"You are not going to believe it."

She gestured impatiently with her hands.

"The Cesarini place. You know the one next door to the Haslams on Traver Road?"

"Oh. My. God." That was all she could manage.

They'd driven past that farmhouse every day to and from school as kids. And every day, twice a day, Mike would come up with some upgrade or change he'd make to the house, the garage, the barn, the driveway, the stables. And every one of those improvements would end with, "That's exactly the kind of place I'm going to own one day."

His dream was going to come true.

"What's making the Cesarinis sell?"

Mike shrugged. "He told the real-estate agent that the kids are all grown and have moved away. His wife wants to move back to Herkimer to be close to her family."

"Wow. But, Mike, how are you going to swing this? That much land has to cost a fortune."

"If this had been a month ago, I wouldn't be able to. Not on my salary. But now that Riley and I are married, the bank will factor in both our incomes. I've already talked with Max's dad. He didn't think there'd be any problem."

Lily wished Max's dad had been so accommodating when she'd asked him for a business loan not long ago. But she would have accepted a hundred no's so that Mike could get the one yes that mattered. Her situation had worked out even without a loan from the bank. And now Mike's would, too.

Dreams really did come true.

And now there it was again. The big farmhouse with its wraparound windows and circle drive. The trim freshly painted and the summer landscaping fading but still peeking through a blanket of autumn leaves.

Mike's dream.

Maybe dreams had been something genetic they'd shared as twins. Lily only knew that weddings were to her what horses had been to Mike. They'd never outgrown those passions.

Her chest tightened around a breath as she wheeled into the drive and parked behind Riley's van.

Suddenly the porch door swung open and Riley stepped out.

"Here comes the bride," Lily said as she got out of the car and headed toward her sister-in-law.

Riley spread her arms wide and they hugged. "I can't believe you're really here. It has been so long."

Lily had loved Riley ever since Mike had first brought her home. She was petite and fair, but with an independent, strong spirit. And Riley was a woman who had tackled grief the same way she tackled life—with love and a lot of down-to-earth practicality. She'd adored Mike. His death had been so hard on her, but she'd kept on coping, kept on healing, kept on living. She'd had two very important reasons—Camille and Jake.

Now she'd found love again.

Lily admired her strength. Sometimes she felt as if she hadn't so much dealt with Mike's death as she had avoided thinking about it.

"I wish I could have come to the office and saved you some steps. You're supposed to be on vacation."

Lily gave a snort of very unladylike laughter. "I'm in town for a wedding, not a vacation."

"As if one wasn't enough, right?"

"Pshaw. I'll just order two of everything." Lily remembered what Max had said. She gave Riley another hug for good measure. "Don't you worry about me. Tonight I'm going to curl up in Dad's chair with a cup of green tea and figure everything out so I can hit the ground running tomorrow. If Dad says one word about bringing home work, I'm going to wrap my hands around his throat. You'll make sure Scott won't send me to jail, right?"

"No problem. You can't plan the wedding if you're behind bars."

Lily braced herself as Riley ushered her through the porch and into the house, keeping up a steady stream of chatter that made the trip through the familiar surroundings a blur. It wasn't until they wound up in the kitchen, with Riley pouring coffee and Lily facing the breathtaking vista through the windows, the sweeping terrain of the farm in all its autumn glory from the stables to the forest, that Lily let herself feel.

A pond and a stream.

"He's not here anymore," Lily whispered.

Suddenly Riley was beside her, pressing the mug into Lily's hands and turning to stare out the windows, too. "I was so torn about selling this place after he died. I couldn't see anything but all the dreams we'd had together. But I made the right choice to keep it. The kids love it here. I love it here. It's everything Mike wanted for all of us, and it's all we have of him. All we'll ever have—except for you."

She turned to look at Lily, a soft smile playing around her mouth. "It took time to accept that we could keep those dreams alive, and keep him a part of our lives that way. I think that's what Mike would want."

"And Scott?"

"And Scott. Took a while. Mike was a brother to him. We talked about a fresh start after the wedding, but, well, Scott's teaching Jake to take care of the horses. They fish together, and Camille loves to ride. Brian's still living over the garage. He's doing really well in college and still helps out around the farm. How could I possibly uproot him after the way he's helped out? This feels like where we're supposed to be."

Lily heard everything Riley said, and it all made sense. But she didn't really understand. Maybe because she didn't feel it. How did one make peace with loss enough to move on?

Had Lily made peace?

She couldn't honestly say. Why had it always been so easy to go about her life and pretend he was still here? When she looked out at the farm, she couldn't feel Mike, but felt only…empty. Was that peace?

"Well, everyone I love seems happy." She found the right words, but they didn't erase that hollowness inside. "Camille and Jake. Mom and Dad. You and Scott. Brian. You've made the right choice, then."

"What about you, Lily Susan? I can say the same exact thing. The kids and I love you. Are you happy?"

Lily met Riley's gaze, saw the concern there, heard everything she wasn't asking.

Lucas. His betrayal. Their broken engagement.

No one had come out and asked yet. They'd been waiting for her to lead them, reassure them.

Lily suddenly remembered Joey's recrimination. *Weddings and funerals. You don't bother coming home for anything else.*

They were worried about her. And, in her big brother's case, worry translated into anger for making everyone worry.

She'd known but simply hadn't wanted to stop long enough to deal with those emotions. Had hoped they'd all buy in to her avoidance and not force the issue. She didn't have it in her to go into gory details. What was the need? Anyone with computer access likely knew all the sordid details of Lucas's stupidity. And that's exactly what it had been—stupidity. Lucas's ego being fed by a beautiful young woman who was using him, making his normal life suddenly crackle with excitement.

Only Riley would push. Gently, of course. Caroline would have, too, only not so gently. Big sisters didn't always feel the need to soften the edges of the truth.

"I'm fine, Riley. I'm moving on with my life. Not as heartbroken as I should be, which tells me everything I need to know." She admitted a deep dark truth she hadn't shared with anyone. "I'm relieved. That may sound crazy, but it's true. I got swept up by Lucas. He was charming and romantic and our lives meshed together, but I wasn't thinking clearly."

"We'd just lost Mike, Lily Susan. No one was thinking clearly."

She conceded the point. "Obviously Lucas wasn't right for the long haul, and I wouldn't want to be married to a man who lacked integrity."

"That's where the relief comes in?"

Lily nodded.

Riley wanted to be convinced. She wasn't. Lily could see it all over her lovely face. And felt guilty. Mike's death had left Riley a widow with two small children. She'd struggled so hard for so long, had learned to move on. That hadn't been easy.

"Don't worry about me. I'm fine. I'm a worker bee. I deal with things as they come up and roll with the punches. I promised I won't stay away so long again." Lily forced a lighter expression she didn't feel. When did she get to move on, to feel like she was on the top of her game again and not feel so burdened by everything? "Now, this is your special event, so we're going to come up with something brilliant."

"Good luck with that. All I can tell you is that I can't have a wedding inside this house. I just can't."

See, even strong people had limits. Maybe Lily wasn't strong. At least not like Riley. What kind of woman would be more worried about the impact on her bottom line than her broken heart?

A woman who was in love with the *idea* of love?

"Then we need other options," she said, taking refuge in the one thing that always made her feel strong. Or used to, anyway. "So talk to me. We'll come up with the perfect event. I promise."

"I hope so because I'm at a loss. All I want is a tasteful second wedding. Scott's on board with that. We want to share our day with all the people we love and make the start of our lives together special for the twins."

"Great—we have a place to begin. And we're still looking at Halloween weekend?"

"It's the only concession I've been willing to make. I want the kids to be a part of the planning, but they've got their wires crossed. Last year we hosted the patrol picnic at Halloween here. Everyone wore costumes and Scott gave hayrides. It was a total hoot. They want a repeat performance."

So, Camille and Jake were patrols. Lily thought about Max's daughter. A lucky little girl to have a daddy determined to love her enough for the mommy she'd lost. That much even Lily could see. A man with integrity. How refreshing.

"That's a little out there," Lily admitted, "but I've hosted Halloween events before. Believe it or not I once coordinated a wedding in a cemetery." She caught sight of Riley's rolling gaze in her periphery and laughed. "I know. But we managed to pull it off. You interested?"

"Um, no. I've tried selling them on some traditional ideas, but no luck. Not even a riverboat on the Hudson and you know how Jake loves boats." Casting an amused gaze at Lily, she set her mug on the windowsill and looked out at the yard.

The stables and paddock were behind the pond to the west of the hill that led to the forest, but there, peeping out from behind the rise... "What about the old barn?"

Mike's first order of business after they'd bought the farm was to build a stable closer to the house as a matter of convenience since he and Riley tended the horses and worked.

There was nothing actually wrong with the old barn except that it was ancient, and too far from the house. Maybe the structure was still sound, after so many years, and the smell of animals would have faded enough so no one would choke, especially after a commercial cleaning crew worked their magic.

Riley's eyes widened. "You think you can do something with it? It would be very picturesque."

It would be about the only place around here that wasn't seeping with Mike memories.

She raised her own mug in salute. "Why don't we go take a look?"

CHAPTER ELEVEN

MAX KNEW he was in trouble the instant he arrived home to find Lily Susan standing inside the reception hall rather than waiting comfortably in the drawing room or study.

The sight of her in a fitted cardigan dress made him catch his breath. That dress, so conservative at first glance, clung to her every curve and left a lot of leg bared. Long, shapely legs he couldn't seem to stop staring at.

So what did he do now? He lived in full-fledged dad-mode, hadn't pursued a woman since meeting Felicia. His dating skills had grown rusty years ago and he hadn't even considered polishing them up...until now. Even though every ounce of his common sense argued otherwise because there was no place to go with this woman.

She must have heard him because she turned around, her eyes focusing on him. Big, gorgeous, sultry eyes that evoked a response in the pit of his stomach, made him uneasy because of where his thoughts had been.

He was in so much trouble here.

"I'm sorry to have kept you waiting," he said automatically, although she'd actually arrived early for their meeting. "I hope James invited you to pass the time somewhere more comfortable."

As impressive as the reception hall was, with its dual staircases and crystal-cut chandelier, it had been designed by his great-grandfather to impress guests, and not to remain in for longer than it took to tug on a pair of riding boots.

Not that Lily Susan looked as if she wanted to sit. She still hadn't said a word. She didn't have to. Her exasperated expression clearly conveyed her mood. Snapping open the daily edition of the *Herald,* she held up his article.

"'Not just for Cinderella—organizing the stylish wedding.' Really, Max? Really?"

"It's a clever headline. I wrote it." Last night, in fact, after he and Madeleine had read *Higglety-Pigglety Pop,* her current favorite book, and he'd tucked her into bed. The article had made it to the newsroom minutes before the 10:00 p.m. cutoff.

"You truly have nothing better to do than document my every move?"

Max had no explanation for the way he felt right now— so ridiculously aware of her. The way irritation made her face beautifully unfamiliar as she stared him down. No easy feat as he stood taller than her despite her heels.

"You don't like the article?"

"I understand reporting on my arrival. Not that I think I deserved the front page, mind you, but that's your business. But what was the point of *this?* Do you intend to channel everything I do into print?"

"Everything you do with the wedding."

"Max, I'm trying to get the press to die down."

Striding toward her, he plucked the paper from her hand. "And I'm trying to capitalize on your celebrity. To give Raymond exposure. Not to mention it's a tough time for print media. I need to keep the *Herald* competitive. You're news."

So was the way he felt right now. Alive. Aware. Of *Lily Susan.* He was so close she had to tip her head back to meet his gaze, and the view from this close vantage point momentarily startled him. This woman was fire. She made his arms ache to wrap around her, to pull her close and feel every curvy inch of her pressed against him.

She would fit him perfectly, he knew, could feel it by the way they stood so close, their bodies almost swaying together in that crazy instant of instinctive awareness.

She felt it, too.

Suddenly Max knew. He could feel it in his gut where it counted, and he had to force himself to take a step back by sheer effort of will, force himself not to do exactly what he ached to do—pull her into his arms.

And change everything between them.

Lily Susan seemed flustered. This woman who played the media so skillfully. Why…because he'd invaded her personal space?

Max didn't know. *He* was flustered.

And like a total idiot, he started running his mouth. "I got the impression you were concerned about the sort of media that might cover this wedding, so I thought I'd give a professional slant. I thought it was the least I could do since you've taken on all this extra work."

Exhaling an unsteady breath, she took another step back. "My hero?"

Silence fell heavily between them. Their gazes locked across the distance, the silence like a physical wall between them. He was reminded of a deer stunned by car headlights. Only right now they were two deer and such physical awareness shone brighter than any light.

Max couldn't tell whether or not she was okay with what was happening. But he knew without question that he wanted to be her hero.

"You do owe me," Lily Susan said, recovering first and

creating even more space for good measure. "And I'm very glad to hear you appreciate the work I do since you seemed to be laboring under the misguided impression I snap my magic fingers, order two of everything and whip up spare weddings out of thin air."

He hadn't thought planning the wedding would be a big deal, true, but he wasn't stupid, either. He'd insulted her with that careless remark. That hadn't been fair, and he didn't like that she felt he'd undermined her work.

Some hero.

"My apologies, Lily Susan. I was uninformed about the amount of work involved. Felicia took care of our wedding, so I didn't know."

"Neither did I, which was frankly a bit disturbing given your mother's involvement in my operation." She motioned around them and shook her head sadly. "You could have had *this* wedding, but you two got married in a hotel. The thought still makes me twitch."

Max curbed the impulse to defend himself, since he knew exactly what she was doing—establishing distance between them. And for the moment, he was okay with that. He'd come *that* close to pulling her into his arms.

Striding to a bench, she retrieved her briefcase and withdrew a folder. "I understand your mother is out. Do you know when she's returning? I'm surprised she didn't want to be here."

"I'm sure she did, but she had a luncheon scheduled. She didn't cancel to prove she understands the difference between being a team player and an intrusive micromanager. She knows I think she wants to take over."

Lily Susan glanced at him, clearly aghast. "You didn't call her that, did you?"

He stifled a grin. "Not quite in those words."

"Oh, my. Another battle, hmm? And here I thought we'd come up with a reasonable working arrangement."

"Assessing motive is all part of dealing with my family," he admitted. "Why do you think I'm so fond of yours?"

That got a laugh, a light sound that managed to keep the awareness humming inside him.

She propped the briefcase on the bench, but kept the folder with her as he led her from the reception hall. "I went through your mother's ideas for how best to lay out our events and she has some wonderful ideas."

"Not surprising. She does have some experience entertaining here."

"You're quite the comedian today, aren't you, Max?" She cast him a sidelong glance. "I wanted you to know she's contributing. She's undertaking the task of getting this place shipshape to start with. Oh, and the flowers."

"Why don't we start this walk-through in the dining room?"

"Fine with me. We've got to comfortably accommodate a hundred and fifty guests. Your mother swears we can do it, but truthfully, I don't remember the dining room being so large. Of course it's been a long time since I've been here."

She strode along beside him, the top of her head parallel with his nose, the perfect height to remain constantly in his periphery. And he was aware of her. The way she took in their surroundings with such interest, the way her pace slowed almost imperceptibly whenever something merited her attention.

They finally entered the dining room.

"I really needed to see the place with fresh eyes." She reached inside her folder for a pen.

Max was fascinated by the way she transformed from

the flustered woman he'd wanted to hold to the professional she was right now. It was a persona, one he'd seen in photos and on video feed, but it was also a defense, he realized.

Lily Susan's comfort zone.

The place she went when she wasn't sure how to respond. He could see the real woman in there, still the smallest bit breathless as she prowled the perimeter of the room, measuring the space with the table plans in her folder.

"If you have any suggestions you want to incorporate, now would be the time. We'll be solidifying the theme today and if all goes as planned, we can confirm with Jamilyn and Raymond later."

"I gave them a heads-up," he said. "One or the other will be available. So you've got some ideas then?"

She circled the long table, her steps both graceful and light, making it so easy to enjoy the view she presented. "More ideas than time to tell the truth. With Overlook, well, let's just say this place is fertile ground for me."

There was no denying that. Anyone who visited her website could see proof of how well she'd always loved the grounds of this place. He'd always known, but now was the first time he ever thought to ask. "Why Overlook?

That didn't seem to be an easy answer for her. She met his gaze, clearly considering. "Because I couldn't get in to Springwood or Vanderbilt," she finally said. "My family was friends with you."

There was a lot more to that answer than she was sharing. Max could feel it in his gut. Lily Susan might be used to dealing with the media, but he was a media man. The instincts might skip a generation, which was why his father had gone into banking, but he could smell a story, wondered what she wasn't sharing.

Max hadn't realized Lily Susan's love of Overlook at the time, hadn't been interested in anything except hanging out where he always felt welcomed. He hadn't thought about how his friendship with Joey would impact everyone in their lives.

He'd only figured that out later during a particularly memorable discussion where his mother had accused him of replacing her with Rosie Angelica.

But for others their friendship had presented unexpected opportunities. For Lily Susan, a connection to Overlook where she could create fantasy weddings. That had amused his mother to no end and the two had struck up an enduring relationship based on business.

"Friendship is like that, I guess," he said simply.

She turned away from a cabinet that housed the china his great-grandmother had brought from Britain. "Like what?"

"It reaches out to everyone around it."

The faintest hint of a smile softened her mouth. She liked that. He could tell.

"I want to tie in to the history of this place," she said, bridging the distance between them, suddenly more at ease.

"That would be the Gilded Age. My great-grandfather completed the work in 1897, a year before Vanderbilt finished his place down the road."

The road being Albany Post Road aka Route Nine. He wanted to impress her, and the history of Overlook happened to be something he knew quite a bit about.

"There were about two hundred mansions along the Hudson at the time," Max explained. "And most of the owners, my great-grandfather included, fashioned their lifestyles as if they were European royalty. They pursued gentleman hobbies like yachting, horse breeding and hunting. And they tried to outdo each other with their country homes. Most went the same route Vanderbilt did—creating homes that rivaled those in Europe. They went crazy bringing things over—art, silk rugs, chandeliers, antiques, sometimes even entire rooms and buildings. My great-grandfather wasn't interested. He was all about redefining American royalty. That's why he used local craftsmen and quarried the stone from Bluestone Mountain across the river."

"I can't believe anyone thought the Vanderbilt Mansion was more palatial than Overlook. I don't see it. Never did."

Like every other kid who'd grown up in the area, she'd taken field trips to Vanderbilt Mansion and Springwood, probably more times than she could count throughout her school years. And now, as a woman, she'd traveled all over the world planning events in some of the most beautiful homes.

But she still liked his home best.

She moved to the Palladian-style windows and stared at the piazza that formed the inner courtyard of the house's three wings. That piazza created the entry point to the neat expanse of lawn overlooking the Hudson River that had given the house its name.

"Why, oh, why can't this be spring or summer?" she lamented more to herself than him.

He'd have obliged her if there had been a way, a juvenile urge to exercise amazing superpowers over the seasons, or greater influence over Raymond and Jamilyn's wedding plans. Since he had neither, he remained as he was, appreciating the sight she made as she jotted notes, silhouetted by the sunlight beyond the windows.

No one but the staff and his grandfather was around this time of day, so the house was quiet. The outside world didn't penetrate through the thick stone walls. His grandfather would be napping in his suite in the east wing and the staff would stay invisible unless summoned. So it was just Max and Lily Susan.

"I'm glad there's enough space to accommodate guests," Lily Susan said. "Every estate is so different. Sometimes it's a real challenge to figure out ways to adequately seat people."

Max supposed for the types of functions Lily Susan planned the accommodations could be interesting. "What did my mother suggest for seating? Because that table won't seat everyone. That much I know."

Lily Susan glanced at the table in question. "Not by a long shot, I'm afraid. Lovely as it is. Your mother suggested clearing out the long table and rearranging the room with smaller tables then opening the parlor for a buffet."

"That'll work? The ballroom's a lot bigger. We could have a seated meal in there. I don't mind a buffet personally, but the guest list is extensive."

"I know, but we don't want to get involved with the ballroom. It's almost impossible to break down the banquet and set up the reception quickly, which means we'd have to entertain the guests in the interim. It's stressful."

"I didn't consider that. Guess that's why you're the expert."

She nodded then flipped a page on her pad. "Gallery, please. Up the main stairs. The route our guests will take."

"Your wish." He gestured in what he hoped was a gallant bow, and Lily Susan moved past him into the hall. She assessed the route on their way upstairs, seeming to take in every detail.

The long gallery ran the length of the second floor and

JEANIE LONDON   113

provided possibly the best view of the river from inside the house. It was a unique feature, a room that was a bit of an oddity as a wall of floor-to-ceiling windows invited the vista inside Overlook, but didn't lend the room any conventional purpose, such as a drawing room or study.

"I don't know if you're aware," Max said. "This room was my great-grandfather's conversation piece."

"What's it used for now?"

"It's my grandfather's conversation piece now. He eats breakfast here every morning to watch the river traffic and invites friends to watch sunsets as they discuss business over port and cigars."

"I can certainly understand why," Lily Susan whispered reverently. "The view is more magnificent than I remember. And I adore your mother's idea about having the cocktail reception here. Oh, why can't this be spring?"

"Then you'd have to deal with the rain and the river blends right into the gray sky. Visually uninteresting. Summer, and everyone would roast. These windows absorb heat. If we were outside, we'd be dealing with mosquitoes at sunset. Not fun."

Lily Susan laughed, a heartfelt sound that chimed through the quiet room and filtered through him in such a physical way.

"My hero. Mosquitoes are not on the guest list." She smiled at him. "You know, Max, I site venues with my couples, but you're very handy to have around in this instance. Normally I do more research because I don't like surprises. But you're saving me all sorts of steps with your inside information. "

He didn't doubt that remotely. Lily Susan had become the most sought-after wedding planner in the world for good reason.

She tilted her head to the side, considering. "Okay,

I'm seeing rustic French countryside. I won't miss the romanticism of this setting, but I don't want to be obvious, either. Raymond's French and Overlook has your family's background to consider. You said your great-grandfather used local resources to build Overlook, but I happen to know he was from Montreal. You can see the influence in the structure, in the furnishings. Not overt, but definitely unique to Overlook. I wouldn't be able to consider this at Vanderbilt Mansion, where the architecture's Italianate and the furnishings were imported from Italy. What do you think?"

Okay, so maybe she hadn't needed his history lesson.

"Sorry, I have no idea what rustic French countryside looks like." Subtract a few more hero points.

"What does it sound like it looks like?"

"I'm visualizing the Loire Valley, which I've only visited once in my life. Close?" He didn't want to lose all his hero points in one shot.

She nodded, clearly pleased. "I'll bet what you're imagining isn't far off. Think elegant, yet not formal. Fields. Farmhouses. Bright flowers. All dressed up."

Resting a hand on his sleeve with a light touch, she guided him onto the second-floor landing. She stood behind him, lifting on tiptoes to place her hands on both sides of his face to direct his gaze.

"Now look straight ahead."

Max couldn't do a damn thing except brace himself because her nearness was having an effect on him. Her voice filtered through him. He could inhale her subtle scent on a breath. Feel the graze of her soft hands on his skin. Sense the warmth of her body radiating between them. Imagine the way her body would melt against his if he leaned back a little.

Only with the greatest effort was he able to shift his

focus to the decor. She'd aimed him in the direction of a corner he'd seen a thousand times yet never really noticed before.

"Tell me what you see." Her voice was a warm whisper against his ear, a sound that evoked a purely physical reaction.

"There's a cast-iron bench with a cream-colored cushion." He got the words out and was impressed with himself. "There's a mirror with a white frame made of some sort of distressed wood that my grandmother brought on a trip. Can't remember which one."

Her hands glanced against his skin again as she redirected his gaze, a soft, tempting touch. "What else?"

Some sort of silky scarf had been draped over the frame, held in place with big silk flowers. A pendant chandelier dangled crystal teardrops from the high ceiling.

"I see rustic French countryside."

She exhaled a laughing breath and stepped back so he could face her. Her beautiful features beamed with excitement. "See, it's already here. Hints of it in unexpected places. That's what's always so amazing about estates that stay in families for generations, or even those that remain privately owned—everyone contributes to the evolution. There's personality. I absolutely adore working in places like this. The events are always fresh, and because of the different floor plans and features, planning events is always challenging in a good way."

Max tore his gaze from her face, making an effort to slow the racing of his heartbeat. He could see the humidor his grandfather had picked up on a trip to Cuba decades ago. Lily Susan's corner, as he would think of it from now on, would have been his grandmother's handiwork, since his mother's tastes ran more along the lines of lavish luxury.

But he understood what Lily Susan meant about the evolution of a home. Places like Springwood, where President Franklin D. Roosevelt had lived when he wasn't staying at the White House, and Vanderbilt's Mansion had been donated to New York State for preservation. The lifestyle was frozen in time, unchanging as the buildings became museums.

That in itself was a unique perspective, one that gave Max his own fresh glimpse of a corner that he'd run past his entire life, and a new appreciation for the uniqueness of his home.

And of the woman who stood so close she was affecting his ability to think.

An image of that photo of Lily Susan on a yacht flashed in his mind. It had epitomized the celebrity Wedding Angel.

But not so much this woman who created blinders with smooth hands, the woman who viewed his house with such enthusiasm and artistic attention to detail.

"So rustic French countryside?" he asked, somewhat distracted.

"Definitely. I can see it." All hesitation had gone. Lily Susan knew what she wanted, and she turned to him then, eyes still molten, only now the gold of sunshine in one of her French fields.

"Madeleine's our flower girl, so she'll lend our setting authenticity. Can't you see her walking down the aisle, dropping rose petals, greeting the guests with *bonjour?*"

The image made Max smile. And in that moment he realized what it was about Lily Susan that captivated him— she wasn't what he expected.

The ambitious businesswoman who reminded him of

his family. The woman kissing her lover on a yacht in the French Riviera. The woman on her knees engaged in conversation with a five-year-old. The woman who could find one unique corner in a house with fifty-four elaborate rooms.

Who was the real Lily Susan?

Because this was the woman Max wanted. Maybe he wasn't supposed to overthink the moment. Lily Susan was home for only a few weeks. She had her life to resume once she rested and found her peace again.

Maybe he was only supposed to savor the moment where he felt alive in a way he'd feared he never would again, and enjoy remembering that he was more than a widower and a daddy. Maybe Lily Susan was nothing more than his wake-up call, so he could remember what it felt like to be a man again— A man who knew what it was to want a woman.

To remember how it felt to live.

After the demise of her engagement, maybe Lily Susan needed a reminder to get back to living, too.

CHAPTER TWELVE

LILY UNLOCKED the front door to her office. Max had followed her into town and was now circling the block to find a parking space. She had a grand total of two minutes to get a grip on herself. Right here. Right now.

Unfortunately, Mara wasn't in the office this afternoon to pose a distraction. She was off meeting with local vendors, running from a menu tasting with the caterer, to a vineyard, to the entertainment company. Ginger had called to say that the florist would be dropping by after her luncheon. Why couldn't Ginger have been at Overlook for the walk-through? Her presence would have forced Lily to keep her mind where it belonged—on business.

A deep breath.

Lily couldn't look to everyone else to curtail her ridiculous reaction to Max. This was her deal, a throwback to the days when her head had been filled with weddings. Of course her head was still filled with weddings, but back then most of her fantasy events had been set at Overlook with Max standing at the altar with his arm linked to hers.

Her perfect groom.

God, she hadn't needed the reminder. Of course she would be stuck in a time warp since she was finally planning an event at Overlook. All these lingering emotions made perfect sense.

What didn't make sense was her stupidity around Max. She wasn't thirteen anymore. Nor was he the reckless teenager he'd been then, either. The man was a widowed father.

She actually trembled when she remembered standing so close in the reception hall, close enough to kiss. If she'd lifted her face… Or was she remembering the way he'd been so close he'd blocked out the world with his broad shoulders?

Was that tremor because she was upset by her reaction? Oh, please, let him not have noticed.

Lily flipped on the lights. Deep breath. She could only deal with one problem at a time. Right now she had a wedding to plan. She needed to get her mind wrapped around the details, not on the man who was on his way up the steps, each long, confident stride proving no matter what twists his life had taken he remained attractive, his agile steps bringing him closer, ever closer…

"Hi again, Lily Susan." That husky voice again.

"Hello again, Max." She stepped aside. She was not going to notice how glossy his black hair looked in the afternoon sun, curling just enough to hint it was almost time for a haircut.

"Are you and Joey still playing in the town baseball league?" She kept the conversation normal while leading him into the viewing room.

He paused in the doorway. "Where do you want me to set up? Desk?"

"The desk is good. I'll spread out these books on the coffee table."

The viewing room had been designed for lengthy visits, with stylish, but comfortable furnishings. This was where Worldwide Weddings Unlimited's clients reviewed proposals and discussed ideas.

"To answer your question, we're not playing in the town's league this season," Max explained. "Scott recruited us for the police-department league. I'm surprised Joey didn't mention it. He's been pretty excited about the whole thing. Playing in a new league makes everyone more competitive. Especially with cops. Joey's been working out so he can keep up. Sarah's thrilled." Max set his laptop on the table then shrugged out of his coat.

Lily was there to take it from him, determined to focus. She would not be noticing the broad shoulders of any other groom. Of course, Max wasn't a groom.... "Joey does look good, but I'm afraid he isn't speaking to me at the moment."

"No comment."

"That's usually my line."

That got a chuckle from him, and the dimple made a cameo appearance. She was quick to put distance between them and headed to the coatrack in the foyer, then grabbed some design books from a shelf and booted the computer.

The audiovisual arrangement was the same in each of her offices because at this stage of the planning process, resources were important. Whether couples were listening to musicians, scanning table settings, surfing websites for registries or watching streaming footage of bridal runway shows, this was where Lily interpreted preferences.

But there was one more thing she needed to do before getting down to business. Heading into the kitchen, she brewed two double espressos and grabbed two bottles of water from the fridge. She needed fortification if she was going to survive a prolonged engagement with Max in close quarters. She needed a moment to regroup and refocus.

"Now we're ready to go." She found Max seated on the couch with his notebook computer logged onto Skype. She set the drinks on the table in front of him then sank onto the couch, as far away as she could while not appearing as if she wanted space between them. But she did. Oh, she did.

Lingering aftereffects of a teenage crush she could handle. But now was not the time to start viewing this man through adult eyes. Not when he'd only grown so much more handsome through the years, and more charming—when he wasn't bullying her into taking on a wedding she didn't want to plan or interfering with her vacation plans.

But he was such a foil to Lucas, who was always "on" for the media, always focused on networking and business opportunities. Lily had admired that, but Max was so easy to be around by comparison, with his quick laughter and caring attention to his beautiful daughter.

No, Lily couldn't gaze at Max through a woman's eyes. Not when she saw the man he'd become rather than the boy he'd been. She hadn't realized until this very second how much she counted on the distance of those years to temper her reaction to him.

Taking a sip of espresso, she sighed as the hot brew worked its magic with fortifying heat.

Max reached for his cup, clearly amused. "I'm discovering a new appreciation for your line of work."

"Glad to hear it." She raised her cup in salute. "The caffeine will alleviate the headache."

"You're planning to get one?"

"A side effect of this part of the process. But caffeine constricts the blood vessels and makes it easier to concentrate." And would remind her that she was a grown woman, not a teenager. "Think of this as preventative medicine."

Then she reached for the first of the display books. "Now let me give you an idea of what I have in mind."

"Do you want Raymond and Jamilyn?"

"Not yet. We'll go through my notes and have some solid ideas to present before getting them online. It'll save time. How does that sound?"

He nodded.

"Let's start with table displays. I want to create a traditionally romantic atmosphere for the bride and groom." On the computer, she pulled up photos of table displays with crystal and silver, floral arrangements swelling with lush peonies, chandeliers and candles on linen-draped tables. She tilted the display toward Max.

"Can you see?"

He inclined his head slowly, and beneath that striking gaze, they were a man and a woman sitting close on a sofa in a quiet room alone. Could he sense she was insanely aware of him? Oh, please, no, no, *no*.

"The whole theme will be very romantic, but here's where I want to veer from tradition." Leaning forward, she reached for a display book of photos from past events she'd coordinated. Even shifting her gaze away from him worked wonders for her heart rate. "I did a wedding once... Where is it?" She flipped pages. "I know exactly what I want. Under normal circumstances, I'd have an impressive presentation to show you."

"These aren't normal circumstances."

There was a threat in there somewhere, a threat that promised anything was possible.

"You wanted breakneck. You got it." She smiled.

Max smiled back.

Their knees were separated by only inches. One false move, and they would be touching.

Scrolling through photos, she fixed her gaze on the display book in front of her, but she could still feel him watching her, knew he hadn't taken his eyes off her.

"Ah, here it is." She turned the book toward him. "Jamilyn is having five attendants, not including our beautiful flower girl." She pointed to photos of long-stemmed bouquets. "What do you think of these?"

"Which one?"

"All of them."

He leaned in and suddenly they were shoulder-to-shoulder. And their knees did brush, lightly.

He didn't pull back. He didn't respond. But the silence only seemed to amplify their closeness. "I'm not seeing uniformity with our wedding party," she said in a rush to distract herself. "I'm seeing a varied color scheme for the flowers. Organic soft shades with more vibrant colors that pop. Violet. Crimson. Blush. Cream. I'll have the florist use different fabrics to drape the bouquets. I can come up with some possibilities for the attendants' dresses after Jamilyn chooses her dress. I'm thinking similar styles but not the same. Variations of a dusty purple, maybe. Nothing extreme like eggplant or lilac. Midrange shades in between."

"Purple was on Jamilyn's list of colors, right?"

Lily nodded and kept up with the babbling. "No orange. No yellow. No fuchsia. She was willing to entertain anything else."

"Do your clients supply these photos for you?" he asked, flipping ahead a few pages.

"I have a photographer on staff."

"This is so impressive, Lily Susan. These photos are art in themselves. You really do have quite an operation." Suddenly Max sat back and loosened his tie. He cracked open the bottled water and took a swig, leaving her grateful for the space between them even while her insides fluttered beneath his praise.

Silly, *silly* fool she was.

With renewed determination, she proceeded to the caterers. They combed through menu after menu, leaning over the coffee table until she could feel her back start to ache.

Their shoulders pressed together.

Their fingers brushed as each of them reached to turn a page at the same time.

Their laughter rang out in the quiet as they sprang apart.

They discussed table arrangements again. "Your mother provided the schematics for how best the caterers could work in the kitchen since it's in the basement."

"Did you know that in the gilded days of my great-grandfather, the staff sent up meals by dumbwaiter?"

Lily shook her head, mesmerized by his striking eyes, even though she remembered hearing that tidbit somewhere before. Why on earth couldn't she seem to get a grip on herself around him?

They discussed the merits of the various local caterers Mara had faxed in. With the Culinary Institute of America located in Hyde Park, she never lacked for innovative menus.

But Lily struggled to keep her head on the details. Instead her concentration focused on the intense physical reaction to a man to whom she had no business reacting, a man of fantasies from a long-ago past that had no place in the here and now.

She couldn't seem to rein herself in, though, and finally resorted to diversionary tactics. "Max, it's time. Will you please get our bride and groom online? Both, if you can. Preferably the bride if you can't."

For a moment, Max stared at her, as if some part of him was sorry to see her get up.

Then, to her surprise, he sent a text message on his cell

phone. Almost immediately, he told her, "Jamilyn needs to get to a computer. Should only take a few minutes."

Finally, abandoning all pretense of propriety, she sat on the floor with her legs curled underneath her. She couldn't sit close to him anymore. She didn't even care if he knew it.

"Bring your computer over here," she said. "That'll save me from having to relocate all this paperwork. I am truly not used to working with so little organization."

That striking gaze swept over her. "You're impressing the hell out of me."

Her insides melted at his praise. He leaned in to log onto Skype, to test the webcam function. She was trapped again in his nearness, a new position from where she could see the stubbled line of his jaw, the strong cords of his neck where he'd popped his top button.

The moment passed. Jamilyn logged on. Max's cell phone vibrated, a muted sound in the quiet. Sliding it from the case at his waist, he glanced at the display then got to his feet in a burst. "I've got to take this call."

Lily waved him off, glad for a reprieve to take a deep breath before the image of a lovely woman with a cloud of soft brown hair appeared on screen, a woman who looked nothing like Lily had imagined a second lieutenant would look like.

Back to business. Thankfully.

Jamilyn would be a beautiful bride. And the anxiety that felt like a pent-up breath inside eased some as Lily presented her suggestions and received more ideas about how Jamilyn envisioned her special day.

Instincts counted for a lot in Lily's line of work and she finally felt as if she was on solid ground. She could translate and create and generally work her magic when she had something to work with. God bless Skype.

She held up photos for Jamilyn to take a look at, attached others to email messages when there was more detail to be seen. They discussed ideas and Lily found Jamilyn delightful to brainstorm with. She was decisive and practical and very appreciative that Lily was willing to fill in the blanks because she couldn't be there to oversee the process herself.

"I trust you with the details, Lily," she said.

Six months ago so much confidence might not have meant as much to Lily, but given the way her luck had been running lately, she found herself appreciating the faith as much as Jamilyn seemed to appreciate Lily's effort.

"I can't believe the Wedding Angel is planning my wedding." Jamilyn giggled, a sound decidedly in contrast with the uniform. "I can't believe I get to sail in and enjoy the party without doing all the work. I've got mixed feelings about that. I should feel like I'm missing out, shouldn't I?"

"You'll be a guest at your wedding, which is exactly what you should be," Lily said, remembering the wording from Max's article. "That's why you hire a wedding planner. But you've got to promise me there won't be any delay with your arrival. You have to come in on Monday because we have licensing to deal with on Tuesday. I can have everything else ready—venue, catering, entertainment, costuming, press—but I can't apply for the marriage license. No power of attorney. No notarized affidavits. You and Raymond must appear before the clerk and then there's a twenty-four-hour waiting period. The end."

"We've cleared everything on our ends, so there shouldn't be a problem."

"Okay. We'll stay in touch. Now if you'll email me the

contact information for your attendants, I'll get with them to see when they can get here for final fittings. I'll post you with a recap so you have everything in print. Sound good?"

"Perfect." Jamilyn saluted with a smile. "And you'll send photos of gowns, too?"

"Hopefully I'll have them to you in the morning. If not look for them by the evening."

Lily signed off, rested her head against the couch and closed her eyes. Okay, they were moving along. She felt nominally more in control. Now, she had to get Denise—who had insisted on turning her bed into an office—to make some phone calls and start transcribing these plans. Then Lily had to check in with Carlisle at her Manhattan office to find out what was going on in Brussels. They hadn't spoken since this morning.

Deep breath.

"We're not done yet, are we?" Max's deep voice jerked her back to the moment.

She cracked an eyelid—only one so she didn't have to withstand a full assault on her senses—to see him walking toward her with those brisk, no-nonsense strides.

"I wish. You wish, too, I'll bet."

"No, actually." To her surprise, he dropped to the floor beside her and leaned back against the sofa. Then he smiled that dashing smile that started up the crazy flip-flopping inside all over again. "Wedding planning is more fun than running the *Herald*. Who knew?"

Lily certainly hadn't because it wasn't until this very moment that she realized she was in over her head with this man.

CHAPTER THIRTEEN

All About Angel—October 24
The Devil Always Gets His Due

Today a photo surfaced on the internet—check it
out at *CELEButante*—that raises an interesting
question. Has the Brazilian runway model (whom
we shall refer to from here on out as Demonico—
suits her well, doesn't it?) who busted up the fairy-
tale romance between the Wedding Angel and her
faithless ex-fiancé, followed the disturbing trend
among talentless females to use their eggs to attach
themselves to wealthy, powerful men and gain noto-
riety? (Reference articles: *Angry Veteran Actor and
Russian Sidepiece* and *Shifty Presidential Hopeful
and Brainless Sidepiece*.)

The All About Angel blog assumed—along with
most wedding watchers on the internet—that the
clock had simply run out on Demonico's fifteen
seconds of fame. (Bad publicity isn't always better
than no publicity, as the saying goes. Particularly
to designer fashion houses, where reputation is everything.)

But judging by *CELEButante*'s photo, there could
be another explanation. The world of haute couture
has no place for a runway model with a designer
belly. And pregnancy certainly explains why De-

monico hasn't been spotted at industry events in any of the four fashion capitals since news of her affair broke. Just when the Wedding Angel thought the dust had settled, she learns selling one's soul to the devil is never a good idea.

Look at the photo and decide for yourself. That belly—a real baby or a food baby? Cast your vote.

LILY FINISHED READING the latest post from the All About Angel blog. The BlackBerry display went dark.

Pregnant?

God, Lily hoped not.

For the sake of the baby. Babies deserved parents who loved them, not to have the circumstances of their conception plastered all over the internet. Lucas and his gross lapse in judgment were both adults who had made their choices. But any baby who resulted from their fling would be saddled with one parent who had no interest in children and another who would selfishly use a child to her own ends. And both who lacked moral fiber.

What kind of life would that be for a child?

She depressed the speed dial.

"Good morning," Mara said. "Did you read it?"

"I did."

"At least the blogger is trashing people who deserve to be trashed. *Demonico.* I'll bet you-know-who is swooning, which makes my vengeful heart happy. Yours, too. Admit it."

Demonico was a play on words for Catalina Delmonico, aka you-know-who's—Lucas's—Brazilian runway model/gross lapse in judgment. Lily's heart was not vengeful or happy.

"Well, there goes our theory that she's the blogger," Lily said.

"My money was on her, too. You don't think she's so desperate for attention that she'd hint at a pregnancy herself, do you? What about your ex-fiancé?"

Lily rubbed the sleep from her eyes, the thought coming at her the wrong way. Lucas hadn't been interested in having children. Lily hadn't been willing to say never, but her lifestyle certainly hadn't lent itself to kids. She loved kids but had been content to put the idea aside because kids deserved parents who loved them and whose lives revolved around family. Not parents who were not even in the same country two months running.

And definitely not parents who had no interest in being a couple—with each other, anyway.

"But why would Lucas invite this sordid sort of publicity?" Lily asked. "He's the one who cheated."

"He was interested in merging with you. Maybe he's trying to force you out so he can take over your end of things?"

Could she have been that wrong about Lucas's character? "But he's trashing his own reputation as much as he's trashing mine."

"Lily, even if he only picked over your connections like a vulture, he'd make out in the deal."

Her sight was adjusting to the darkness, and she could remember being a young girl lying in this very bed, waiting for the moon to come out, willing herself to sleep on the nights when she knew it wouldn't. She wasn't sure why the dark had always made her feel so alone, especially since Mike's room had been on the other side of the wall.

Then she remembered… "Hang on, Mara."

Flipping back the comforter, Lily stepped into her slippers and crossed the short distance to the dresser. And it was still there, inside the top drawer. A filigreed night-light in the shape of a bride. Lily wasn't surprised that her mother hadn't gotten rid of it. She'd been so thrilled to find it at a craft fair all those years ago.

"It was made for you, Lily Susan," she had said. "I knew you'd love it."

And Lily had. She couldn't remember why she hadn't taken it with her when she'd moved out of this house, all she could remember was being so eager to leave.

Now she couldn't even remember why.

Using her BlackBerry as a flashlight, Lily plugged in the light and chased the shadows away. She felt better.

Going to stand at the window, she yawned widely. God, she was tired. More tired than when she'd gotten here if that was even possible. "I don't see Lucas pulling something like this."

"You didn't see him cheating, either."

No argument there.

"Whether you-know-who is pregnant or not, my name shouldn't be linked to hers." Lily's annoyance gained steam. "Today is the Pingel/Bauer event in Brussels. My bride doesn't need this sort of nonsense on her wedding day."

"I don't think she'll be surfing the web before she walks down the aisle, so we're good."

"No, we're not good. Maybe she'll update her Facebook status or tweet after the ceremony. And even if our bride doesn't get online, one of her guests is bound to. And with the media paying attention to this idiot blogger, they'll probably give this post mileage. It's not fair."

"But what can you do?"

The inability to fix a problem rubbed wrong. "Someone knows who this person is. I'm going to call my attorney and have her advise me. Someone had to sign up for that account, and I don't care what privacy protection they have."

"Are you sure you want to do that?"

Lily rubbed her temples. Sun wasn't up yet, but the headache was. She needed caffeine. "No, I'm sure I don't want to do that, but I have to do something."

"If the media gets a hold of it…" Mara exhaled hard. "Lily, they'll be all over it."

"I keep stalling for that exact reason, but I'm tired of being kept emotional hostage. And the media is already all over this. If Elaine tells me I have to go to the police so they can find out who's responsible—" Lily leaned her forehead against the wall, resisted the urge to beat her brains out. "The police. I'm not thinking straight. I'm planning a wedding for my sister-in-law and she's marrying a policeman."

"Think he can help?"

"At the very least he'll help me figure out what my options are without getting the press involved."

"Sounds like a plan. Get 'em, Lily."

But Lily didn't so much feel encouraged as she did tired. Not when she realized why she hadn't thought about calling for advice before now. Not so long ago, she wouldn't have had to think. She would have simply picked up the phone and called. Mike.

CHAPTER FOURTEEN

"Are we almost there, Daddy?" Madeleine asked, eager to try on her flower-girl dress.

"Almost, I told you Madame Lily Susan's office was in town, near the *Herald*."

"It never takes this long to get there."

That made Max smile. He could hear the sulk and one glimpse in the rearview mirror revealed the mutinous expression his daughter wore. "There's the bridge. We're almost there."

The Poughkeepsie Railway Bridge spanned the Hudson River. It had been built in the mid-1800s, an engineering marvel during an era when people relied on ferries to cross the river. The bridge had remained in service until a few decades ago, when a fire had ended its long and illustrious career.

But like much of downtown Poughkeepsie, the bridge had been given new life recently when it had been refurbished into a pedestrian walkway with a majestic view of the river and the cities on both sides.

Madeleine wasn't interested, and not even a discussion of the day's happenings at school could distract her, and by the time he pulled in front of Lily Susan's office, his daughter was sliding out of her seat belt and readying to hop out.

He managed to keep a grip on her as they crossed the street. Max wasn't sure whether it was the dress itself, knowing Camille would be having her dress for Riley's wedding fitted or the mystique of visiting Madame Lily Susan, but his daughter's enthusiasm was barely contained.

In contrast, he was bracing himself to see Lily Susan. To feel the gut-wrenching awareness the minute he laid eyes on her. To watch her blush beneath his gaze and try to keep distance between them as they reviewed musicians' demo CDs and tasted wedding cakes and sampled champagne and wines to complement the menu.

To wreck his whole day because he couldn't think about a damned thing except how much he wanted to end this torture, pull her into his arms and kiss her. *Finally* kiss her.

He was attracted to her. She was attracted to him. But she wasn't ready. He wasn't wrong about this, and if he made a move too soon, it could have long-term repercussions. Not only wouldn't he stand a chance with her, but family affairs would also be agony. He'd only been kidding himself that they might enjoy a few stolen moments together before she left. No way would that be possible. They'd be tripping over each other for the rest of their lives. Even though she didn't come home often, those ties between their families ran deep. He couldn't stand the idea of a future of being thrown together and having to pretend she didn't matter.

Between him and Lily Susan a kiss would not be just a kiss. It would be so much more. He knew it deep down, couldn't pretend otherwise. He had no clue what the future might hold—nothing seemed possible, or practical, given their situations—but he knew how he felt. Knew he wanted a chance. No matter how much he burned for her, his timing had to be spot on.

He didn't want her to only be attracted to him physically—he wanted more. And if he had to wait…he'd have to wait. Unfortunately, they were working on borrowed time.

Five weeks and counting.

Then she'd be gone. And he'd lose his opportunity.

"Let me ring the bell," Madeleine said.

"Please." He reminded her automatically while stepping aside so she could stretch up on tiptoes to press the doorbell.

Her eyes widened and she gasped when chimes sounded, and he couldn't stop himself from running a palm over her silky hair. She saw beauty in even the smallest things, and for so long, viewing the world through Madeleine's perspective had been his lifeline.

The door opened and Lily Susan was there, looking as lovely as she always did, a bit breathless as if she'd rushed to answer. Today she'd swept her hair back, giving him a better look at her finely boned face, her jaw perfectly curved to invite his fingers to cup that smooth skin…

"Bienvenue, mes amies." She spread her arms wide in welcome then she and Madeleine exchanged pleasantries that even Max could understand with his own limitations.

Lily Susan motioned them in. "I've got another very excited young lady—and her not-so-thrilled brother—upstairs in the workroom."

Madeleine scooted around Lily Susan, but Max was forced to wait until she moved to get inside, feeling somewhat at a loss as his French wasn't as up to snuff.

"Bonjour." He knew that one.

Lily laughed, a sound as lyrical and lovely as she was. He liked the sound of her laughter. Hadn't thought to enjoy something so simple, or so beautiful, again.

"I appreciate your effort, Lily Susan. Madeleine doesn't have many people to practice with."

"Neither do I." That smile again. "Did you understand?"

"A little. You're well. She's excited. Beyond that…"

Lily Susan inclined her head approvingly. He moved to pass her, and there it was again, that rush he felt the instant they stood close, the awareness of every inch of her as if his own body had been wired to react.

The reaction was so physical, he instinctively glanced at her, sure that she felt it, too. Giving her head a slight shake, she seemed to be pushing aside the feeling. Her chest rose and fell on a fluttering breath.

No question she felt it, too.

But Lily Susan was so skilled at suppressing her feelings. Would she ever be ready to act?

"Thanks so much for bringing Madeleine by, Max," she said as if the moment had been nothing more than a figment of his imagination. "Outfitting the kids all at once will save some time."

"Not a problem."

"Riley had to run back to the *Herald.* She didn't think she'd be long. There was breaking news that required some decisions and some dummies to work on. At least I think that's what she said. Does that sound right?"

He nodded.

"Good. She told me to tell you everything is under control. You don't need to make an appearance."

"Okay, then. Thanks."

They both sounded so casual, so in control. But the distance between them made all the difference in the world. His chest eased up its death grip around each breath.

Lily Susan called out in a singsong voice, "We've got guests."

Taking Madeleine's hand, she climbed the stairs, leaving him to follow behind, his gaze clinging to her shapely bottom as she made her way up with light steps. The pants she wore were tailored, not tight or clingy, but those pants didn't leave a curve to his imagination.

Fortunately, distraction came in the form of Riley's kids and a seamstress.

"Hey, Mr. Max." Jake extended a hand and Max shook, stifling a smile. This kid took being the man of the family seriously and had ever since Mike died. Max wondered how he'd make peace with Scott moving onto his turf.

"How's the fitting going?" he asked.

"They're killing me. I don't know why I can't wear my baseball uniform. Pop Scott is wearing his uniform."

"I heard that, Jakie, and I'm telling Mom what you said." Camille didn't miss a beat.

"I'm pretty sure Mom already knows how Jake feels." Lily Susan diffused that exchange with laughter and redirected impressively fast. "Wait until you see Madeleine's dress. *N'est-il pas belle?*"

"Oui, madame!"

Jake shook his head and looked mournfully down at the shiny dress shoes that apparently went with his suit. "I don't know how they expect me to ride in the hay wagon in *those.*"

"I feel your pain, buddy," Max whispered.

That got a smile, at least.

"But what's this about a hay wagon?" Max asked. "Last I heard you were planning a wedding."

"It is a wedding, Mr. Max," Camille explained. "It's a Halloween wedding in the barn."

Jake nodded. "Hay, stinky horses and everything. For real."

"Wow," Max said. "Guess that's what you get when you hire a fancy wedding planner."

"We're not having stinky horses at Uncle Raymond's wedding, are we, Daddy?" Madeleine asked.

"I don't think so. Let's ask. *Sommes-nous,* Lily Susan?" He knew that one, too.

"Not one stinky horse," Lily Susan confirmed to his daughter's obvious relief. "Now come tell me what you think of Camille's dress. Doesn't she look gorgeous? She picked it out herself. *Que pensez-vous?*" she asked Madeleine.

"Elle est belle."

Camille shifted her gaze between them. "What does that mean?"

"It means, little twinnie, that you look beautiful."

Camille nodded, but glanced between them again, clearly unsure if she liked that someone so much younger could do something she couldn't. Or maybe it was that Madeleine shared something with Aunt Lily Susan that excluded Camille.

The seamstress had been pinning a hem and abandoned the task good-naturedly so Camille could bask in some appreciation. Everyone oohed and aahed appropriately over the green dress that he guessed was casual enough for a barn wedding.

"How's she going to climb into the hay wagon in that?" Max asked Jake, who spread his arms in entreaty.

"I hope you're wearing shorts under that dress, Camille."

"Shut up, Jake."

"What color nail polish, do you think, Madeleine?" Lily Susan narrowed her gaze at him, a silent reprimand for egging on her nephew.

Madeleine cocked her head to the side, considering. "Orange, or maybe yellow."

"I said orange, too." Camille beamed. "My bouquet has orange and yellow flowers in it."

Madeleine seemed pleased that Camille approved and stood her ground alongside when the seamstress moved in to finish pinning. Max took a seat on a bench where he could view the proceedings from a distance.

The seamstress's name was Frances. She didn't seem much older than he was himself, but appeared quite skilled at what she did. She made quick work of pinning and tucking with Lily Susan's help.

"So you've decided to have the wedding in the barn?" Max asked. "That's an interesting choice."

"Atmosphere," Lily Susan said. "We're calling it the Halloween event. We didn't want anything as passé as costumes, but we still want the theme. Right, guys?"

Both kids nodded.

"We're decorating the barn with all kinds of autumn stuff. Pumpkins and leaves and cold apple cider."

"And we're having a soda-pop bar," Camille informed them. "A candy bar, too."

"And stinky horses," Jake added.

Lily Susan winked at him. "But no stinky horses inside the barn. They're only for the hayrides. Wouldn't be a Halloween event without hayrides, would it?"

"Nope."

"Tell them about the cookies, Aunt Lily Susan," Camille urged.

"We're going to have the best party favors ever. Sugar cookies in the shapes of letters. We're going to spell messages and put them in pretty boxes with ribbons. After the guests figure out the message, they can eat the cookies."

"And I get to eat all the broken ones," Jake said, and that look on his face pretty much guaranteed there would be broken cookies. Lots of them, if Max guessed right.

"You know, Madeleine, we could use your help with those cookies, if your dad will let you come."

Madeleine spun toward him, positively frantic for permission. "I can help. Can't I, Daddy?"

"That sounds like fun. You should probably find out when and where they'll be baking," he suggested, then kept his mouth shut and let his daughter get the details.

Lily Susan explained how they were going to take over Rosie's kitchen—with her assistance, of course—to bake letter cookies for fifty guests.

There was no doubt in Max's mind that Lily Susan could have hired a bakery for the job, but he liked how she involved the kids. He hadn't expected that from her, but there was no denying she not only seemed to enjoy the twins, but was also good with them. And her caring extended to his daughter.

"Can Madeleine help us with the pinecones, too?" Camille asked.

"Of course, if she'd like," Lily Susan said. "We're decorating with them. The barn. The centerpieces—"

"We're going to tie little tiny ones on name cards and on the toasting glasses." Camille could barely stand still and Frances steadied her with a hand before she fell off the dais.

Lily Susan smiled. "Memo to self—remember the pinecones. I don't have them yet, and I know Mara doesn't."

"We have pinecones, Madame Lily Susan," Madeleine said. "You can pick them near the river in our yard. We have baskets to carry them. And we even put peanut butter and birdseed on them for the squirrels and birds."

"Cool," Jake said.

Max wanted to intervene to let Lily Susan off the hook with his overly eager daughter. He wasn't thrilled about the idea of another personal visit to Overlook with the memory of their walk-through still fresh. The memory of how he almost pulled her into his arms. He knew Lily Susan didn't have the time for a personal visit. Not with two weddings and cookie baking.

"That's so generous of you, Madeleine. And we do need lots of pinecones. Think the squirrels will mind sharing?"

Or maybe she did have time.

"Oh, no," Madeleine responded earnestly.

"Then thank you so much for the lovely invitation. Don't you think we should probably check with your dad?"

Madeleine ran to him, imploring. "Can we, Daddy? Can we?"

Max stared into his daughter's beautiful green eyes, struck, as he always was, by the disconnect between being an adult and a good parent. All too often the two didn't line up. Like right now when he hated to be the bad guy, hated disappointing Madeleine with even the tiniest heartbreak. Especially when the reason was nothing more than he didn't want to test his restraint around Lily Susan.

Then again, how was he to convince Lily Susan to let down her guard if they didn't spend more time together?

"If Madame Lily Susan can squeeze us in, then she's welcome to come." He tossed the situation back, a challenge. "She's supposed to be relaxing on her vacation."

"Yay!" Madeleine spun around. "Will you come, please?"

There was no way for Lily Susan to refuse such a polite invitation, even if she'd been able to resist his challenge. *"Oui."* She narrowed her gaze over the kids' heads before getting back to business. "Feels good, little twinnie?"

Camille hopped from the dais then twirled to make the dress fan around her. "Perfect."

"Great. You couldn't possibly look more beautiful. Start thinking about how you'd like to wear your hair. We'll have the stylist in for a dry run next week, okay?"

Camille nodded, and Lily Susan stepped away from her niece and crossed the room with quick steps. "Your turn, Madeleine."

Max heard his daughter's quick intake of breath as she squeezed her eyes shut tight. Lily Susan made a great show of extracting the garment bag from a wardrobe.

She unzipped the bag to reveal a white formal dress. There was reverent silence. Even from Jake.

"Okay, ready?" Lily Susan asked with a smile.

"Oui, madame!"

"Then take a look."

His daughter gasped, and to say she was thrilled would have been a dramatic understatement. "It's mine?" she breathed on an exaggerated sigh.

"Oui." Lily Susan held it up in front of her. "You have to try it on so Madame Frances can make it fit properly. Do you want your daddy to help you? We have a dressing room."

Madeleine didn't even glance his way. "No—you."

Lily Susan smiled and they disappeared together.

"So when are you going to try on the girl's dress," Jake asked.

"You wish, dude."

He snickered. "Yeah."

"Sorry to break it to you, Jake, but it's bad luck for any man to try on the bride's dress before the wedding. Can't have bad luck now, can we?"

"Why not?" The roguish look on Jake's face gave Max a new appreciation for Riley. This one had to be tough to keep a lid on. Max hoped Lily Susan was right and this was a boy thing or else he was in trouble himself. Madeleine already had him wrapped around her finger without trying. God forbid she figured out how to try.

"Ta da." Lily Susan emerged from the dressing room, arms spread as she introduced the flower girl.

Madeleine appeared, in all her white-satin glory, her glossy dark curls swinging as she twirled for her appreciative audience. After the oohs and ahs died down, she explained, "It's just like Aunt Jamilyn's dress."

"A perfect miniversion for the perfect flower girl." Lily Susan got Madeleine up on the dais for Frances to size.

"Is it bad luck for a guy to try on a wedding dress before the wedding?" Jake asked.

"You'd like that, wouldn't you, little rodent?" Lily Susan grinned and Max suspected she'd heard the entire exchange. "Tell you what we can do. Since we don't want bad luck, but even I think Mr. Max deserves to try on a wedding gown, we'll go for the next best thing."

Max wasn't sure what to make of that, but it didn't sound good. She went into the wardrobe and pulled on a top hat and some sort of lacy veil.

He knew what she planned to do before she got to him and would have protested on principle alone, but Lily Susan was suddenly in his personal space, and the only thing he was aware of was the slight warmth of her body as she stretched forward to fit the tiara on his head, the brush of her fingertips against his hair as she arranged the veil. Her full smile was so close that all he'd have to do was shift his balance for their mouths to meet.

Their gazes met for an instant, and Max knew right then and there that he wasn't the only one in danger here.

Then she straightened and plunked the top hat on her head. "Grab my cell phone, twinnies. I've got to have something to tweet today. Might as well lighten up the mood with a laugh at my expense."

His expense, too, it looked like. But Max didn't mind one bit as the kids vied to get the perfect shot, and he posed with a goofy smile on his face.

But as Jake and Camille discussed which was the best photo for their aunt to tweet, the phone rang.

"Jake, just look at the ID and see who it is," Lily Susan said, not bothering to get up from where she was handing Frances pins again.

"Just a number."

"How many numbers? A lot?"

Max knew what she was asking—if there was a country code.

"Yeah."

"Dang." She cast an apologetic look at Frances and started stabbing pins into the big pincushion. "I have an event in Brussels today. I can't ignore it. Pick up, Jake, please. Tell them I'll be right there."

She was on her feet when Jake pressed the phone against his shirt and whispered, "It's Lucas. He wants to talk to you."

If Max hadn't been watching, he'd have missed Lily Susan's reaction completely. She blanched at the name.

The ex-fiancé, and soon-to-be father if media reports were correct.

But the reaction was gone as quickly, and Lily Susan was smiling at her nephew. "Thanks, I'll take this call out here."

She sailed through the door, and Max could hear her light tread on the steps, knew she didn't want to be overheard.

She wasn't gone long, but the smile didn't return with her.

"Important?" he asked in a low voice.

"No, not anymore."

Max guessed what she meant. So did Jake, too, apparently. His eyes widened. "Was that the deadbeat, no-good ex-fiancé?" he asked, excited.

"Jake!" Camille nailed him with a blow on the arm that made him jump away. "You're not supposed to repeat that. Uncle Joey said." She scowled at her brother and went to stand with Madeleine. "Boys can be so stupid."

Madeleine nodded in a show of solidarity.

Lily Susan ruffled Jake's spiky blond head. He rubbed his arm where Camille had punched him, and Max credited Riley with the fact Jake hadn't swung back. "It's okay, kiddo. Your Uncle Joey's right on this one."

"Then why were you going to marry him, Aunt Lily Susan?" Camille asked.

Lily Susan sighed. "Because we worked well together, and I thought that was enough."

Her answer obviously satisfied Camille's curiosity, but left Max considering what she said.

We worked well together.

Had she meant as a couple or literally? They had worked in the same business, and for some reason, Max suddenly couldn't see the woman who had put a veiled tiara on his head to amuse her nephew, or who would make time to pick pinecones to please a little girl, being part of a couple with a man who'd betray her.

Max didn't know. But to his surprise he did recognize something familiar—grief. The signs were all there. The way she drowned herself in work, the breakneck pace she kept, the constant running from family and avoiding any discussion of her broken engagement. True, Lily Susan worked nonstop on a good day, but she hadn't come home in forever. Max wasn't wrong about this. He knew the symptoms intimately.

He caught her after she herded the twins into the dressing room. "Listen, if you don't have the time to collect pinecones tomorrow, don't worry. I'll explain to Madeleine."

Then Max waited, wanting her to take him up on his offer, but hoping she didn't.

"A chance to walk along the Hudson on a Sunday?" She smiled. "I wouldn't miss it. This is my vacation."

He inclined his head, appreciating that she didn't want to disappoint his daughter. A lot, in fact, because as he watched Madeleine twirl in the mirror, her excitement tangible, the sight grabbed him by the throat. She was so starved for a woman's attention.

True, he'd made sure she'd had women in her life. Claire, whom he'd brought over from France and lived at Overlook with them. There was Rosie, Felicia's mother, his own mother, Sarah, Riley, Caroline. And each of them fitted in as a small piece of the puzzle, but not one of them could replace Felicia.

Now here was Lily Susan, with all her savvy around the kids, who was both the woman he wanted and the woman he didn't want.

He already had a family of businesspeople. He wanted a real family. That had always been part of the attraction to the Angelicas. He loved his own family, cared about each of them, but he wanted more than business and money to be the glue holding them together. And for one fleeting moment he'd had it, too.

He understood Madeleine's attraction to Lily Susan. She was larger-than-life yet a kindred soul—an Angelica who spoke French and created magic. Max was sure the package couldn't get any more attractive in his daughter's eyes.

Even so, Lily Susan didn't seem all that happy to him. Sure, she was ambitious and motivated enough to build an impressive business at a very young age. But she had sacrificed all the important things in life for the things that didn't ultimately make people happy. Had she realized that after her ex-fiancé's betrayal? Or did she think she was happy with her jet-setting, nonstop working life?

If she thought so, Max would have to change her mind.

CHAPTER FIFTEEN

LILY GLANCED one more time at her BlackBerry display.

Wedding preparation is so much fun! Tasting yummy cake. Sipping lovely bubbly. Visiting amazing locations. Is there any place more beautiful than walking along the Hudson River on a brisk, sunny afternoon? There's no place like home;-)

But she really wanted to tweet:

Mental exhaustion robs the joy from everything good in life. It muddles the senses, makes everything feel like a catastrophe and makes it damned near impossible to withstand the charms of even the most unsuitable of men. So skip whatever you've got on the agenda today. It's Sunday. Take a long nap.

She pressed the send button then stared at the doorbell. She couldn't bring herself to ring it. Not yet. All she wanted today was a little peace and quiet and a lot of pinecones. Was that really so much to ask?

The only thing working in her favor right now was the fact that it was Sunday, which meant she probably wouldn't hear from her attorney. Or Lucas, either, with any luck, which she hadn't had all that much of lately, admittedly. Scott had advised that the best bet was to have her attorney draw up a cease-and-desist letter to send to the hosting company of the blogging service. Once the company knew they were facing potential legal action, they would investigate what was written on the All About Angel blog and likely take it down.

A lot of phone calls and faxes later, Elaine had finally sent the letter. Lucas didn't feel this action was nearly enough, as he'd told her during yesterday's telephone conversation, but Lily didn't care what he thought. She grilled him to find out if he was behind the All About Angel blog, but he'd called to let her know that he didn't like being dragged into this mess by some random blogger and planned to file a lawsuit. He didn't care that this blogger was trashing her reputation, but he cared now that he'd been dragged in. Panic seemed a natural response to impending fatherhood. Good old Lucas. Lily didn't think his anger was an act.

God, she was tired.

She hit the doorbell. Within a minute the door opened and the butler appeared.

"Please come in, Ms. Angelica," he said, stepping aside so she could enter. "Mrs. Downey asked me to let her know when you arrived."

Lily opened her mouth to tell him she was actually here to see *Miss* Downey, but she would have had to raise her voice because the man had already retreated halfway across the reception hall.

Lily went into the adjacent salon. She'd always liked the double parlor arrangement of these rooms. They were actually two twin rooms—the drawing room on one end and the music room on the other, each flowing into the other through a wide archway with elaborate moldings. Lily had seen the design before, in Europe, New Orleans and other places that had now blended into memory. At least she still had the energy to appreciate decor.

She stopped in front of the French doors beside a marble fireplace. Forested acres of the estate blocked any view of the river from this part of the house. The vista here was wilder than most of the grounds, less manicured with the lawn melting easily into the forest. Untamed patches of shrubbery and fallen autumn leaves created small oases beneath the splintered sunlight from the trees overhead.

This place had once held such magic for her.

She'd planned a wild woodland wedding with attendants dressed as fairies on this very spot. She'd always been the bride in these elaborate ceremonies. And Max the groom.

Shoot. Her. Now. Even she couldn't explain why Overlook had inspired her. She knew it wasn't the stuff—the big house, the cars, the fancy furniture. Even now she wasn't much of a stuff person. She had a nice apartment on the Upper East Side, but it wasn't large by anyone's calculation—especially not Lucas's. But Lily loved the place. She had an amazing view of the park, and for the amount of time she spent there, her apartment suited her lifestyle. She didn't even own a car.

Funny, but Overlook hadn't diminished in her mind. She remembered the first time she'd visited her elementary school as an adult. The chairs had seemed teeny tiny and hallways that had once felt endless she suddenly crossed in a few strides.

But she could still look at these grounds and envision a thousand ways to create fantasies. Maybe her attraction came down to nothing more than that it was the first place that had opened her eyes to circumstances so different than those she'd grown up in, circumstances where anything and everything had seemed possible.

She supposed she had Max to thank for that.

He had bridged the distance between two very different worlds for Lily. If the heir to the Downey dynasty could sit on her living-room floor playing Nintendo with Joey or kill her dad at chess, then there was no reason why she had to wait for school field trips to visit grand estates like Overlook, or the Vanderbilt Mansion or President Roosevelt's Springwood, no reason why she couldn't reach for the stars and grab them.

"Lily, dear."

She turned as Ginger swept into the room, a woman at one with her surroundings. She was understated luxury personified with her tailored pantsuit and stylish scarf.

"I know you're here for an outing with Max and Madeleine. Everyone heard all about it at breakfast."

From Madeleine, Lily assumed, since Max had seemed pretty eager to get her off the hook for the pinecone excursion. Was he as eager to avoid their chemistry as she was? There was no denying it when the air between them practically sizzled. She knew that's all it was—physical attraction. She'd been alone since Lucas, spending all her time working. As usual. And Max was a very handsome, very charming guy whom she'd once fantasized about.

Was it really any wonder she responded to him? But she wasn't looking for a fling. She wasn't even looking for a man. She didn't want to think about men—that only brought painful memories of Lucas and how poor her judgment had been. Sheesh. She could have married him and made the biggest mistake of her life. What had she been thinking? Lily didn't know, but she'd learned her lesson the hard way and she wasn't about to make another mistake.

Felicia had died two years ago. As much as Max had adored his wife, he was still a man, and from what her mom had said, he hadn't so much as dated since.

Still, she liked that Madeleine was so excited and was

glad to have made the time for her. Maybe this could be her vacation. An afternoon vacation. Why not?

"I hope you don't mind that I had James head you off, dear. There are some details I wanted to discuss and I didn't want to hunt you down tomorrow when you're already here now."

Hunt down being the operative term, since Lily's life sans bridal crew had degenerated into one of nonstop errands.

"Of course not." She kissed Ginger's cheek. "What's up? No problems with the florist, I hope?"

For all the mock weddings she'd planned on these grounds in her youth, Lily didn't possess the tactical expertise Ginger had entertaining in her own home, a resource she simply couldn't overlook. And to Ginger's credit, she'd been contributing as a part of the team.

"Come with me, dear, and I'll show you."

Ginger led Lily into the dining room and Lily immediately spotted the details up for discussion.

Both ends of the table had been laid out with formal place settings of the same china, silver and glassware. But the different centerpieces changed the entire look. One had the organic shades they'd chosen for the wedding— dusty violets, earthy crimsons, lush greens, blushes and creams. The florist had cleverly created a harvest arrangement with real eggplants, bunches of purple and red grapes set amidst crimson roses and lush greenery that was both colorful and rustic.

The second setting had only blush peonies swelling from crystal vases with wood accents and greenery. The display lacked color, was almost stark, but when set against the china, silver, crystal with the teardrop chandeliers above, the effect was rustic yet very elegant.

"Oh, my," Lily said. "I see."

"I knew you would. I know we've already chosen the colors, but when I got the florist here, I didn't like the color on the table nearly as well as I thought I would."

"That peony centerpiece is definitely simpler, but if they line the center of the tables with all the silver and crystal, the effect will simply be stunning."

Ginger nodded. "I thought so, too."

She went to the sideboard and retrieved two votive holders made of fragile clear glass. "If you agree with the peonies, then I think we should add these." She set them on the table and lit both. "Lots of them sprinkled all the way down the tables. I like how they sparkle against the silver, and we'll need the light. Trust me, this room will become dark after the sun sets."

Lily folded her arms over her chest and imagined the dressed tables around the room. "I do trust you, and I think the room will be gorgeous. But what about the gallery for the cocktail hour? Can we use harvest centerpieces there? I really like this."

A smile spread across Ginger's face. "And that's exactly why we've made such a good team all these years. Attention to detail. We're kindred souls because that's exactly what I was thinking."

"Wonderful then. Let's do it."

Ginger was obviously pleased with the response, so eager to have her contributions acknowledged that Lily felt another pang for having ignored this location for so long. Even Mara came into the city on a regular basis for inquiry review meetings, and had the chance to feel as though she was a part of the Worldwide Weddings Unlimited family, even if her operation was limited in scope. Not so with Ginger. The renovation had been the first time that she'd had a chance to feel included for four years.

That said, Lily also knew the situation was compli-
cated. While she'd known Ginger wanted to keep a hand
in the office, there had been no way to know that Ginger's
involvement in the renovation would spark this interest
to be involved in more than the financial aspects of their
operation.

Lily hadn't known because she hadn't been around.
There had been too much going on for so long. Was that
why she hadn't felt inspired in so long?

She took a deep breath when Ginger stepped out of the
room to arrange with her butler to transport the harvest
arrangement to the gallery.

She refused to stress out so early in the day, but that
muscle below her eye was twitching again.

True, she was busy, but too busy? The only thing different in her life the past few years had been her involvement with Lucas. He'd been the perfect solution, the
perfect opportunity to combine business with pleasure,
to have a friend...well, a business partner with benefits.

To have a life.

That came at her sideways.

Lucas hadn't been the perfect groom in any way.

"Have you made a decision about the ceremony yet?"
Ginger asked on their way upstairs.

"No, but we've got to. We're almost out of time. I think
our best option is the double parlor. We could have the
ceremony in the ballroom, but then we'll be scrambling
to set up the room for the reception during dinner. Not
sure why we'd want to do that when I very much like the
idea of Jamilyn and the wedding party making grand
entrances down the staircase. Getting the musicians at
a vantage where they can see the procession might be
tricky, but— If only the weather was warmer. Every wedding I ever envisioned at Overlook involved the grounds."

"We could even work with this weather," Ginger agreed. "But in another month, even an unseasonably warm day will still be too cold for much time outdoors."

Another month. With still so much to do. Her eye twitched again for good measure. The whole point of this outing with a little girl and her dad for pinecones had been to do something enjoyable while accomplishing something, too.

More combining business with pleasure.

All she'd done was work since she'd gotten home. Nonstop. No slumber parties with Caroline. No movie nights with Riley and the twins. No sit-downs with Joey to address whatever his beef was with her.

No time to visit Mike at the cemetery.

By sheer effort of will, Lily wrested her thoughts on track. "Which is why your idea about the gallery works. And if the weather is unseasonably decent, we'll throw open the French doors in the double parlor and ease up our space restraints."

"Invite the outside inside."

"Exactly."

Ginger slanted a sidelong glance and flashed that pleased smile again. "I'm glad you're back, dear. You've been missed."

Lily hadn't expected such candor from Ginger and wasn't entirely sure how to respond. She settled on honesty. "Thank you. And I've been missing all too much myself. I hadn't realized it. Not until this visit."

"You sound surprised, dear. You've devoted yourself to establishing your reputation and building your business. That sort of dedication comes with a price, but now you're established. You don't have the same demands on your time, and it takes time to notice that things are changing."

Lily wondered if that's what Ginger had been doing in

her own life. Involved with her family, rearing children, keeping up with charitable endeavors and social connections. Then her boys were grown and starting their own families. That had freed a chunk of Ginger's time. Was it any wonder she'd embraced the renovations with both hands?

After James had relocated the harvest centerpiece, Lily asked him to let Max and Madeleine know she would be with them shortly. She didn't feel right about running so late, but she also didn't feel right about rushing Ginger, who clearly needed some attention. And since she'd been making an effort to be part of the team, Lily suspected Max would agree that diplomacy was the better part of valor.

They went through all the details of the cocktail portion of the wedding before Lily finally headed to the drawing room, where she was greeted by Madeleine and the baskets.

"Bonjour," Madeleine said, looking absolutely adorable dressed for their outing in a peacoat and matching beret.

"Bonjour, ma fille chérie. Please forgive me for running late." Lily knelt and kissed the child's upturned cheek in welcome and resisted the urge to explain.

Keeping an excited little girl waiting for business?

The very idea struck her as backward, and she couldn't place the blame solely on Ginger's shoulders.

Madeleine shrugged and ran to grab the baskets, leaving Lily to face her father.

She stood slowly, bracing herself to meet that striking gaze and those chiseled features. He looked kind of stoic but, sure enough, as if on cue, her insides sort of melted.

"Max." She inclined her head. "Thanks for hosting."

"So my mother got a hold of you." Not a question.

"Just some decisions to be made with the floral arrangements. I should have asked her to wait until after our outing. I'm afraid I didn't realize how long it would take."

He shrugged. "You're here now."

Something about him was almost disbelieving. Why? Because he thought she'd actually stand up his daughter after accepting an invitation? Or because she'd accepted the invitation at all?

Lily didn't get a chance to consider the answer because Madeleine was suddenly handing her a large wicker basket, and Max held out her coat.

"These gloves are for you so your fingers don't get pricked," Madeleine explained, the perfect minihostess and tour guide as she led them out the door into the brisk, and beautiful, Sunday afternoon. "I'll take you to all the good trees. We have lots of them. Some have big pinecones and some have little ones. Which ones do you need for Camille's wedding?"

That made Lily smile. "Actually we need both. Big ones. Little ones. Teeny tiny ones, too. We can use all sizes for our arrangements. And we need to remember some for the birds and squirrels, too. What size do they like?"

"Big, so they get lots of peanut butter."

"Then we'll make sure to give them the biggest ones we find."

Max strolled quietly behind them as they traversed the area where the grounds led into the forest.

"I was looking out at this very place, remembering one of the weddings I wanted to plan here." Lily knelt to rummage through some pine needles, glad for the gloves.

"Uncle Raymond and Aunt Jamilyn's wedding?"

Lily shook her head. "Pretend weddings."

"I'll have to show you Madame Lily Susan's website," Max added. "She has lots of pictures of weddings. Some from when she was your age."

"Really?" Madeleine said breathlessly.

Lily smiled, feeling a little breathless herself to know Max was so familiar with the content on her website.

Which was downright stupid. Not only had Max personally witnessed her youthful weddings, but the man was also a publisher, who was reporting on her stay in the area.

"When I was your age, I liked to dress up and play bride. Your grandma used to let me visit your house and my mom used to make me beautiful wedding dresses."

Those dresses were still all neatly stored away in the attic of her parents' house. She might go through them while she was in town. Maybe her publicist could use them for something. Or... "If you ever want to dress up as a bride, Madeleine, for Halloween or a play at school, please let me know. I have lots to choose from."

Mom would love that.

"Merci, madame!"

"There's something about weddings that capture the imagination no matter what age a girl is. See, Max, I wasn't such an oddity."

"*Oddity* isn't the word I would have used."

"Hmm. Not sure I even want to ask."

He'd bent to pick up some cones, but Lily could see a hint of the dimple in profile. "Obsessed."

There was nowhere else to look, so she watched him stand in a display of lean strength, the jeans pulling taut against strong thighs. "Well, I can't deny I like weddings, now can I? But I prefer to think of myself as passionate and focused."

"Those work, too."

She didn't get a chance to reply because Madeleine cried out, "Oh, look at all these pinecones."

"You've hit the jackpot." Lily kneeled beside her and offered her basket. "You keep this up and we'll have to make a trip to my car to empty our baskets. I brought a box. I hope it's big enough."

Madeleine laughed and enthusiastically loaded up the basket. "Whoever fills their basket first wins."

"The race is on." Max meandered ahead to the next pine grove at a snail's pace. A very handsome man with his hiking boots and low-slung jeans. A man in his element. Or was it just her interest in him that made him seem that way?

Both Lily and Max slowed their collecting by unspoken consent, and when they reached the river, the wind picked up, lifting Madeleine's dark curls off her shoulders and whipping them around her face.

"We forgot to pull your hair up," Max said. "Come here, pretty. I've got a pony."

It took Lily a moment to realize that Max's *pony* was actually a hair elastic that he slipped off his wrist. Madeleine ran to him, a sort of automatic hop-skip. Compliance with an obvious measure of let's-get-this-over-with-so-I-don't-lose-the-race. She was such a darling little girl.

Lily remembered the twins at this age, so enamored of everything, still not quite settled into their personalities. Now, at the ripe old age of nine and a half, they'd gotten the hang of life and had formulated some decided opinions.

Max swept the beret from Madeleine's head and collected the dark curls, his long fingers so tenderly working the windswept strands into a fat ponytail that he secured low on her nape.

"Is that better?" he asked.

She nodded, and he barely got the hat on her head before she rushed toward the next stand of trees.

"Squirrel-size." She held up a massive pinecone.

Lily laughed and the feeling—genuine, heartfelt—welled up from inside her.

Glancing at the steely waters of the Hudson River, her own tension melted as she took in the amazing vista.

The river felt like home. She could remember field trips to the many parks between Poughkeepsie and Hyde Park all through her elementary years. Sneaking down to the Main Mall as a teen. Her first time driving over the Mid-Hudson Bridge. Captaining the crew team as an undergrad. Watching Joey and Max play a thousand baseball games at the various diamonds along the river.

Watching fireworks from the middle of the burned-out railway bridge long before it had been renovated into the Walkway of the Hudson. In those days one treaded very carefully and tried not to hyperventilate at the sight of the Hudson flowing a hundred and twenty-five feet below through the ties.

The insanity of youth.

Those years were ahead for Madeleine. Lily wondered how Max, who so lovingly filled the roles of dad and mom, would weather that era when it came.

And would he tackle life's challenges as a single parent, or would he become another woman's perfect groom?

"Do you ever get tired of the view?" she asked, refusing to even venture down that road. Max Downey wasn't the man for her. He wasn't a man she could sleep with and never see again—not that she was into one-night stands. But Max came with attachments. His family and hers had history. Chemistry would fizzle out and that would leave years of awkwardness at family gatherings. Besides, she was in no condition to judge if they could be good together. Look at the mess she'd made with Lucas. She didn't know how she could trust herself right now. Not until she'd had time to rest and clear her head so she could think clearly. Not make such poor choices. It was simply too soon. No matter that chemistry said otherwise.

He gave a light shrug, followed her gaze with those piercing eyes. "Not tired. I would say that I learn to appreciate it more with age."

"I suppose it's easy to take for granted when it's your backyard."

"I've lived my whole life in this house."

"And spent so much time at mine. I could never figure that out. What was the attraction, if you don't mind me asking?"

Max considered her, thoughtfully it seemed, almost as if he was gauging how honest he wanted to be. "You had everything I wanted in my life. I didn't know what it was back then, but I felt it with your family even when I didn't have a name for it. It's the most important thing in the world."

"What on earth did my family have that yours didn't?" The very idea seemed impossible while standing here, on the family estate where three generations of Downeys had lived behind them, with the view of the majestic Hudson River in front of them.

"They have their priorities straight."

"Wow. That wasn't what I expected."

His gaze had shifted from her to Madeleine, who was drifting closer to the overhang with every step she took. Not dangerously close but he knew she wasn't paying attention. She was five. Max was on her in two long strides then one touch on her shoulder redirected her.

"What did you expect me to say?" he asked.

"I'm not sure. Maybe I'm not even sure what you mean. Priorities straight. It can't be love because I happen to know how much your mother loves you and your brothers. I remember how difficult it was for her when you all left for college. You have no idea how much she missed you."

A smile played around his mouth. "I know she loves me. I love her. But you've got to understand there's a lot of business cluttering the family. There are obligations and opinions about how each of us conduct ourselves and manage our obligations. That sort of pressure creates distance. We're every-man-for-himself around here. It's never as simple as Joey deciding to follow in your dad's footsteps and take over the hardware store. Your family says, 'Cool.' And when Caroline says she would die before sorting through nuts and bolts because she wants to be a nurse, you all say, 'That's cool, too.' Mike wants to be a cop. Lily Susan wants to plan weddings. No problem. Everyone supports everyone else. Your family has their priorities straight."

"So you're not a rebel, then?"

"Is that what you thought?"

"Yes and no," she admitted. "I didn't really know. Joey was no help whatsoever. He's older than I am. I was never a confidant or a contemporary. I'm still not."

"He loves you."

"I know, but he's a protective big brother. Not like—" She couldn't get the word out of her mouth. It was there one moment and stuck the next.

Not like Mike.

She wasn't going there and redirected fast. "You know, Max, I think I've seen what you're talking about with your mother. She's a closet CEO and always has been. I could never figure out why she didn't have her own career. Not that she doesn't accomplish amazing things with her charities and organizations. She does a lot of good work that reflects well on your family."

"That's exactly what I'm talking about. That's her role. Social. Charitable. Philanthropic. Maybe if she'd married into the family now—not forty years ago—she might have claimed some family business interest of her own. But she was groomed to take over my grandmother's place and had no other options."

"If her past year at my local office has been any indication, that may ultimately change."

Max looked amused. "So I noticed. Hence one of the very reasons I asked you to plan Raymond's wedding. Between Madeleine and the *Herald,* I don't have the time to rein her in."

"I'll have you know that she is contributing invaluably to Raymond's wedding and as a team player. Not to mention the renovations she supervised at my office the past year, Max. Seriously. You may think that renovating and redecorating may seem right up her alley, but she has a marvelous head for business. She made the renovation budget stretch to the point of screaming in very creative ways."

"Is that why you never bought out her shares?"

Lily nodded. "I understood she wanted to be a part of something that was her own, and I care about your mother. She believed in me when no one else did. I owed her the same."

His gaze was on Madeleine again—his daughter was still determined to fill her basket first. "You spend so much time away from your family, Lily Susan. I could never figure that out. What's the deal there, if you don't mind me asking?"

He turned her curiosity around and pointed it at her.

She would be unfair not to be as honest. "I love them all very much. I keep in touch. They come to visit me. But I won't lie. They can be overwhelming. Everyone's involved in what everyone else is doing. There's a lot of pressure with that, too. Just so you know." Especially when they didn't approve of what she was doing. "I had things I wanted to accomplish, and I couldn't do that here." She waved a hand around to encompass everything from Overlook and Hyde Park to her dad's hardware store in the Valley.

"Are you happy?"

That question took some consideration. "You know, at any other time in my life, I might have had an answer for you. But not right now. I don't really know what I am beyond tired. And stressed. I'm very tired and very stressed."

They walked along in silence for a few minutes, the wind whipping around them, cold despite the bright sun. Madeleine turned back to them, raising her basket high.

"I win!"

"Thank you," Max said simply.

"For what?"

"For being honest with me. For accepting Madeleine's invitation. It means a lot to her."

"Thank you for sharing your beautiful daughter. And for satisfying my curiosity." Her smile suddenly seemed to cover her face. She liked that she'd pleased this man, so much more than was smart. "And for the pinecones."

CHAPTER SIXTEEN

LILY WAITED in the office for Mara's return as long as she could before finally having to leave. She was due at Riley's to inspect the cleaning crews' work in the barn. They had finished this weekend, and now her family volunteers were wrapping up with the last of the nitpicky details before Lily and her vendors could get in to start setting up. She'd hoped to take the decorations that Mara had picked up, but it looked as though it wasn't meant to be. Lily would simply make another trip.

Life had degenerated into ticking minutes, where she crammed as many details as she could into each one. Her time on the road was spent on the phone to confirm myriad details—photography times, installation of electrical outlets, checking that the napkins matching the chair ties had arrived, verifying the times for the hair and makeup people to arrive. Sleep, when she managed some, was a means for her to dream up solutions to whatever problems had arisen with any one of the two local weddings or the other six events in production all over the world.

There were always problems. Too many out of her control.

As she locked the office door and headed down the steps, Lily took a chance and depressed the speed dial.

Mara picked up before the second ring. "Good afternoon and welcome to Lawsuits Are Us."

"What are you talking about?"

Silence on the other end of the line. Not good. "Mara?"

"You haven't been online have you?"

The bottom fell out of Lily's stomach. "Oh, God. Now what?"

"Forget I said anything."

"I wish. Let me have it."

"'Demons versus Angels—the lawsuits,'" Mara began to read. "'Brazilian runway model Catalina Delmonico has sued Interbay Press, LLC, owner of blog.ging.com for libel and is seeking ten million dollars in damages. The lawsuit, over an independent blog hosted on the defendant's blog.ging.com server, cites that the flawed registration process has allowed vicious lies about the plaintiff designed to defame her and cause harm to her career to be published under the condition of anonymity that protects the defamer and violates the plaintiff's civil rights.'"

"This fire is never going to burn out and I'm going to roast in this mess for all eternity."

"I'm sorry, Lily. For making jokes and for running late. Are you okay?"

"Does that woman really think her career is worth ten million dollars?"

"I guess this means she isn't pregnant. She should unload all clingy T-shirts from her wardrobe or do some crunches. I saw the photo and she does look thick around the waist."

Lily appreciated the attempt to make her feel better. "Lucas called me specifically to tell me that if that woman was pregnant, he didn't know anything about it. Think I should believe him?" She didn't give Mara a chance to reply. "Doesn't really matter, does it?"

"Not from where I'm standing."

"Where are you standing by the way? I waited in the

office as long as I could. Where are the rest of my decorations?"

"I'm so sorry. I'm on my way back now. The party supply store sent the wrong size boxes with our order."

"Please tell me everything worked out."

"It did. Just took time to sort through. But on the bright side, Lily, be happy that the blog from hell is finally out of commission. It's about time someone was held accountable for the unsubstantiated trash being published about us. If those posts had run in print, your attorney would have slapped a ten-million-dollar libel lawsuit against the publisher a long time ago."

"I'm sorry the cease-and-desist letter my attorney sent didn't do the trick." Lily almost tripped over the curb getting to the door of the rental car she'd picked up. Finally. A sporty little MINI-Cooper since all she did was drive nowadays. The muscle below her eye was twitching. "I'm in hell."

"No, you're on vacation."

"I'm vacationing in hell, then."

There was laughter. "Be that as it may, you can relax in the hot weather. Close your eyes and pretend you're on a beach in San Remo."

She slipped into the car and popped in the Bluetooth. "Please tell me that you're on schedule with the Eversham/Raichle event." *Please distract me while I drive.* "I need to hear that one wedding is working out the way it's supposed to without any aggravation."

"Eversham and Raichle are quite happy and everything is on schedule. Anything else going on?"

"You mean other than attorneys and lawsuits? Nothing earthshaking. I haven't heard yet from Zian and he promised he'd touch base after the Chin/Lime reception was over."

"Come on, Lily. He's probably still clearing out stragglers who don't want to leave the open bar. We tasted that signature drink Chef Josh created for the couple at the last inquiry review meeting. I had to flag a taxi so I could get to my hotel. I didn't trust myself to walk two blocks. If we were guests, Zian would be dragging us away from the bar, too. I'm sure he'll call as soon as he can."

"So I should go with no news is good news?"

"Absolutely." That was Mara, ever the optimist.

On an up note, everything else happening in the field today seemed to be holding its own. Lily had already had her daily conversation with the main office. But for some reason, the act of discussing work wasn't having its usual calming effect.

Especially as Lily drove beneath the overpass of the railroad tracks and recognized where she was.

"Damn it." The curse was out of her mouth as she saw it.

"What?" Mara asked.

"Not you. The cemetery."

"Oh." There wasn't much more to say than that. Mara understood the significance. "Let me tell you about the supply house goof-up. That'll distract you."

"Thank you."

Mara launched into a tale about the boxes packed with items that in no way resembled what they'd ordered for the soda bar and the cider stations for Riley's wedding.

Lily listened, but she could no more peel her gaze from the cemetery than she could have driven blindfolded. There it was stretching out behind a black iron fence, gravestones in all shapes and varieties of stone and manner of decay for as far as she could see.

Why on earth had she driven this way? She didn't have time to stop for a long-overdue visit right now, so why?

Once Salt Point Turnpike had been a back road to the Valley that bypassed traffic on Routes 44 and 55. But she hadn't driven this way since she'd been home, not until she had time to stop.

An insane impulse to wave and yell, "Hi, Mike!" gripped her, and she tightened her fingers on the steering wheel, a physical effort to control her insanity.

She had to be losing her mind.

Mara was still talking in the background.

"I'm sorry," Lily said. "I missed that last bit."

A sigh. "What was the last thing you remember?"

"The part about the boxes for the cookie favors."

"Okay. They were the right style of boxes, but you'd have had to stuff your niece or nephew inside to fill one up," she said, then—darling she was—kept up the chatter until Lily pulled into Riley's driveway, where she recognized every car, truck and unmarked police cruiser crammed in the circular drive.

"I'm here."

"You good?"

"I am. Bless your heart, Mara. Thank you."

"Good luck, then. I hope you find the barn in tip-top shape and you don't have to do a thing but order everyone around."

Lily actually laughed—it was a weak, fragile sound, but a laugh nevertheless. "Talk to you later."

After disconnecting the call, she reached in the backseat for her bag. She would have changed at the office had she not been in such a rush to get out. Knocking on the porch door, she waited. No one answered.

"Hey, people," she called out, trying the latch. Finding it unlocked. Lily let herself in, calling out again. Apparently everyone was at the barn. She changed into jeans and sneakers in the guest bathroom and headed out to join her family.

They'd turned decorating the barn into a party, too. Before she'd even gotten through the stable gate, she could hear the music blaring. Lily couldn't say she was surprised. Not with her family. Any excuse to be together and have fun.

They have their priorities straight. That Max had recognized the importance of family spoke volumes about him, about what he valued. She didn't want to know what it said about her. She let herself through the stable gate and crossed the paddock, the music growing louder with every step. Her sense of being a stranger was growing, too. So this is what she'd become in the years since she'd left home—a woman who arranged other people's weddings.

Always a bridesmaid, never a bride, as the old saying went. Only Lily wasn't even the bridesmaid. She was grunt labor.

Shaking off the thought, she headed toward the big doors that had been thrown wide open, activity beckoning from within.

Lily shouldn't have been surprised to find Max inside with the family. She spotted him first, up on a ladder washing a shelf. He wore a pair of low-slung scrubby jeans that didn't do a thing to make him look any less attractive.

"Lily Susan." Mom spotted her. "I told you we'd all help you."

Mom didn't look much different than she always did, with her hair wrapped up in a kerchief and an apron around her. Lily gave her a kiss.

"And I appreciate everything you all do."

Everyone was engaged in some activity. Even the kids

were hard at work, with Camille and Madeleine placing long-stemmed artificial flowers in the milk cans that Lily had salvaged to use as decorations.

"Wow, the place looks great," Lily said.

"Glad you're here. Mom's giving orders like a tyrant." Caroline cast a worried glance around, clearly making sure their mother wouldn't overhear, which was unlikely given the volume of the music. Carrie Underwood. "But I want to know what we're going to do if the temperature drops. We'll freeze in here."

"Pshaw." Lily waved her off. "Not a chance. That's why the wedding's during the day. We'll be out of here before the sun sets, and once the fresh hay gets here, we'll have plenty of insulation." She reached inside her bag for her ever-handy notepad. What would her life be without her lists? "I suppose I could order some space heaters in case." She'd have to bring in the appliance people to find out what would work safely in this environment. She didn't want to burn down the barn.

God, no more fires at weddings. She could see the headline already.

Is the Antibride burning a path straight to hell?

And not with Max and Riley on the premises. Neither would miss a detail and the *Herald* would get an exclusive.

Caroline shrugged. "Did you check the weather forecast?"

"Sixty-nine and sunny."

"Then we should be all right."

"Here's hoping." Lily hung her bag over a railing and surveyed the area. She had to come up with a floor plan before the rental company delivered the tables. They were scheduled to arrive in the morning. Now that the barn was cleared out and the dilapidated tractor and rusty equipment gone, she could actually see the space she had to work with.

"Camille, Madeleine, I need your hands," Mom called out. "Come help me with these lights, please."

The two raced to her assistance, and Caroline laughed. "The girls are so helpful. Not so much with the boys. Scott took Brian and Jake with the horses to graze at the stream."

A pond or a stream.

"This was such a brilliant idea, Lily Susan." Riley kissed her cheek, curly hair contained with a bandanna, a beaming smile on her face. The perfect bride. "I want you to be the first to know that we've decided to turn this into the party barn. We're kicking off a new tradition with the wedding and every year we're going to host an annual Halloween party here. Mark your calendar to make sure you're in the country."

"Will do." Lily laughed. "So that's how you're getting around the twins and the Halloween party."

Riley nodded. "It's all about compromise and negotiation. We can meet everyone's needs if we make the effort."

"Glad to hear it. Although I'm not convinced Jake won't show up in costume. He wanted to wear his baseball uniform."

Caroline gave a snort of laughter and Riley shook her head.

"That's a good thing. He was attempting to compromise because I want him to wear a suit and he wants to wear his Halloween costume."

"What's he dressing up as this year?" Lily asked.

"A sumo wrestler."

"Should have let him wear it," Caroline said before taking off with her spray bottle.

"Would have made for some interesting photos," Lily agreed. "Don't have any of those on the website."

"Yet, right?" Riley grinned. "You do have an office in Asia."

"I've got to figure out the table layout first."

"Do what you need to do and work your magic. We've got the rest under control."

"Not yet, you don't," Joey's voice boomed over the music. "Not until I'm here."

"You're late," Max yelled from across the barn. "Work's all done. You missed it."

"Damn shame that." Joey shrugged. "Got busy at the store. Couldn't get out until now."

"Glad to get you whenever we can have you," Riley said.

"Thanks for helping," Lily added, about to hug him.

Joey leveled a cool gaze her way. "You don't have to thank me, Lily Susan. I'm here because I'm part of the family."

I'm not here for you.

That was the implication, anyway. Riley frowned at him, and Sarah made a beeline from across the barn. But Lily knew her brother. She knew if he hadn't backed down by now, he wasn't going to. Not until he'd had his say. He'd continue blasting her with hostility whenever he got a chance.

She was going to have to deal with him eventually, so her choices were before the wedding or after. She was tired of tiptoeing around him. "What's the problem, Joey?"

"Which one?" he grunted in a voice that seemed to barely contain his anger. "The fact that you can't make the time to visit your family? Or that you got engaged to some guy and couldn't be bothered bringing him home to meet anyone? Or that you expected us to fly all over the damned world to attend your wedding to some guy we've never met? Or that you don't say one word about how you're doing after you cancel the wedding? Or that you don't care that your parents are worried about you? Or that you've got an internet stalker you're involving the law with but didn't tell anyone about?"

All Lily's energy seemed to drain away that fast. God, she was tired. Maybe her iron was low? Anemia could certainly explain the way she felt.

"Oh, wait," he added, his tone dripping with sarcasm. "You could tell Scott and Max, but the rest of us had to read about it in the newspaper."

Sarah appeared at his side and placed a hand on his arm, a silent plea for him to stop. She looked stressed, and he didn't even glance her way.

"I'm sorry," Lily said. "You shouldn't have had to read about this in the paper, but please try to understand. I've had a lot going on since coming home. I've barely seen anyone let alone had time to catch up when all I've been doing is work."

"All you've ever done is work. What's new about that?"

"Cut her a break, Joey," Sarah said. "She's busy and tired."

Caroline and Mom came over.

"Calm down, Joe," Mom said. "Now's not the time."

He shrugged off Sarah's hand. "I'm not going to calm down, and I'm not going to cut her a break. She doesn't give a damn about this family or about how everyone's worried about her."

About how *he* was worried about her.

It was all over him, in his hurt anger, in his frustration. In the vein throbbing in his temple.

Riley vanished, herding Camille and Madeleine past

the knot of adults. Lily could overhear her telling them, "It's okay. Uncle Joey's just upset."

"I'm sorry," she repeated. "I wasn't trying to keep the situation a secret. I've refused to give some anonymous blogger a lot of my attention. Unfortunately, I was finally forced to do something. I asked Scott for his opinion, and he gave me good advice. I acted on it. That simple."

"Lily Susan didn't know an article was going to run in the *Herald*," Max said, the voice of calm reason.

She knew exactly what he was doing—running interference. She gave him a quiet smile over her shoulder, so he knew she appreciated the effort. Not that it would assuage Joey.

"I don't understand what's wrong with you, Lily Susan. Don't you care?"

Sarah made another attempt to drag him away, but when he shrugged her off, she tossed her hands in the air and stormed off. "This is uncalled for."

Caroline whispered something to Joey that Lily couldn't hear, and he visibly relaxed a little, enough so that it didn't look like that vein in his temple might burst.

But Lily hated the way she felt. Joey and Caroline, her big brother and sister. Joey and Caroline. Mom and Dad. Lily and Mike.

Not anymore.

"Of course I care," she said. "I kept my problems to myself because I didn't want to worry anyone."

"What are you talking about? You don't think everyone's been worrying about you anyway? Engaged to that loser. Canceling your wedding. You never come home. Mom and Dad have to chase you when you're in the country to make sure you're still alive. It's like you're not even a part of this family anymore."

"That's enough, Joey," her dad's voice bellowed from

behind her, loud enough to make her jump. "You shut your big mouth and you do it now. You hear me?"

Lily knew that tone. So did Joey. He scowled but finally shut up.

"It's okay, honey-bunch," her dad said, coming up next to her and patting her shoulder with a beefy hand, a strong, familiar hand that was always so capable at handling everything from tools to wiping away tears.

And in that moment, standing there facing all of them—her angry brother and everyone trying to calm him down, demand order or run interference... It hit her.

Joey was right. She didn't feel a part of this family anymore.

CHAPTER SEVENTEEN

MAX STOOD in the middle the family he loved, not sure who was more upset right now. Big Joe and Joey both looked ready to explode. Rosie and Caroline were trying to calm them down. And Lily Susan...

She'd stepped away, but that small distance appeared to be a chasm between her and the people who loved her. The people she loved. Her media facade was in place, her face so unreadable... Max knew from her sheer lack of expression that she was hurt. He couldn't say how he knew, but he wasn't wrong.

The urge to go to her, slip an arm around her waist and nudge her closer to her family gripped him. He wanted to be the one standing beside her. It was a crazy impulse, one that wouldn't be appreciated by Lily Susan or Joey at the moment, so Max did the only thing he could to diffuse the tension.

"Come on, Joey." He grabbed his jacket from where he'd hung it over a stall rail. "I need stuff at the hardware store."

Joey was so entrenched in the moment that it took a second for him to realize Max had spoken. "What about the store? What are you talking about?"

"We need to run to the hardware store," Max repeated. "I need sprinkler heads."

Joey shook his head as if he wasn't sure he'd heard

right. "You have a groundskeeper who maintains your irrigation system."

"Yes, I know. His name's Karl. He asked me to pick up sprinkler heads."

"Yeah, and you want some PVC, too," Big Joe said. "It'll take some time to figure out what you need, but it'll save you the extra trip." Code that translated into: keep Joey away for as long as it takes him to calm down because if I get my hands on him…

"We'll get PVC, too. Joey, we're out of here." Max glanced at Rosie. "You'll keep your eyes on Madeleine until I get back?"

She waved him off. "I've got her. No worries. Just get that immature Joey out of here right now. You have my permission to beat him if he doesn't calm down." Narrowing her gaze at her eldest son with a look that should have killed him on the spot, she added, "Riley took the girls to the pond if you want to let Madeleine know you're leaving."

"Thanks. Let's hit the road, Joey."

For a moment, Max thought Joey might argue and stand his ground, but he finally tossed his hands in the air, and scowled at Lily Susan, whose expression had been set in porcelain.

That distance was her defense, Max realized. An invisible wall between her and the world. He'd seen it firsthand at the airport when she'd been swamped by reporters.

The woman he'd come to care about was behind that wall. Did she feel ganged up on? By people who were worried about her. She stood her ground, didn't let anything slip through that careful mask.

He didn't get a chance to consider that thought any further because they reached the pond, where Riley and the girls were feeding ducks.

"Uncle Joey and I have to run to the hardware store," he told Madeleine. "We'll be back soon. You want to stay with Camille?"

Madeleine nodded and tossed another handful of cracked corn at the ducks, laughing as it bounced off their sleek heads and sprinkled the surface of the pond.

"They're dive-bombing to get it," Camille shrieked.

Riley met his gaze with an expression that seemed to ask, *Everything okay?*

Max nodded then headed up the hill toward the house and his car. By the time they reached the driveway, Joey had found his voice again.

"Now I'm the bad guy. What's new?"

"Feeling sorry for yourself?" Max clicked open the locks and hopped in the driver seat. "Where's that coming from?"

"I'm not feeling sorry for myself and you know it." Joey made an exasperated sound. "Come on, man. How many times do I have to stand back and keep my mouth shut? Our parents are worried about her."

Joey was worried.

"She's been gone for years. You know that, Max. How long am I supposed to keep playing nice and pretending nothing is wrong?"

Max maneuvered around Big Joe's Cadillac and pulled onto Traver Road. "Did you think attack mode was going to resolve the problem?"

"Our parents aren't young. They took a hit with Mike."

With Mike. A euphemism that everyone in the family had adopted. No one seemed to be able to bring themselves to use Mike's name with the word *died* in the same sentence.

Didn't Max do exactly the same thing when he said Mommy-up-in-heaven?

"I know my parents still have Riley and the twins," Joey continued. "But it's not the same as having Lily Susan around. She's their strongest connection to him. She was Mike. Mike was her. It's a twin thing. You know what I'm talking about."

Max did.

He also knew grief. Firsthand, in all its ugly glory. He'd lost more than he'd ever be able to comprehend.

She was Mike. Mike was her.

Max couldn't even fathom what that could have been like. He'd watched Riley struggle to deal, the long, difficult road to healing, a road that had taken her and the twins clear across the country for years before she'd been able to face the life she and Mike had made together.

Max had learned so much, from both her struggles and her strength. Sometimes he thought that was one of the few things he'd had in his favor to help him learn to cope when he hadn't even wanted to try. He'd had Riley in his corner with her experience and empathy. He'd had so many loving people to help him out along the way. But he and Riley also had some really compelling reasons to fight their way back—their kids.

Lily Susan had been alone.

"I hear what you're saying, Joey. And I'm certainly not making excuses for your sister's behavior, but something's up with her. I feel it in my gut."

"You mean the loser fiancé cheating on her?" Joey scoffed. "That was the best thing that ever happened. Even if she hasn't figured it out yet. Not that I would have minded getting out of the country for the wedding. I paid all that money for a passport for nothing."

"Take a vacation." Max slowed to take a crazy turn on a road filled with them. "But I'm not talking about the loser. Something else."

"What?"

Max frowned. "She's pretty high-strung."

"Yeah, got that part, genius. Running a business will make you crazy on a good day. And she's running an über-business. Your family at least divvies up the workload. As far as I can tell, Lily Susan is running the show herself."

"She has staff—"

"I'm not talking about delegating. She's got offices all over the world, and even though she has people executing, she's still overseeing every detail, making all the decisions. Your family doesn't operate that way. You each pick a business and run it. You may consult on the big stuff—company vision, VIP hires, whatever—but you deal with the day-to-day stuff yourself. Can you imagine running every advertisement by your family? You'd wind up shooting yourself."

"That's the truth."

What Joey said was true. Had Lily Susan expanded beyond her ability to manage? Unlike the *Herald* or the family hardware store, the Wedding Angel *was* Worldwide Weddings Unlimited.

"Her entire business revolves around her vision, her creativity, her expertise. I don't see how she can delegate that," Max admitted, remembering when she'd placed soft hands on the sides of his face and aimed him at a small corner in a massive estate to get him to use his imagination.

She was a creative woman, a strong woman, a loving woman. He'd seen all these sides of her during these past weeks together. But the woman he'd left standing in that barn had been untouchable, unreadable behind that perfectly poised expression.

Was she a sensitive woman, too?

A woman who'd been forced to hide a marshmallow center from the world, so she could deal with the media and achieve her dreams? A woman who had maybe given up a little too much along the way? A woman who had been rocked by loss and hadn't had a loving family to help her find her way back from grief?

That thought struck him hard.

"Joey, do you really think Lily Susan doesn't care about the family?"

"She sure in hell isn't acting like she does."

"That's not what I asked."

Joey shifted. "She cares. But she doesn't show it. Although I could be wrong. It's been known to happen from time to time."

Now it was Max's turn to snort. "Yeah, right."

"She's running away and our parents have to keep chasing her. Even when she's here she doesn't talk to us."

"Yet, she knows everything's that's going on around here. You all keep her up on things."

"She does ask about us," Joey admitted.

Max saw that at the dinner table the first day she'd been home. She wanted to know everything going on with everyone, but didn't mention a thing about herself. "Why would she ask if she didn't care?"

Joey shrugged, but his interest piqued. "No clue, so we're back to my question. If she cares, then why is she acting like she doesn't?"

"It's like she's on the outside looking in."

"No argument there."

"Well, maybe that's the question to ask. Why doesn't she feel like she's a part of the family anymore?"

Silence.

Max shifted his gaze off the road to find Joey staring at him, wide-eyed.

And there it was. Neither of them had to say another word. They'd been friends since sixth grade. There were things Max admired about Joey Angelica, things he positively couldn't stand. And vice versa, no doubt. But Max knew Joey, and right in that moment, they were both thinking the exact same thing.

Mike.

"Well, hell, Max," Joey said. "You are way smarter than you look." Then he clapped himself on the forehead. "And I can't believe I am so stupid."

Rhetorical. Max didn't say a word.

"You remember what they were like." There wasn't a trace of anger left in Joey.

"Your mom used to call them peas in a pod."

Joey nodded, was staring out the windshield as Max passed the elementary school. They'd all gone there. Every one of the Angelica kids. Two generations. Max wondered what Joey was remembering. He could practically see Mike and Lily Susan, another version of Jake and Camille, only so much younger than Joey and Caroline that they were the little family darlings. Everything they did was cute or reckless or mischievous.... Which was Joey's point. They did everything together. Even Lily Susan's crazy weddings. Poor Mike got roped into playing a role every time. He could never tell her no. And if he did, someone always guilted him into agreeing. Usually Joey, who didn't want to play groom himself.

"Maybe my baby sister hasn't figured out how to be a part of our family without Mike," Joey said thoughtfully.

"Makes sense. You guys have all been together riding the ups and downs. She hasn't been here."

Joey didn't reply right away, and Max's head was so filled with the thought as he maneuvered through the Valley, with cars pulling out on both sides of the street during traffic hour, that he didn't say anything until he pulled into the customer parking spaces in front of the hardware store.

"You already figured out I don't really need any sprinkler heads, right?"

Joey still didn't reply, and Max put the gearshift into Park and glanced around to find Joey smiling.

"What?"

"You've given Lily Susan a lot of thought." Not a question.

"Hardly a surprise since I've been around your sister more in the past three weeks than I have in the entire time I've known her."

Joey was watching him with an almost disbelieving expression.

"What?" he asked again.

"Oh, nothing, man. Nothing at all."

But Joey's smile was a lot more than *nothing at all*.

CHAPTER EIGHTEEN

"DID YOU AND Uncle Joey win, Daddy?" Madeleine asked.

Lily pulled the cookie sheets from the oven then nudged the door shut with a hip. Bracing herself, she turned to find Max standing in the doorway behind her. He still wore his baseball uniform, the fitted lines molding every inch of him. He was toned, healthy, not overly muscular but athletic. A blast from the memorable past. She had no problem envisioning the way he'd looked all those years ago, a teen or a college student home for the holidays, wearing a similar uniform with one team logo or another, looking just as attractive.

The dirt and grass streaked all the way up one leg, suggesting he'd slid somewhere. Catching the ball? Sliding into a base? Lily didn't ask. She was glad for the hot cookie sheets that needed to find a place to cool in an already crowded kitchen, which gave her an excuse to tear away her gaze from the man who looked far too attractive for her peace of mind.

"We won." Max strode across the kitchen, nodding her way. "Uncle Joey hit a homer."

"That should make him happy," her mom said from her place at the table.

"You know it," Max agreed, pressing a kiss to the top of Madeleine's head. "I wasn't sure if you all were done yet so I came straight here."

"Not quite," Lily admitted, an understatement.

Max nodded, glancing around the kitchen and adjoining dining room, where cooling sugar cookies in an alphabet of letters dominated the terrain of the baker's rack, countertops and windowsills. The table had been turned into an assembly line. Mom rolled out dough over the floury surface. Camille, Jake and Madeleine used cookie cutters to cut out letters. Lily lined them on the baking sheets then shifted them into the oven to cook for nine minutes before taking them out and trying to find a place to let them cool.

"I had no clue wedding planners did this sort of thing." Max fixed her with a curious gaze that made her heart throb a slow beat. "I'm learning a lot about your work."

"I saw a similar idea in a magazine once and thought it was clever. I've always wanted to make the idea mine but hadn't come across the right event." She gave him a casual smile, refused to acknowledge her awareness of him, refused to encourage her own body's mutiny. "I thought a Halloween wedding in a barn sounded perfect."

"It is perfect," Jake said around another mouthful of broken cookies.

"You're going to pop if you eat much more," Rosie warned.

Jake rubbed his belly and pushed out his stomach. "Lots more room."

"Looks like you got a food baby." Camille rubbed her hand over her brother's stomach, and Madeleine laughed.

Max's dimple flashed, making it impossible not to notice the dirt smudging his stubbled jaw. "And this looks like a lot of work. I'm surprised you didn't have a bakery make everything with all you've got going on right now."

"Where would the fun be in that? It's a big job, so I knew I'd need lots of help." She grinned at her little helpers, three excited kids who were currently trashing the dining room with floury hands and enthusiasm. "I've got to squeeze in the fun when I can on this trip."

Something about that appeared to amuse him, but Lily didn't wait to try and figure out what. She headed to the table instead and sorted through cookie cutters in the shapes of letters. "We need more vowels. Madeleine, how about some *O*'s because you're the only one with an *O* in your name? Jake, you can make *A*'s."

"I can do *I*'s," Camille offered.

"I have an *I*, too." Madeleine eagerly reached for another cookie cutter and slid it toward Camille.

"We all have *I*'s." Jake rolled his gaze. *"A-N-G-E-L-I-C-A."*

She deflated visibly, but Lily distracted her with a special task after checking the first batches of cookies cooling on the baker's rack. "Madeleine, will you help me start the boxes after you're done with your *O*'s?"

"Oui, madame."

"Merci," Lily replied, heading to the chair, where she'd stacked the flattened boxes.

"Do you mind if I clean up since it looks like you're going to be a while?" Max asked Rosie.

Mom inclined her head in the direction of the stairs. "Go on. Use the guest room."

"Thanks. I'll be back."

He crossed the room with long-legged strides, and Lily had to resist the impulse to watch him go, knowing the sight of him from behind would be as appealing as the front view. She was hopeless.

"I'm done," Madeleine said, wiping doughy hands on her apron.

"Wash up then you can give me a hand. Or two."

She skipped away from the table, ponytail bouncing with every step. Lily couldn't help but smile.

This was a vacation moment. These kids made everything fun. They were a bright spot in her hectic days, exactly the sort of enjoyment she'd hoped to have lots of on this vacation. She'd take what she could get, though, and be grateful for the distraction. Especially with the thought of Max showering in the guest bathroom upstairs, Lily needed one.

Madeleine popped open boxes, so obviously eager to please. On so many levels Max was blessed with this little one. He was luckier than most dads—maybe because he'd lost so much. He'd almost lost his daughter, too.

The thought came at Lily sideways, tugged hard as she watched Madeleine's small hands wrestle with the decorative box with determination on her face.

They have their priorities straight.

Looked as though he had his priorities straight, too.

"That's the last of the dough," Mom said, heading into the kitchen to deposit the rolling pin in the sink. "I've rolled out absolutely everything. There isn't another letter in the bunch."

"Not even one more *I?*" Camille giggled.

"Not half an *I,* silly girl." Mom tweaked Camille's nose. "Not even the dot on top of the *I.* Let's get this table cleared and we can start making messages."

"Grandma Rosie, Jakie broke another cookie."

"You better stop eating all those cookies, Camille," Jake retorted. "Or you'll get a headache and puke."

Migraines were an unfortunate reality for Camille. Usually after too much excitement, sugar or chlorine. Riley couldn't quite get a lock on the triggers yet.

"We'll have no headaches or puking today, thank you very much," Rosie said in a tone of voice that didn't offer wiggle room. "Not another bite or we won't have enough cookies for the guests. Now bring me the trash can, will you, Jake?" She dusted loose flour into piles, distracting the kids so they could get on to the next task.

Lily wasn't sure what it was that struck her about the sight of her mother and the twins, but she could suddenly see the way her mother had been years ago, standing over the very same table, helping Lily and Mike do any of the thousand things they'd done together.

Lily suddenly remembered that crazy tooth-decay science-fair project. Mike had talked Rosie into taking their baby teeth from the tooth-fairy stash, long after Joey had spoiled the magic by revealing who the tooth fairy really was.

What decayed a tooth faster: soda, fruit juice or milk?

Mike's inspiration for the project was rebellion after being told he couldn't drink soda at night. He'd been on a crusade to prove that soda was actually a better choice than the healthier alternatives Mom offered.

And he had gotten more weight for his argument when his experiments had proven that fruit juice had the worst effect on teeth. Of course she had told him to drink milk then brush his teeth before bed—there was no swaying her once her mind was made up. But he had gotten a week of riding lessons at summer camp that year because of his resourcefulness. He'd won first place at the school science fair with his project and had gone on to compete at the county level to win another ribbon.

So many memories.

Somehow the image in front of her was all wrong. The twins were too young and Mom too old. And Lily was standing on the outside watching them, not a part of them.

She shook off the thought and helped Madeleine finish the boxes to speed the process along.

After getting copies of the messages and the cooled cookies onto the middle of the table, she told the kids,

"Each of you get a message. This will be like we're playing Scrabble."

The messages were simple and straightforward wishes for the new Mr. and Mrs.

Happily ever after.

Hugs and kisses.

Lots of love.

Lily was standing at the sink, washing her hands when Rosie came up beside her and said, "It was really sweet of you to take the time to involve the kids in the preparations."

Lily looked at her mother then, really looked. She was such a beautiful woman, but age had softened her face. The gray wasn't so noticeable until Lily peered closely. Otherwise Mom's golden-blond hair looked lighter than it had before. But there was more and more gray each time Lily saw her.

"I'm glad we had some fun together," Lily said. "My visit hasn't been like your trips to the city. We always get out and do stuff then."

"This has been a working trip, no question. But things will settle down a little after the wedding this weekend. You'll only have one thing to focus on then."

Lily wouldn't count on it. Maybe after the vacation was over and she got back to normal life.

"You're so good with the kids." Rosie stared thoughtfully across the counter, watching them. "I wish you spent more time with them. They grow up so quickly."

"That's the truth. I think I see it even more because I'm not here every day."

Mom nodded. "So where does a family fit in with your life plan, Lily Susan? I thought you'd decided you wanted one when you became engaged."

"It wasn't like that with me and Lucas, Mom. You met

him. We weren't a white-picket-fence couple with two-point-five kids."

"I know. You were a career couple." She waved a dismissive hand, not disapprovingly, but she didn't fully approve. Not by a long shot. Lily knew it by instinct. "What about now? How has everything that's happened impacted your plans?"

A nice way to dance around the situation of a cheating fiancé. Lily knew Rosie needed reassurance, felt bad she hadn't offered any before now. But she didn't have an answer because she didn't really have a plan. Or one that extended beyond accomplishing her business goals. She'd simply wanted to come home, rest and regroup.

"I'm fine." She reached for the dish towel to dry her hands. "Don't worry about me. I'm moving on and very grateful Lucas was indiscreet before the wedding instead of after."

"A blessing there. I agree. So you go back to being a single career woman now? Is that what moving on means?"

"I don't really have a plan, to be honest." She wasn't going to lie. This was Mom. Somehow talking to Mom had always been easy. "Not beyond resting while I'm home and letting all the media drama die down, so I can return to business as usual."

Lily could tell something about her answer bothered her mom. It was there in the way her mouth tightened. The way her breath exhaled on a tiny sigh. Imperceptible responses no one would notice, except someone who knew her so well.

But to Lily's surprise, her mother didn't pursue that line of questioning. She only asked, "How are you after yesterday?"

"That's a pretty way to phrase it." Lily forced a laugh.

"Joey's an idiot. Not that I'm arguing his point. Please know that. I understand why he's upset. I don't understand why he couldn't address his issues with me before he felt the need to attack me publicly."

"True. My guess is he didn't want to talk over the phone."

"He knows where I live."

"You think he should have had to chase you?"

"He's the one with the beef." But even as Lily said it, she knew her response was nothing more than an automatic defense. "No, I don't think he should have to chase me, but I've been busy with work. You know that. Our relationship hasn't suffered. We've managed to find time to have fun and talk and address whatever issues come up."

"Because your father and I chase you."

"Ouch." She didn't have a defense for that because it was true.

"Jakie, that isn't one of Mom's messages," Camille said. "That's not even a real word."

Lily seized the opportunity to escape. She went into the dining room. "Hey, guys. What's going on? Did you finish putting together all those messages already?"

"Aunt Lily Susan, Jakie's being gross."

Jake shook his head. "Nuh-uh. I'm making my own message. Like Madeleine."

"I'm not gross, Jake." Madeleine stood her ground. "I made a special message for Mrs. Riley. See, Madame Lily Susan, it's in French. *Je t'aime.*"

I love you.

"That's a beautiful message," Lily agreed, "And Mrs. Riley will love it. We need to mark the box so it doesn't get mixed up with all the others, and you can give it to her special. Camille and Jake, you guys, too. You can make special messages for Mom."

"I got one already." Jake stood back so Lily could see what he'd arranged with the letters.

"Jacob." She stifled a laugh. "Camille's right. *Penie* is not a word."

"Told you." Camille pumped a fist in the air triumphantly.

Jake blew her off with a snicker. "Oh, yeah, it is, Aunt Lily Susan. *Penie*'s a word. It's a boy word."

Lily didn't have an answer for that one. She only bit back more laughter, so reminded of Mike. His son was so much like him, a mischievous little charmer.

"Do you really think your mom's going to want to eat *penie* cookies on her wedding day, Jake?" Lily asked.

Jake snickered. "It'll make her laugh."

No doubt there. Riley would have to be good-natured to put up with these two without sprouting gray hair.

Mom intervened to put an end to the discussion. "If you want to make your mom laugh at her wedding then write a joke message. One without body parts."

They resumed the assembly line. Kids assembled the messages. Lily packed the cookies gingerly into the boxes. Mom secured the boxes with bows that had little pinecones attached to the ribbons.

Lily thought they'd finished all private conversations, but as they met at the counter where they were stacking the favors, Rosie whispered, "I accept that you're fine, Lily Susan, but are you happy? Because that's what I want for my family. I want all of you to be fine and happy. Nothing less." She met Lily's gaze with familiar eyes that seemed to reflect all the love she felt inside, and always had. "So if you're happy, I'm happy. Are you happy?"

Was she?

Lily was saved from replying when Max reappeared, still damp around the edges from a shower. His cheeks were pink from where he'd shaved. His Henley shirt hinted at all the hard muscles below, and he looked so handsome in that moment, he took Lily's breath away.

Her mom glanced between them and narrowed her gaze. Not so long ago Lily would have been able to reassure her mom. But not now. Right now she honestly couldn't say what she was.

And somehow Mom knew it.

CHAPTER NINETEEN

THE SUN HAD barely risen on Riley and Scott's wedding day—a day that promised perfectly crisp autumn weather both bright and clear—and Lily was already dealing with nonsense. Not wedding nonsense thankfully, but the never-ending-nightmare-of-her-life nonsense.

She'd opened her eyes this morning to find tweet after tweet from her followers, expressing concern and offering best wishes in support after an online celebrity-reporting site had launched photos of Lucas's ex-fling, clearly *not* pregnant, leaving the Piazza Hotel in Manhattan with a man who wouldn't allow himself to be photographed.

Everyone assumed the man was Lucas, of course. The headline: *Is the Mystery Man a Mystery?*

Lily hadn't tweeted a reply, but had allowed herself a quiet morning—and caffeine—before trying to wrap her brain around this latest bomb. But even now, with the brain cells firing and a few more details knocked off her wedding checklist, Lily still hadn't decided how she should respond. Or even if she should.

Heading toward the paddock, she paused to open the gate only to find Max coming down the slope in her wake. She blinked, and for a split second couldn't reconcile the sight of him looking so completely gorgeous, casually dressed in jeans and a tweed jacket, with the time and place.

"The wedding doesn't start for a few hours," she said,

shaking off her surprise. "What are you doing here so early? Wait a minute. Did my dad ask you to keep an eye on Joey?"

A slow smile spread over that attractive face as he covered the distance between them. "No, he didn't."

"Then why are you here?"

Max didn't answer right away. Instead, he leaned against the wooden fence and crossed his arms over his chest. "Riley told me you were on your way to the barn."

"Do you need something?"

He shook his head. "Just wanted to see how you were doing. Offer my help if you needed it."

It took Lily a second to put two and two together. "The mystery man."

He nodded.

"The mystery man is a mystery." Lily let the gate fall shut.

"So you don't think he's your ex?" Max got straight to the point. "Why else would he cover his head with a jacket so the paparazzi couldn't get a photo to identify him?"

Lily wasn't entirely sure why Max thought this was his business. She wanted to ask, but continuing to avoid it wasn't going to do a thing except keep the whole stupid mess simmering in the back of her brain while she tried to work. She needed to come up with an official response soon, anyway. *No comment* would work for the press but not for her Twitter followers, who were kind enough to care.

"Knowing the way the ex-fling operates, my guess is this is an attempt to manufacture more press. I mean why else would she file a lawsuit she can't possibly win?"

"Makes sense."

She didn't want to discuss this, especially not with

him, but in the quiet predawn, with the first birds awakening and the air scented with cool pine, she found him all too easy to talk to. "I spoke with Lucas while we were fitting the kids' outfits." When she'd found out her idiot big brother had been running his mouth in front of the kids. "He mentioned that he'd changed his plans so I wouldn't have to worry about running into him during designer week. He sent his assistant, thought it best to lay low since news of the lawsuit broke."

"You believe him?" Max asked.

Lily considered that. Hooking an elbow over the rail, she stared into the paling dawn, at the freshly raked lawn leading from the house to the stable. At the wooden cart filled to the brim with clean hay. Soon there would be an archway there, too, decorated in crimson and green hydrangeas, big leathery leaves, pinecones and orange twinkle lights to mark the site where Riley and Scott would exchange vows then start off life as man and wife with a hayride to the stream.

"Doesn't matter what I believe anymore. Lucas claims he dumped the woman when he found out she'd tipped off the press to their whereabouts. I do believe that. Despite his faults, he's an incredible businessman, and his reputation has taken a beating because I'm so visible to the public. He's the bad guy."

"Rightfully so, as far as I'm concerned."

Lily couldn't suppress a chuckle, and appreciated Max's family loyalty. "He's angry—at himself and his lack of judgment—for letting a woman get the better of him because his ego needed to be stroked. Suggests weakness on his part. No, I really don't see him risking more damage to the company he has built from the ground up for a woman so clearly focused on furthering her own self-interests."

"That makes sense, too."

And it did. They'd always had business in common. A career couple, her mother had called them.

Lily stared at Max, a man who cared. A man who would get up early on a Saturday and drive all the way from Hyde Park to check on her.

A man she'd always cared about even though he hadn't really been a part of her life in a long time. He was the sort of man she would want in her life if she was choosing.

And staring into the beautiful dawn, a day filled with promises, not only for Riley and Scott, but also for everyone lucky enough to open their eyes on a new day, Lily knew without question that she hadn't been happy in a long time.

There was her answer.

"You okay?" he asked and the concern was there in those piercing eyes. "Got a lot to deal with today."

He wasn't referring to Lucas, but Mike. "You're very sweet to think of me, but I'm good. Glad we got this media nonsense out of the way before the festivities begin. Not that I expect anyone to bring up that foolishness on Riley's big day. Not even Joey." She smiled, hoping to reassure him. "By the way, thanks for dragging him away the other day."

"Don't mention it. He's only upset because he cares."

Her mom had said the same thing. She hadn't needed to. Lily knew. So many people who cared. Even Max. "I've been away too long. Got a few things to clean up now that I'm back."

He only nodded, seemed to understand.

"And I appreciate you making a trip all the way here to check on me."

"My pleasure, Lily Susan. I hope you take time to

enjoy the day. You get to be a guest for a change. Sort of, anyway."

"*Sort of* is right." She rolled her eyes.

Silence fell between them, filled with such expectation, as if neither knew what came next but didn't want to disturb the moment, didn't want it to end.

At least she didn't.

No, in that moment, Lily felt expectation, and an excitement she couldn't remember feeling in so long.

For a man who had no place in her life.

"I've got to inspect the barn," she said quickly, somehow not able to meet his gaze. Not when the thoughts racing through her brain were all about the reasons why his lifestyle didn't work with hers, about what his mouth might feel like if they kissed. "Thanks, Max. I really appreciate you coming by."

"My pleasure, Lily Susan."

Then he reached for her hand and brought it to his lips.

Her heart stalled in her chest, quit on the edge of a beat, as his warm mouth brushed her skin.

"I'm glad you're okay." He turned and headed to the house.

For a stunned moment, Lily watched him retreat, not registering much more than the attractive sight he made and the way her insides tingled.

It was only when he took the back stairs two at a time and disappeared inside that Lily managed to shake off her daze, too.

God, she had to get a grip. She needed to focus, to work. She had every reason to be happy. No heaters were necessary because the weather was cooperating. The barn should be perfectly comfortable once the sun rose. There would be sixty people inside, lots of excitement and movement, hope and well wishes, a celebration of everything Lily loved about weddings.

She walked across the paddock, following the path the bridal party would take in a few hours. She made note of the various places to point out to Gabrielle, who would be involving the guests in a formal photo shoot outside the barn, immortalizing this family gala.

Lily had pulled in her own photographer, hadn't been willing to trust Riley's memories to anyone less talented and skilled than Gabrielle—who had been Worldwide Weddings Unlimited staff for years and created visual art with her talent.

The barn was a work of art itself, Lily decided as she pulled open the door and flipped on a light, illuminating the scene in breathtaking glory. She skimmed her gaze over every detail, claiming this moment for herself, the deep breath before the plunge, the moment she got to see her vision in form before the action started.

The tables were round eight-tops, and were packed in close, but still allowed enough room for movement and interaction.

White linen draped the tables, and the centerpieces featured Madeleine's pinecones among huge white peonies and sprigs of holly berries. The effect was earthy and woodsy, perfect for the country setting.

Each wineglass had a tiny pinecone tied around the stem with ribbon that matched the favors doubling as place cards. Those decorative boxes, filled with their homemade sugar-cookie messages, sported personalized cards with the guests' names, and on the flipside was the message Made with Love Especially for You.

All true. Lily remembered the chaos in her mother's kitchen and a windy day on the grounds of Overlook, a sweet hostess and her too-charming father.

Twinkling orange lights decorated the railings, a sparkling adornment that extended around the barn, outlining the loft and each service station.

The retro soda bar made a cheerful addition, with its pinstriped canopy in bright green, glass jars of long straws and a glass cooler case that held row upon row of brightly colored bottles in every flavor.

There was another beverage station that would serve coffee, tea and cold apple cider in glass urns. Baskets of crimson hydrangea and shiny green apples decorated the table, perfectly suitable for bobbing or eating. But Lily didn't imagine anyone would be interested in the latter with the nearby dessert bar featuring hand-dipped ice cream and child-size pumpkin baskets to fill with all sorts of retro Halloween candies—Mary Janes, Tootsie Rolls and Hershey miniatures.

The wedding cake would be displayed on another table. It wasn't actually a cake, but a tiered masterpiece of cupcakes in all flavors. Riley hadn't wanted the traditional bride-and-groom topper, so the baker had decorated the top tier of cupcakes with saddle straps and placed a spun sugar saddle on top. Lily had decorated the table with huge sprays of crimson hydrangea.

Absolutely perfect.

"It's so different than the last wedding you planned for me, isn't it?" Riley whispered.

Lily turned to find her sister-in-law standing in the doorway. "Aren't you supposed to be enjoying a leisurely morning coffee? You know, chatting with your mom and stepdad and gearing up for the day?"

"I got the coffee. I sucked down a whole cup while wrangling with your nephew about having Pop Tarts for breakfast."

"Who won?"

Riley grimaced as if Lily should know better than to even ask the question.

"I don't imagine that went over too well."

"Um, no. The little rascal. Told him I wouldn't even keep them in the house for snacks if he didn't back off." She met Lily's gaze. "Max told me you were good, but I wanted to check for myself. Gave me a chance to get out of the chaos."

Lily laughed. "So, what do you think?"

Riley raked a thoughtful gaze over the interior. "It couldn't be more perfect. Two perfect weddings. I don't know how you do it. The kids will be thrilled."

"High praise indeed." But she'd expected Riley to be pleased today. This wedding had been designed exclusively for her. It suited her personality and her wishes.

The last wedding had been Mike's wedding.

Lily had been new in the wedding-planning business back then, had worked hard to please her brother, who had wanted to please his beautiful bride. So they bypassed the chapel and were married in Shakespeare's Garden on Vassar's campus, where the wedding party followed Mike and Riley, who'd ridden in a horse-drawn carriage through the campus.

"Thank you," Riley said simply.

"You're welcome."

"Your brother was the love of my life." Riley stared into the quiet barn but there was no missing the glint in her eyes. "I never thought I could love again, and I was at peace with that. I've got our children and we'll always be his family. But I'm learning love comes in all shapes and sizes and no two loves are ever the same. I'm so very blessed. And grateful. You know how wonderful Scott is. He couldn't possibly love us more."

Lily didn't have words, couldn't have gotten them out

around the thickness in her throat if she had. Riley had tackled Mike's death the same way she tackled life— practically and with so much strength. She was such a wonderful mom to the twins, and Lily needed Riley to know that she was grateful, too.

But she couldn't seem to get the words out. Instead, she gave her a big hug. And in that moment, Riley became an anchor, an example of balance and grace, and Lily managed to shake off her drifting melancholy and find a smile.

"Now, my beautiful bride, let's get you to the house for a little pampering, okay? Gabrielle will be here soon to start taking pictures of the preparations. I'll have to be ready by then, too. And no more wrestling with my nephew, got it? I'll deal with getting the little rascal into his monkey suit if I have to sit on him to do it."

Riley took a deep breath, suddenly looking every inch a fluttery bride. "Promise me you'll do more than work today. This is a family event, and you've worked so hard to make it happen. I want you to enjoy being together with everyone. It's been too long. Will you promise me?"

Leave it to Riley to be worrying about others on her special day. "I promise."

CHAPTER TWENTY

LILY FULLY INTENDED to keep her promise to Riley. By the time the photographer arrived at the house, Lily was dressed, made up and ready to have fun. The bride was photographed in her bedroom, attended by her daughter and mother, who'd arrived from Florida earlier in the week.

Riley's wedding dress was uniquely suited to a second wedding on Halloween in a barn—full-length but flowing and casual with a cotton lace overlay. Her curly hair was pulled off her face and left to drape down her back. There was no headpiece or veil, only her smile and the sparkle in her crystal blue eyes, which were her most beautiful accessories.

The florist arrived.

Bouquets—check.

Boutonnieres—check.

Serving-table arrangements—check.

Fresh sprays for the archway and chairs—check, check.

The groom arrived. One handsome cop set to take on a ready-made family—check.

Camille ducked out of Riley's bedroom to get her almost stepfather settled in Jake's room on the opposite side of the house. "You can't see Pop Scott until you walk down the aisle," she informed her mom. "It's tradition."

"Love of weddings seems to be a generational thing." Riley met Lily's reflection in the mirror.

She laughed. "So it would seem. Just make sure you do as she says. We don't want to spoil the romance."

Riley rolled her eyes but looked quite willing to be swept away by all the tradition and excitement.

Lily sent Gabrielle to photograph the men getting dressed. She intended to document the preparations in a series of candid photos to fashion into a hardbound book as one of her wedding gifts, so Riley and Scott could share these special moments leading to the ceremony. Camille would like that.

Excitement mounted as they prepared and photographed the wedding party, which was small with only bride, groom, Camille as maid of honor and Jake as best man. Riley's mom and stepdad would walk her down the aisle—or over the paddock, as it was. And there was a casualness to the proceedings that wasn't typically a part of Lily's work. She didn't hesitate to step into the kitchen to grab a cup of coffee. She shared the laughter even as she was ordering everyone around.

She felt a part of the fun as Camille talked Riley into abandoning pearl earrings for a pair of her own flashy danglers to spice up the wedding dress.

She actually got misty-eyed when Jake showed up to let Riley see that he'd put on his suit, from tie right on down to the shoes that squeezed his toes.

"Pop Scott didn't even have to pull his gun," he said proudly, Mike's grin on his face. "It's your wedding present."

Riley knelt to hug her beautiful children, this beloved family that had been through so much in the years since Mike's death.

And Gabrielle, skilled professional that she was, captured each and every second without interfering.

Lily took the opportunity to slip away and clear her

own misty gaze. The bride was allowed a few tears. The parents of the bride, and guests, even. But not the wedding coordinator, not even though she was family. Hurrying down to the barn, she conducted a final inspection.

The band and sound system—check.

The caterers and food—check.

The bakery and cupcakes—check.

The ushers, consisting of her nephew Brian and several young men from a youth volunteer program Scott ran through the police department, arrived for instructions about seating guests—check.

Guests were already being seated by the time she made it inside and found her niece frantic.

"What's wrong?"

"My shoes are slippery and I slid down the steps." All that on one halting breath.

"Are you okay?" Lily sank to her knees to survey the damage. "No blood. That's good."

"I've got a big hole. And I need to look perfect for Mommy's pictures."

Definitely a trauma on such an exciting day. There was scuffed skin exposed through a tear in the otherwise pristine white tights. But the damage to Camille seemed minimal, so Lily reached onto the counter and grabbed a napkin to dry Camille's cheeks. "No getting upset, little squirrel. We can fix this."

"We can't fix this big hole."

Lily stood up and took her niece's hand. "I know a secret."

Camille glanced up curiously as they headed into the family room, where Lily had stored all her gear.

"There's no such thing as an accident if you're prepared. That's a good life lesson I want you to remember. Okay?"

"Okay," Camille promised, even though Lily was fairly sure her niece had no clue what Lily was talking about.

She withdrew a shrink-wrapped pair of tights in Camille's size. She winked. "This is why they pay your aunt the big bucks."

Camille wrapped her arms around Lily, catching her around the hips in a tight hug. "Oh, I love you, Aunt Lily Susan."

Smoothing a hand over the silky blond head with her elaborate updo, Lily said, "I love you, little squirrel."

And there were tears, right below the surface, ready to make an appearance without permission.

Lily helped Camille quickly change her tights and they rejoined Riley in time to greet Chief Levering, Scott's boss and Poughkeepsie's chief of police, who would officiate.

"Good to see you, Lily Susan." He gave her a hug. "It's been a long time."

Lily skipped right over mention of the last time they'd met. Chief Levering had been Mike's boss, too. "Thanks for taking part in the festivities. Is Deb already seated?"

He nodded. "Keeping a spot warm for me."

"We're all set with the paperwork. Riley's parents will witness after the ceremony, since our maid of honor and best man haven't reached the age of majority yet. Sound good?"

Chief Levering nodded, then Lily steered him toward Scott for last-minute instructions before she sent the men outside.

"We're almost ready to go," she said. "How's everyone doing here?"

"How do I look, Aunt Lily Susan?" Camille twirled. She met Lily's gaze and winked. Gabrielle snapped off a few more shots.

"Perfect. You couldn't possibly be more beautiful." And with any luck, a smile would be another part of Jake's wedding gift to Riley. "Let me see you with your bouquet."

Camille scooped up the bouquet of white flowers interspersed with bright orange and yellow and greenery the same shade as her skirt.

"Perfect."

She herded everyone inside the hall outside of Riley's bedroom so she could get the men outside without being seen. And then Lily directed them out the front door for their trip around the house and down the slope of the yard to where the groom waited, looking dashing and handsome in his police blues and brass, Jake beside him, the smile not yet in place though he looked adorable in his suit, the wedding rings clutched inside a fist.

Lily stopped everyone before they came into view, giving Gabrielle a chance to move ahead of the procession. Then she cued the band and almost instantly, the music faded and transformed into the familiar strains of Pachabel's *Canon in D*, the beautiful music swelling into the crisp autumn day. The guests stood and turned toward the house.

Lily smiled at Camille. "You're on, little squirrel. Smile pretty."

Riley kissed her daughter before she stepped forward with a bright smile.

"I'm grateful, too," Lily whispered to Riley.

"Thank you. For everything." Riley's tears seemed to be waiting to make an appearance, too. Exhaling sharply, she blinked them back and said, "Okay, I can do this."

Her parents looped their arms through Riley's, giving subtle support, and they stepped around the corner as Camille reached the rows of chairs.

Lily hung back, spotting Max, who was holding Madeleine in his arms so she could watch the procession. But Max was probably the only one in the crowd who wasn't watching the bride. His gaze caught Lily's across the distance then swept appreciatively over her, a look that made her stomach swoop in eager reply. Lily willed her body to behave, but the chemistry was there, too real to deny, too strong to fight.

The past and the present seemed to blur in that moment, her memories of fantasy weddings colliding with the man who gazed at her with awareness, not the imagined attention of her youth.

The guests all turned to follow Riley's journey. Not Max. His gaze still held hers unreservedly, searching for something, seeking, and Lily had to tear her gaze away, force herself to focus, to see whether the videographer had circled the guests to get the prime angle of the archway.

Riley took Scott's hand and smiled down at both twins, while her parents retreated to their seats and Chief Levering told everyone to be seated.

Lily didn't join the guests, wasn't sure why she hung back. She could barely hear the chief, could only follow the service because she knew the ceremony by heart. The twins performed their roles brilliantly. Camille took Riley's bouquet when Jake presented the rings to Scott. This would be the wedding they would always remember, their yardstick for perfect weddings that they took with them through their lives.

They hadn't been around for their parents' wedding, with the Cinderella carriage on the blooming grounds in the spring. They had pictures to show them, like they had of the father who'd loved them so very much. They'd been so young when he died. How could they even remember him?

Thankfully autopilot kicked in when the guests cheered the new couple on their hayride and she occupied herself with directing the guests toward the barn, where the doors were thrown wide and the music spilled out and the refreshments began flowing. Where guests gasped aloud in surprise at the transformation of the barn into a fantasy reception hall, where people lined up, clamoring to take a turn on the hayride, and their laughter made the most beautiful music of the day.

Lily supervised, one moment rushing into the next until the hours passed in a blur. There were formal photos and introductions and video guest interviews and toasts and dinner and dancing and two-sided tape, when Jake, who was dancing with Riley, pulled out half of her hem with his heel.

"I told Mommy you'd fix it," Camille said after tracking down Lily, who was outside directing her nephew Brian to let the horses graze while he went inside to eat. "That's why they pay you the big bucks."

And there was more laughter. Everywhere she turned someone was laughing loud enough to be heard over the music and chatter.

And there were compliments. Lots and lots of compliments all directed to her. About everything from the apple-cider bar to the flowers to the weather, as if Lily had control of that.

"Excusez moi, madame," said a familiar male voice in a horrific French accent as Lily turned away from the front man of the band, who was also master of ceremonies. "I understand that you've forgotten an important promise you made to the bride."

"Oh, no." Lily turned to Max. "What's that?"

Max surprised her by catching her full against him and waltzing her onto the dance floor as the trendy pop tune slowed to a ballad.

Lily had no choice but to follow his lead, breathless from the strength of his arms around her, from the feel of his body so close every hard muscle seemed to mold against her.

Lowering his head, he pressed his cheek to hers and whispered against her ear, "To have fun."

Why was he tempting her this way? He should know better than to play with fire, and what was erupting between them was nothing short of combustible.

"Riley…" It wasn't a question. But she managed to find some tiny shred of reason inside that wasn't focused on the warmth of his body or the clean male scent she inhaled with every shallow breath. "She told you to dance with me?"

He tipped his head enough so she could see his face, and from this close, and unfamiliar vantage, he was breathtaking. "I don't need anyone to tell me to dance with a beautiful woman."

The young girl who had once dreamed of this man paying attention to her was apparently still alive and living inside the adult she'd become. She melted from the inside out. What did she even say to that? Not that he gave her a chance to reply. No. He had her off guard and he knew it.

And he took advantage.

Leaning into her, he bent her low over his arm. All she could do was go full-bodied with the motion, feel every inch of his hard thighs against hers, his arm an anchor that held her with such unyielding grace.

There was a split second when she literally stopped breathing, the past and present colliding again in that crazy way. Hadn't she imagined dancing with him before? At her fantasy weddings? Or had she simply wanted to dance with him at Caroline's wedding or Joey's or Mike's? How could they possibly have attended so many family functions and never once danced together?

"You know what's happening between us, Lily Susan?"

A gasp slipped out before she could think to hold it back. A loud gasp, by the amusement transforming his expression.

What was he doing? He couldn't talk about their chemistry, mention what kept flaring between them every time they saw each other. How could they keep their reactions under control if they gave it substance, brought it out into the sunlight?

Or Halloween twinkle lights, as it was.

"We're ignoring the heat, Max. We were ignoring it, so we wouldn't get burned."

Leading her into a slow spin, he bought himself time to make sense of what she'd said, to come up with some way to overcome her objection. She knew Max so well, knew what he was doing. Then she was twirling toward him, suddenly up close and personal again, her pulse rushing a slow, heavy beat that had nothing to do with the music.

"Why shouldn't we go up in flames?" he asked.

"Because fire is dangerous."

"Some chances are worth taking, Lily Susan."

God, why wasn't she surprised? She should be, but she wasn't. When had this man ever played by the rules?

He was a Downey, for goodness' sake. He lived at Overlook, yet he'd spent practically half his life at her house.

"Think about it, Max. It only makes sense." She sounded breathless and pleading, not remotely rational.

"You're a dad with a beautiful little girl and a life here. I don't even live close. What can we possibly do with that?"

He seized the moment, urging her into another dip. He helped her straighten, encouraged her closer until she could feel his warm breath against her temple when he said, "I don't have an answer for the logistics. I only have how I feel."

His gaze poured over her face, a bold look that proved his words. Obviously he didn't care who might see.

"Isn't that the perfect place to start?" he whispered as the music faded, robbing Lily of a chance to reply because suddenly her dad was there, grinning that wide grin, clapping Max on the back.

"You win an award for getting her to slow down long enough to have some fun," he said. "Swing by the store and I'll set you up with some sprinkler heads. On the house."

Her dad and Max both howled at that, leaving Lily a moment to steady her pounding heart. Or try to. Her thoughts were racing. Max had changed everything with a few words, and she had no chance to sort through her reaction, no chance to do anything but step into the circle of her dad's arms and remember what it had always felt like to feel safe here.

To feel loved.

"You must be pleased, honey-bunch," he said. "Your wedding is a success. I knew you could do it."

"Thanks, Daddy." She kissed his cheek. In her heels she was as tall as he was. "But I had a lot of help."

"You're good at what you do, and I'm very proud of you."

"That's so sweet."

"I mean it." He rested his cheek against her temple. "I've missed having my little girl at home."

And that was the crux of it, Lily knew. He didn't say another word, just enjoyed the opportunity to spend time with her, making the most of the moments she allowed him because she'd been so stingy with her time.

She could change that, and would. There were so many things to consider, if she'd only slow down long enough to consider them. Her family. Pleasant Valley.

Max.

She thought she understood where he was coming from. He was a man. The love of his life had died long before their life together should have been over. And she was a woman. One he'd known forever. A woman he thought was beautiful.

Somewhere deep inside her unfolded, a place she'd ignored for a long, long time, but her reason screamed a warning. She wasn't his kind of woman, for so many reasons. Not the least of which was that she wasn't what he admired above all—a woman with her priorities straight.

That would be her dad and mom and everyone else he liked in her family. Not his mother. Not her. Here she was, completely and totally attracted to the man of her wildest dreams, the man she'd always been completely and totally attracted to, and she couldn't trust what she felt, couldn't trust her reaction to him. Didn't know whether or not the way she felt was real. She was so good at deceiving herself.

Are you happy? her mother had asked.

Finally, she could answer the question.

No. She wasn't happy.

Her dad guided her around the dance floor. Not with the smooth, athletic strides that Max had before him, but with a familiar motion that was all strength and security wrapped up in his burly hug. Her dad was getting older. Her mom was getting older. The twins were growing up and she was missing everything. Caroline and Riley were more sisters than Lily and Caroline, despite the blood tie, because proximity counted. Joey was angry and had to wait so long to address his issues with her that he'd simmered to the point of combustion.

No, she wasn't happy. If Mike had taught her anything at all, it was that life was precious and shouldn't be wasted.

She'd had a near miss with Lucas, but had gotten lucky. She'd wasted too much time on that man, getting sucked into a semblance of a life and telling herself it was good enough.

It wasn't. Nowhere near enough.

So what did she really want? Lily had everything she'd always wanted in her life—Worldwide Weddings Unlimited, travel, fantasy, success.

So why wasn't she happy?

"Mind if I take this pretty lady off your hands, Dad?" Joey.

Lily held her breath as her dad bowed out gracefully, giving Joey a warning glance before disappearing between the couples on the crowded dance floor.

Surely Joey wouldn't be a jerk in the middle of this special occasion. Of course, he'd confronted her in this very barn in the middle of everyone only a few days ago. Lily opened her mouth to start evasive maneuvers, but Joey headed her off by saying, "I'm sorry for going nuts the other day. I should have dealt with the way I felt a long time ago."

She met his gaze. Her big brother. He was getting older, too. There were sprinkles of gray in his sideburns, a few wiry hairs in his eyebrows that made him look so much like their dad.

"You shouldn't have had to chase me." She remembered her mom's words. "I've stayed away way too long. It was selfish."

He liked that. Lowering his head to hers, he softly head-butted her forehead in a gesture from when she'd been a little girl begging for attention from her older brother. "It started out as being worried about you after Mike. And then there was the guy. All right, I admit it. It was a power thing." He chuckled, clearly not worried at all about whether or not they'd put this behind them. "It's my right as the oldest to give anyone who's even thinking about joining this family a walk around the block."

Meaning give them hell. And no one had gotten in without it. Not even Riley.

She hadn't given him that chance with Lucas. That walk around the block that proved he cared and would have let Lucas know that she wasn't alone in the world, that she would have backup if he behaved poorly.

"I love you, baby sistuh," he said with a grin. Their dad's grin. Mike's grin. Jake's grin. "Remember that."

He didn't wait for her reply because the song was over and they were getting shoved to the edge of the dance floor by the kids, who were raring to dance now that the tempo picked up.

And why should he wait for her reply? He knew she'd forgive him. They were family. Nothing should get in the way of family. Nothing was ever so monumental that it couldn't be let go. Nothing too hurtful it couldn't be hugged away.

Family.

Lily wasn't sure what happened then. She glanced around the room, at Riley and Scott laughing as they made their way to the cake table to distribute their tiered cupcakes under the head caterer's promptings, because the kids could wait no longer for the hand-dipped ice cream no matter how much soda and candy they'd already had. At Camille and Madeleine hanging onto Jake for dear life on the dance floor because her nephew was ready to bolt. At Brian, who had brought his girlfriend and was dancing cheek-to-cheek, two college students in love. At Mom and Dad laughing with Chief Levering and his wife Deb at their table. At Max chatting with Caroline and her husband Alex over bottles of orange soda.

All Lily could see was the one person missing, the person who should have been here because if he were, they wouldn't be having this wedding. The entire event would have been just some Halloween patrol picnic.

CHAPTER TWENTY-ONE

MAX KNEW THE INSTANT he saw Lily Susan slip outside that he shouldn't have pushed her. She wasn't ready to deal with what was happening between them. And now he'd upset her and had probably ruined any chance he might have had for her to take him seriously.

Joey noticed her fast exit, too, and showed up at the table as Max excused himself.

"Something's wrong," Joey said. "We were good a few minutes ago, I swear."

The very last thing Max wanted to do was explain how he'd made a play for Lily Susan. Not now. Not when everyone was so worried and they were beginning to get a handle on the problem. But he didn't get a chance to say anything. To his surprise Joey waved him on.

"You go," he said. "I'll make up some excuse about where she went. Don't worry about Madeleine. I got her."

Max understood. If everyone noticed Lily Susan was gone, they'd worry. And today wasn't the day for worrying.

He slipped out the side door as the master of ceremonies was sending the guests to the cake table.

This was his fault. With everything going on, today was the last day he should have confronted Lily Susan about what was happening between them. Pure selfishness on his part. He hadn't been thinking. He'd been feeling—how good she felt in his arms. How much he wanted to get her someplace alone and dance, hold her close and kiss her. Finally kiss her.

Turning the corner of the house, he found Lily Susan maneuvering her rental car out of the driveway. She pulled out and headed toward the Valley, leaving him scrambling to get into his car so he didn't lose her.

Thankfully, he'd parked on the grass between the road and the garage to keep out of the way.

They were halfway to the Valley before Max even caught sight of her. She was taking turns fast in a rental car that was small and environmentally friendly. The car of a woman who spent a lot of time in Europe. He could easily see her whipping through the chaos on the streets of Rome or Paris.

Slowing, he hung back so she wouldn't see him as she merged with traffic. She didn't make the turn for her parents' house. Her office? He considered calling her on the cell, but when she turned off Route 44, Max thought he knew where she was going.

And sure enough, a few miles later, the blinker went on, and she pulled into St. Peter's Cemetery.

Maybe he wasn't the reason Lily Susan had gotten upset, after all. And maybe he and Joey hadn't been that far off the mark with their speculation, either.

This cemetery had been around since long before his great-grandfather's time, a sprawling place behind an iron fence the city of Poughkeepsie had grown up around. Downeys were resting all over the wooded acreage, but not Felicia and their son. No, Max had honored her parents' wishes to let them rest with the Girard family in their hometown a few hours' north. Even though it wasn't as simple for him and Madeleine to drop by in between holidays, he knew his in-laws were comforted. That counted.

Max eased his SUV through the entrance, not wanting to be noticed yet unwilling to lose sight of Lily Susan, although he had no doubt about where she was headed.

To his surprise, though, she didn't drive down the winding lanes toward Mike's grave site. Nor did she head toward the office and the chapel. Instead, she pulled her rental off the lane. The brake lights flashed and faded. She didn't move again.

Five minutes passed. Ten minutes. After fifteen, worry won Max's battle with patience. He could see her silhouette, unmoving, as if she were staring down the lane.

Decision made, Max's heart rate ratcheted up as he shoved open the door and stepped out. His footsteps crunched over dried leaves as he covered the distance between the cars and he was glad for the noise. He debated whether or not to call out so as not to startle her.

The sight of her, so beautiful in her designer dress, but with tears flowing freely down her cheeks, all her usual poise not only gone but also broken, did things inside him that proved how much he cared about this woman.

"Lily Susan," he said softly through the open window. No response. "Lily Susan."

She turned toward him, so locked in her anguish she didn't seemed surprised to find him there.

"I don't even know where he is." The words were the barest whisper, filled with tears. "He's here somewhere, and I don't know where he is. I haven't been here since the funeral."

St. Peter's Cemetery was huge, no question. That she hadn't thought to head to the office where there was a locater guide told Max everything he needed to know.

"He's not far. We can walk from here." He was already easing the door open, taking her hand, helping her out.

She walked beside him without a word, gliding along

the grass in high heels as if she were crossing a ball-room, allowing herself to be steered around grave sites, her warm hand in his, so trusting.

The afternoon hush was broken only by the occasional sounds of wildlife in the trees, birds that hadn't yet abandoned the area for a warmer climate, the sounds of passage crackling dried leaves on the ground.

And there it was. A simple white marble gravestone with two angels with outstretched wings on top.

Mike's memorial looked like a party compared to other grave sites. There were the usual flowers, but along with the fresh flowers fading in the metal holder there were signs of frequent visits. Camille and Jake's most recent school pictures. Four small plastic horses with their hooves pressed deep into the grass to keep them upright. A bright pinwheel that caught a breeze every so often and spun silently. A bottle of Guinness Stout. Gifts from those who loved the man whose name was immortalized in marble, the beloved man who rested here.

Michael Jacob Angelica
Beloved Husband and Father
4/4/1975–2/2/2008
Always in our hearts

Lily Susan stood transfixed at the sight, and Max let his hand slip away, retreated as she sank down, resting back on her heels, her fancy dress spreading around her.

He had no frame of reference for what she was feeling. He'd experienced losses, but he'd learned that loss was unique, the way love was unique.

Mike was Lily Susan. Lily Susan was Mike.

No, Max had no way to know how she felt. He only remembered two little blond kids from his own youth. So inseparable he'd always called them the girl twin and the boy twin. So like Mike's kids. Each their own person yet so completely the same. Two halves of a whole.

No, Max couldn't truly fathom how Lily Susan felt. He'd lost half his heart and soul when Felicia and their son had died.

Lily Susan had lost half of herself.

"He's not here." Her whisper barely broke the afternoon quiet.

And Max glimpsed a small part of what Lily Susan was feeling. Of what she'd been running from.

"Mike never left," he said simply. "This is a memorial, nothing more. Mike was Riley. And Camille and Jake. He was your mom and dad. And you. He was everyone who loved him. You haven't forgotten him, have you?"

She shook her head, the tears flowing freely again, though she didn't look away from the gravestone.

"You remember every crazy thing you two ever did together. You remember every nasty word he ever said when you were bullying him into being a groom in your make-believe weddings. You remember every sweet thing he ever did. What was that thing he used to do at night? He did it every time I was over and Rosie herded you two off to bed before everyone else because you were so little."

"Foot crumbs." Those broken words were barely audible even in the quiet, but Max remembered.

"That's it. I remember. As soon as your mom would tell you two to get ready for bed, he'd tear through the house and jump into your bed."

"Without wiping his feet," she said a little stronger now. "I hated anything dirty touching my clean sheets."

"Sounds like something Jake would pull on Camille, doesn't it?"

She only nodded, but he could see a hint of a smile in profile, the slightest softening of her mouth.

"Mike will never leave because you remember everything about him. You were a part of him, Lily Susan. His twin."

"He was my better half."

Max went to her then, knew if he didn't she might never find the strength to stand. He knelt beside her, forced her to face him, braced himself to see the anguish in those eyes.

"Mike won't ever leave because you have him here." He rested his hand on her chest above her heart. "And here." He brushed his fingers across her forehead. "You remember everything he was and just because he's not at Sunday dinner every week or harassing you on the phone doesn't mean you'll ever stop loving him."

Her sobs broke then, an intrusion in the hush of this place, welling up from so deep inside her that she shook as Max pulled her into his arms, cradling her against him, lending his strength when she couldn't find her own, refusing to let her get lost in her grief.

He whispered her name over and over against her hair, inhaled her light fragrance with every breath, tried not to notice how perfectly she fit into his arms even when she was boneless from grief.

When her sobs finally faded, he reached into his pocket and pulled out a handkerchief to dry her cheeks. She finally lifted her gaze to his, and he knew she'd found herself again.

"You're very sweet, Max."

Sweet wasn't exactly what he was looking for from her, but he'd take what he could get right now. Getting to his feet, he extended his hand. She slipped her soft fingers within and he helped her rise.

Still he didn't reply, didn't want reality to intrude on their closeness.

She pressed a kiss to her fingertips and brushed her hand along those marble angels and Max knew she was ready to leave. Neither spoke as he led them back to the cars, but when they got to her rental, he felt compelled to break the silence by asking, "Are you okay? We can drive back in my car if you want. I'll come back with Joey to get yours."

She shook her head, exhaled a shuddering sigh. "I'm a mess, Max. I'm not happy. I haven't been since...I don't know when. And it's not Lucas." She waved off the notion with an impatient hand. "That was a blessing in disguise. I think I only got involved with him because something was missing and I didn't know what."

Max could see the truth in her words, felt a profound relief to hear her admit that there was a problem. Especially as she was recovering herself, and the vulnerable, real woman who had melted in his arms to be comforted vanished in bits and pieces, placing more and more distance between them.

He didn't know how to keep her with him, though he wanted to say something that would. His conflict must have been all over his face, because she said, "I can't deal with how I feel about you now. I'm sorry. Not until I figure out what's broken inside me and fix it. Riley healed. She's beginning a whole new life today, and I don't question that she loved my brother with her whole heart and soul. That she still loves him. I don't think I have her strength."

"You have the strength, Lily Susan. You'll find it as soon as you stop running."

She only frowned at him.

"Running from grief. It'll follow you wherever you go.

Trust me. Riley will tell you the same thing." She'd escaped to Florida for two years before making peace with Mike's death.

Lily Susan didn't reply. He couldn't tell whether or not she believed him because she inhaled deeply and a visible calm came over her, fragile perhaps, but impenetrable all the same. The distance between them was complete. The Wedding Angel had returned.

Max wanted the woman he'd held in his arms, the real Lily Susan, the woman so few people ever saw. He was determined to find a way to have her.

"Okay, it's all good."

"You're going back?"

She nodded, almost grinned. "This is my family, remember? We planned the party to last until the sun goes down and after, if necessary. I'll come up with some excuse for leaving."

"Find Joey before you say anything to anyone. He was going to come up with a reason. You'll want to keep your stories straight."

Her expression softened at that, and he could see through the veneer enough to know she was pleased her big brother had covered for her.

She held up the rumpled handkerchief, clearly undecided about returning it when she saw all the makeup.

"Can you tell I've been crying?" She tipped her face up to his, eyes fluttering shut for inspection. "How do I look?"

He found himself smiling, hopeful in a way he couldn't remember feeling in so long. The makeup was entirely gone, and in its place the natural sun-kissed glow of the real woman.

Pressing a kiss to her forehead, he whispered, "Beautiful."

CHAPTER TWENTY-TWO

Finally taking the vacation! Yay! Limiting work to only a few hours a day and leaving the rest to my enormously capable and always appreciated staff. You rock! See you when I return to reality in five glorious days—I'll be hitting the ground running.

LILY PRESSED Send and posted to her Twitter account, but what she really wanted to tweet was: Taking a deep breath to clear my head and get my priorities straight. Wish me luck—I need it.

What had happened to the woman who didn't believe in luck, good, bad or otherwise?

The only thing Lily knew for certain right now was that life had gone off track somewhere along the line and she needed to get it back on again.

Allowing herself to come down off the little wedding and refresh herself for the big wedding was her first step in doing that. She didn't care that there were still a thousand details to follow up on. Mara and Denise could call and check that the gowns were on schedule as easily as she could. Right now she needed a breather. Period. The timing seemed perfect as the twins had moved into her parents' house while the newlyweds headed to Canada for a honeymoon.

Work couldn't be blown off entirely, of course, not with so much going on. But Lily managed to condense her workday into a few hours to oversee and delegate the things that couldn't possibly await her attention. But she only spoke with her staff and didn't once deal with a vendor or even visit the office.

The rest of the time she spent driving the twins to and from school, being shown off to teachers and classmates, sharing lunch in a deafeningly noisy cafeteria, helping with homework so they could go to the park or the mall or curl up in front of the television in a nest of blankets for a Disney-movie marathon.

There was lots of giggling and her mother was in her element, too, nurturing everyone with their favorite meals and nighttime cups of cocoa with lots of marshmallows.

She slept late one morning. Of course, she'd had to drug herself with nighttime acetaminophen, but once the groggy feeling had worn off, she actually felt refreshed, as if she'd actually rested rather than merely slept.

She even talked Riley into letting the twins skip school to visit Mystic Seaport, a maritime museum in Connecticut Lily had loved visiting on field trips, a place that had inspired the many nautical-themed weddings she'd planned since.

She also remembered staring out to sea on those field trips, knowing Europe and the rest of the world was out there somewhere across the waves and wishing she could weigh anchor to get there. To sail into the great wide unknown.

Once that had seemed such a romantic future, so full of possibilities. Now it made her wonder why she always wanted to be someplace other than where she was. She found it very curious that when she'd finally gotten someplace else—a world full of someplace elses in fact—she wasn't happy.

And she wasn't. She had to make peace with Mike's

loss, determine how much that factored into her discontent. Because Max had been right when he said she'd been running. She stayed away so she could pretend everything was exactly the way she left it. But she couldn't honestly say she was happy with her life before Mike, either. Rather, she'd been ambitious and too busy to even ask the question.

Now, when the kids were at school and Rosie was doing the payroll for the store, Lily surfed the web and researched the grieving process. She recognized some of the symptoms, read up on how learning to cope was a process, one that would take time, but she was determined. She remembered what Riley had told her about how the farm was all they had left of Mike and the dreams he'd had for their family. If Riley could learn to make peace, Lily could, too. Mike would never want the people he loved to struggle. He'd want them to live.

And she wasn't living. Had she ever really? All she ever did was work. Was that really all she wanted from life? What were ten thousand Twitter followers when she could sit in a blanket nest and play footsies with Camille and Jake?

"Max called again," her mother said. She'd been holed up in the home office all morning. "On the landline. He said you're not picking up his calls."

He'd narced on her? "That's not true. I spoke with him earlier in the week and told him I was taking a few days off and would be unavailable. I don't want to think about the wedding. At least not more than I have to."

All fact. She'd thanked Max for his kindness and caring while she'd been upset. She appreciated his help, but she simply couldn't deal with what was happening between them. She'd been up front, had asked for time to sort out her head. She had no clue how long that would take.

Rosie set the bank-deposit envelope and checkbook on the kitchen counter and came to stand in the open doorway of the back porch. She eyed Lily thoughtfully, not saying a word that her feet were on the coffee table as she worked on her laptop.

"Is that the only reason?" Rosie asked.

"Sure, why else would I pick up his calls?"

She narrowed her eyes. "Just so you know, Joey already told me."

"Joey told you what?"

"That he thought something might be going on between you and Max."

"This is why I don't come home more often," Lily said peevishly. "Just so you know. And make sure Dad understands, too, so he doesn't blame me when I vanish again."

Rosie exhaled heavily and came to sit on the nearby ottoman, which Lily probably should have been using to prop her feet instead of the coffee table. "He only told me that he thought you and Max might be developing an interest in each other."

Why had Lily made peace with her brother again? "What on earth makes him think that? Did Max say anything?"

"Not that I know of."

"Then this is speculation."

"Your brother isn't an idiot, Lily Susan. He has eyes in his head. He and Max have been friends a long time."

"I hate to disagree with you but, yes, Joey is an idiot. Because there isn't anything to see."

"He sees the same thing I see." Her mother arched a skeptical eyebrow. "I hope you don't think I'm an idiot, too. We've all been watching that boy try to find his way since Felicia died. We help when we can and pray for him when we can't. He has had a lot to deal with and he's healing. It takes time."

Lily hated thinking about Max coping with so much heartache, and the way he tried to be everything to his little girl.

And because she was a coward. She had to force herself to ask because she didn't want to hear what her mom was going to say. "Okay, what is it you think you see?"

"He's alive. For the first time in so long I barely remember. He's interested in life again."

"That's a wonderful thing," Lily agreed neutrally.

"Something has his attention."

"If you're implying that I have his attention, Mom, I'll remind you that we're planning a wedding together. He needs me at the moment. That's all."

"He doesn't need to plan the wedding with you, does he?"

Setting the laptop onto the love seat beside her, she faced her mom squarely. "Listen to me, Mom. Max is involved because he's worried about his mother. You know Ginger. She can get out of hand sometimes. He didn't want her to take over on his brother-in-law's dime."

"I know. That's why he hired *you*. Do you really think with everything he's got on his plate he cares about the details?"

"Well, when you put it like *that*..."

"I'm not sure why you seem so surprised, Lily Susan. You've always had a crush on him."

For people who claimed to want her to visit more often... There simply were no secrets in a family like this one. "Mother, I was a child. And what does my childhood crush have to do with Max helping me plan the wedding?"

"He's a wonderful young man who's still a little vulnerable. Especially to a woman who thinks the moon and the stars hang on him."

"You think I still have a crush on him?" How could she deny it when even she'd been surprised by her response to him? That her feelings could be so transparent made her inwardly cringe.

"Are you saying you don't?"

Lily suddenly remembered a line from *Moonstruck,* one of her all-time favorite movies. "I should have taken a rock and killed myself years ago," Cher, playing the lead role of Loretta Castorini, had said.

Boy, did Lily understand the feeling. "Mother—"

"I only want to know if you're planning to hurt him."

"How can I possibly hurt him?"

"By not taking his phone calls for one thing."

Well, she couldn't argue that now, could she? "Why would you think I'd even do that? And why are you so worried?"

Her mom didn't reply right away, looking so indecisive that Lily braced herself.

"It's not that I think you would hurt him intentionally, Lily Susan," Rosie explained. "But as I said, you've had an interest in him for a long time. You might dismiss your feelings more easily than he might. I thought you needed to know. And I'm worried because your father and I are a part of the reason you're handling the wedding."

Somehow that didn't surprise Lily. "How big a part?"

Her mother gave a small shrug, looked decidedly sheepish. "Max was debating what to do. He wanted to ask for Ginger's help, but he had those concerns. We suggested you because you were going to be here for Riley. We wanted you to stay as long as we could keep you here."

"I knew it."

"All I'm asking is that you be kind. If you're not interested in him in a real way, that's fine. But don't ignore him. He's had a very rough road, Lily Susan, and he's so wonderful. You couldn't possibly ask for a more loving or kind or loyal man."

Lily honestly couldn't think of anything to say. What could she say?

Her family was crazy on a good day?

She'd brought this on herself for not visiting more often?

Rosie seemed to recognize that no answer was forthcoming, so she stood and headed through the door. "And for the record, your father and I would approve of Max."

Meaning they hadn't approved of Lucas.

She retrieved her bank deposit envelope and desktop checkbook and disappeared from sight, leaving Lily staring after her, totally unsure what to do with that entire exchange.

Her family was still backing Max.

They didn't trust her to handle the situation kindly. Because they all knew something was sizzling between them.

Thank you, Joey. That stupid brother of hers. But even as the thought entered her mind, Lily knew he was only worried about her and Max. Two people he cared about. And she'd much rather have her stupid big brother concerned about her in his stupid nosy way than have him not care.

Or not be here at all.

Resting her head on the cushion, she closed her eyes and tried to block out the memory of dancing with Max, their bodies almost touching, that dimple as he bent over her in a dip, blocking out her view of the world except for his handsome face. She couldn't shake off the memory of him. Or how she felt in the cemetery when she'd come completely unglued in his arms. His voice throaty and low. His caring kindnesses.

Okay, so they had chemistry. She'd have to be dead not to notice. But their chemistry couldn't be translated into real life. Maybe for two other people but not for her and Max.

The logistics completely didn't work even if they were inclined to give in. She would be in town for only three more weeks, and they were not a couple who could have anything but a responsible relationship. Anything else would only serve to create awkwardness every time they ran into each other. *Forever.* There was no question about whether or not he'd remain involved with her family.

When he finally met another woman he could love— and he would because he was a handsome man with his priorities straight and a Downey to boot—he'd find a woman who would be a good mother to Madeleine, a woman who would be around to attend school functions, not one who worked around the world and couldn't manage to get home for years on end.

But Lily had to ask herself if that's really what she wanted. Now that she recognized the reason she'd been avoiding home, she could choose to do things differently. Did she really want to be the single, celebrity aunt who wasn't a real part of anyone's life, who only came home every now and then and dropped into everyone's lives for a fantasy holiday?

Another fantasy—like the weddings she created.

And they were fantasies, no question. One beautiful day filled with excitement and possibilities, immortalized forever digitally. After the wedding came the marriage and the real work, the real life, the days in and days out, when couples lived up to their vows or not. *For better or worse, in sickness and in health, forsaking all others...*

Ugh. Lily squeezed her eyes tightly shut. Technically Lucas hadn't betrayed anything but his integrity and her trust. She'd been spared the vows.

But she'd seen real life with couples who did live up to the vows. Her parents. Max's parents. Joey and Sarah. Caroline and Alex.

Mike.

Felicia.

Riley and Max had been forced to find the strength to go on for the sake of the beautiful little people who depended on them.

To heal and find love again.

"I'm learning love comes in all shapes and sizes and no two loves are ever the same," Riley had said.

Max was too vital a man not to find another love, one that could translate into real life. He deserved that kind of love. Her mother was right—Lily couldn't ask for a more wonderful man. She had always known that. And Madeleine deserved someone *real* to love her, too.

Lily's phone vibrated.

Glancing down, she half expected to see Max's name on the display, but the landline from the Poughkeepsie office flashed. Lily should have felt relieved.

"How bad?" she asked.

Mara chuckled on the other end. "Now that's awfully cynical, Lily. What makes you think it's bad?"

"Because we've already spoken today and you know I'm taking a mental-health break so you wouldn't have called unless something bad had happened. Which leaves, how bad?"

"Not earth-shattering, but it needs attention."

Mara launched into the tale of why the A-list entertainment company that she preferred to work with couldn't go to contract even though they'd already tentatively agreed to provide musicians for Thanksgiving Day.

"That means I have to drop to my B-list, which I'm not particularly comfortable with," she explained. "Not for such a high-profile event. But given the insanity of the lead time there's no way around it. The band is brand-new with this company, so I knew you'd want to hear them live. I asked to arrange a time and it turns out they're in town today cutting a demo. I thought I'd give you a call in case you don't want to lose another week tracking them down again."

Lily was already on her feet and slipping on her shoes. She glanced at her laptop, decided against leaving it out since the twins would probably be home before she returned and her entire life was stored on the hard drive. "That's perfect, Mara. Have I told you how much I appreciate you lately?"

"Not since your last Twitter."

Lily laughed. "Well, I do. Will you give them a call and tell them I'm on my way?"

"Done."

Lily had wanted to keep her real life at bay until Monday, but a few hours of business wouldn't kill her. Even if she hadn't wanted to get out of the house after that conversation with her mom—which she did— entertainment was key at any wedding, particularly the master of ceremonies, the person who kept the schedule moving along smoothly.

They'd been so lucky with their vendors thus far solely because most couples didn't book full-scale weddings on Thanksgiving Day. Lily wasn't going to push her luck at this stage of the game.

"Mom, will you pick up the kids at school today?" she

asked as she passed the office. "Mara called. I've got to run an errand. Can't wait."

Rosie appeared in the hallway before Lily could get out the door. "You're running away because of what I said, aren't you?"

That's twice Lily had been accused of running in less than a week and she didn't like it one bit. Probably because it was true. Well, it had been true about Mike, but not now. Her reputation in this family could stand some work.

"I'm not running. The entertainment for Max's wedding fell through. I've got to go check out another band pronto."

Her mother glared at her, clearly disbelieving.

Lily glared right back. "*You* got me into this, thank you very much. But it's *my* reputation at risk if the event turns into a disaster."

"Oh, go work, then." Her mother huffed and waved her off. "I'll make your excuses to the twins."

"It's your fault," Lily replied as she ran out the door, car keys in hand. "So be nice."

And the next thing she knew she was racing through Friday traffic, putting all thoughts of Max and her crazy family out of her head in the sort of vacation from real life that felt all too familiar.

Work.

She made the recording studio in record time and listened to the band run through an entire set. And to Lily's relief and utter delight, the band proved to be far better than she'd have ever expected to find at a B-list entertainment company.

They could provide configurations to fit the entire wedding, from ceremony through reception, from a duo to nine pieces, acoustic or electric. They had a Grammy-nominated guitarist and their repertoire was extensive and would accommodate a variety of preferences and requests. They could play brass and woodwinds, which would work perfectly for the ceremony and solve the problem of space because they were willing to break down their configuration.

The only question Lily had is how this band had wound up with a B-list entertainment company. And it turned out that the band was actually an established one based out of Massachusetts that had recently extended their travel base, hoping to book gigs in Manhattan.

Her lucky day.

Lily contracted them then and there, and they were equally thrilled to get their foot in the door with Worldwide Weddings Unlimited.

She headed out of the recording studio and pulled out her phone, intending to update Mara, but once outside, Lily found a small crowd on the sidewalk waiting for her.

One glimpse and she knew who they were.

There was no earthly reason for the press to be here. She couldn't even figure out how they'd found her since she hadn't even known she'd be here until a few hours ago. But there they were with their cameras and their questions.

"Lily, do you have an official statement?"

"How will the accusation impact the weddings Worldwide Weddings Unlimited has in production?"

"Do you expect lawsuits or criminal charges?"

The mention of criminal charges snapped Lily from her surprise. "I'm sorry," she said. "I'm afraid I don't have a clue what you're referring to. Would someone care to clarify?"

"I will," said an accented voice, and the crowd parted

like the Red Sea to reveal a striking woman wearing a business suit.

Lily blinked once, twice, but the woman sauntered toward her as though she were crossing a runway, all lanky curves and smooth strides. Lily would have known the woman anywhere though they'd never met in person.

Lucas's gross lack in judgment—Catalina Delmonico.

Definitely not pregnant.

She approached to the rapid-fire sound of camera shutters, meeting Lily's gaze with arrogance flashing in those fiery dark eyes.

"You need to stop your nonsense," she demanded haughtily.

The sheer amount of media experience Lily had should have counted for something, but she was still staring blankly when the woman whipped out a letter from an envelope and thrust the paper in front of Lily's face.

She recovered then, enough to skim the document written on an attorney's letterhead.

A cease-and-desist letter claiming Lily was the All About Angel blogger.

CHAPTER TWENTY-THREE

MAX WAS IN THE newsroom laying out the dummies for the next edition. Even though he'd been trying to stick with Riley's schedule the week had still been insane. He made a mental note to tell her she didn't get any more vacations no matter what.

He was over vacations—especially after Lily Susan had blown him off under the pretense of one. Although he supposed that only working a few hours a day from her parents' house did qualify as one to the Wedding Angel.

On one hand he was grateful she saw the need to start paying attention to her personal life. On the other hand, he objected to being shut out of the process so completely.

With only a few weeks left before Thanksgiving, he was working on borrowed time before Lily Susan left and he lost any hope of convincing her to give them a chance.

"Mr. D.," an assistant said. "Got a call for you from George on line six."

Max went to the switchboard to take the call from one of his senior beat reporters. He listened to George's fast account of the confrontation that had taken place on the steps of a recording studio only a few blocks away.

"She accused Ms. Angelica of being the All About Angel blogger?" Max asked incredulously.

"Presented her with a cease-and-desist letter right there in the street. Made a grand show for the media, and while Ms. Angelica skimmed the letter, Catalina Delmonico gave a soliloquy about the damage the slander has done to her reputation because she is most obviously not pregnant. She made a few digs about vengeful women who couldn't keep their men happy and concluded by quoting 'Hell hath no fury,' if you can believe it."

Max could believe it all right, like it or not. Accusations and ugly confrontations were the last thing Lily Susan needed to deal with right now. "What did Ms. Angelica do?"

"She rallied fast, and kept it simple. Told everyone that if she was the blogger this was the first she'd heard about it. She thanked the press for the warm reception and offered an exclusive after being advised by her attorney about how to deal with Ms. Delmonico's slander. Got some laughs, I can tell you."

Max didn't think Lily Susan would be laughing, and the urgency he felt to drop everything and find her made it nearly impossible to think straight. He told George to come in and write the story then handed the phone to the switchboard operator. He wanted to talk with Lily Susan and find out exactly what had happened so he could manage the coverage. Breaking news would be going live on his competitor's websites soon.

Max didn't care about breaking the story. He cared about damage control. He cared about Lily Susan. The *Herald* would be one news source with the plain facts because he knew the headlines would get sensational fast.

Wedding Angel confronted by ex-fiancé's ex-fling.
The Wedding Angel's desperate bid for attention.
Angel vs. Demon: live and uncensored.

He touched base with his editor-in-chief then headed to his car, trying Lily Susan's cell. She didn't pick up. So he made a few more phone calls as he drove the blocks toward her office. The last person to see her was Rosie when she'd gone into town to handle some problem with a vendor.

Joey was the only one in the family who'd heard about the confrontation. "Dad had to go pick up an order from the supply house, so he doesn't know yet. If you find her, let me know. Everyone's going to be worried if she doesn't show up."

"You got it," Max said.

Her car wasn't at her office, either.

Not sure what to do, Max drove toward Pleasant Valley by way of the cemetery. If she wasn't there, then maybe she'd gone to Riley's place. He knew the twins were staying with Rosie and Joe, so maybe she'd gone to the farm for some privacy.

One thing Max did know, he wasn't heading home until he found her, so he called Claire and told her to take Madeleine down to dinner with his grandfather and whoever else may be eating in tonight. He'd try to make it home for their bedtime story but couldn't promise.

Lily Susan wasn't in the cemetery, either, but he found her when some uncanny sense of premonition prompted him to glance in his rearview mirror as he was cruising through the Valley.

Her rental car was parked behind Chick's Tavern.

Chick's in the Valley was a hole-in-the-wall tavern that had been around as far back as Max could remember. Long enough to become sort of a Pleasant Valley institution, where anyone who lived in the area had passed through at some time or another. Chick knew everyone in town and everyone knew Chick. Max didn't think anyone had a clue what his real first name was.

Max fired off a text to Joey before he went inside.

Found her. Tell everyone not to worry. She's with me.

He didn't mention where she was. Since the hardware

store was down the block, he assumed that parking behind Chick's meant she didn't want to be found.

Max found Lily Susan sitting in a dark corner alone, long hair tumbling around her shoulders and practically glowing in the low light. She leaned back in the chair, twirling the stem of a wineglass in her hand. An ice bucket held a bottle of champagne.

"Hey," he said quietly, not to be overheard by the happy-hour patrons looking to start the weekend. "You good?"

She glanced up at him as if she wasn't at all surprised to find him standing here.

"I'm toasting my life. Would you like to toast with me?" She didn't wait for a reply, but hopped up and headed toward the bar, noticeably unsteady. "Chick, I need another glass."

The balding, middle-age man who owned the place set a glass down on the bar with a barely perceptible nod. Lily Susan was smiling, however, when she headed back to Max.

She didn't sit down, but reached for the bottle. Max got there first.

"Please, allow me." Pulling the bottle from the ice, he checked to see how much was left. A lot more than he'd expected.

"Are you working on your second bottle?"

"God, no." She bent over enough so he got a prime glimpse of the smooth swell of her breasts as her neckline dipped, and whispered, "It's awful. Like my life. I'm sorry."

Max didn't like the sound of that at all. This whole situation was ripe for disaster. He had no clue how long ago she'd gotten here. He did know that she was big news right now, and if she'd been thinking clearly, she wouldn't be running the risk of having photos of her drinking at the local watering hole splashed all over the news.

He had no way of knowing whether or not anyone in the bar was with the press or if anyone might have recognized her. Instead of pouring himself a glass, he grabbed the bucket.

"Let's toast in private." He steered her toward the bar. "Chick, anyone in your back room?"

Chick inclined his head at the swinging doors that led to the kitchen and the rear entrance. "All yours."

Lily Susan didn't resist when Max shouldered open the door then held it open while she strolled through. The private room was used for small local meetings, card games and the like. He got Lily Susan inside and pulled the door shut behind them.

Setting the ice bucket on the table, he filled his glass. "So what are we celebrating about your life?"

"What a spectacular failure I am."

Max discovered a few things then. Lily Susan had been impacted by the confrontation with her ex's fling and she was a serious lightweight in the drinking department.

"I won't argue spectacular." He sat next to her at the table. "But I'll argue the failure part."

"That's very nice of you, Max. So we'll toast you, too. That's the kind thing to do. Cheers to Max Downey, loving, responsible, loyal and general all-around nice guy. Hear, hear." Raising her glass, she saluted him and sipped.

Max was glad to hear she had a decent opinion of his character. That was something to add to their chemistry. Respect. All good so far. Sinking back in his chair, he brought the glass to his lips and sipped. "This is bad."

"I know. It's all Chick had. I'm guessing he doesn't do a whole lot of toasting."

Max could say the same about Lily Susan. "I heard what happened at the recording studio."

She gulped deeply this time, thick, dark lashes fluttering shut as she pulled a face. "Mom could pickle beets in this."

"Are you okay?"

"Just ducky, thanks."

"I'd like to help however I can."

She grinned. "That's nice of you. We should toast again."

"Not necessary." His fingers brushed her hand, grazing skin against skin, and directed her glass back to the table. "You might pickle your insides if you drink much more."

"No arguments there."

"Do you have any idea why people would think you're the blogger?"

"No clue. I don't know how the press knew. I don't know how anyone knew where I was. I don't know anything anymore."

The press part Max could guess since the ex-fling had already proven she liked media attention. "Why were you down at a recording studio? I thought you were on vacation."

"I was. This is all your fault, Max Downey. You and your stupid wedding." She scowled with great animation, and Max decided he would get her tipsy again sometime. On good champagne. A picnic at the river, maybe. Champagne, even the bad stuff, broke through Lily Susan's polished veneer until there was nothing left but a lovely woman who was candid and funny and so very, very real.

"What does my stupid wedding have to do with why you were downtown on your vacation?"

"Because of your stupid entertainment. Mara couldn't

go to contract because nobody wants to work on Thanks-giving Day and the only band we could get was from a B-list company so I had to hear them—how could I not?—and they happened to be in town today, so I went even though I was supposed to be on vacation."

All that on one long, exasperated breath. Max couldn't help smiling. "I guess it is my fault then. I'm very sorry."

"Oh, I'll bet you are."

"I am. I'm a loving, responsible, loyal and general all-around nice guy, remember."

"I know. You're Mr. Perfect as far as my parents are concerned. They approve of you." She narrowed her gaze and pursed her mouth in disapproval. "They'd probably approve of me, too, if I brought you home."

It took Max a moment to make sense of that, and his heart began to pound with a slow, hard beat. "Who wants you to bring me home? Your parents?"

"Oh, please. Don't act like Mr. Innocent. I know you're in on this whole thing. Mom admitted it."

"Admitted what? That you want to bring me home?"

"Not me. Joey. He told them. Well, Mom anyway."

Max shook his head, as if he could shake loose a few brain cells and understand what she was talking about. "Joey told your mom what exactly?"

"That we have chemistry."

Max couldn't imagine Joey ever using those words, but he could imagine Joey figuring out that something was up between them. "And your parents approve of me?"

"Don't be ridiculous, Max. You're more a part of my family than I am. Didn't you get the memo? Everyone loves Max. And now everyone is worried about you. 'Don't hurt Max.' Like I'm some sort of…Brazilian runway model." She shoved the glass away so fast that he caught it while tipping over. Then she dropped her face down onto her outstretched arm and heaved a dramatic sigh that ruffled the silky hair covering her face.

"I don't think you're a Brazilian runway model." He wrapped his fingers around hers and gave a reassuring squeeze. "And no one needs to worry about me. I'm ducky."

"Maybe you should tell *them* that because I don't think they got the memo."

"You could bring me home and make everyone happy. What do you think of that idea?"

"What…about making me happy?"

"You'll be happy, too."

She tugged her hand from his and brushed aside enough hair to stare him down through one eye. "You sound sure of yourself."

"I am. Because what we feel for each other doesn't come along every day. I think you'll agree. We'd be foolish not to give *us* a chance to see where we can go."

"Us." The word fluttered out on a breathy sigh, a sound that managed to reveal everything she wasn't saying. It seemed she liked the way it sounded as much as he did. "How can there be any *us?* I'm leaving in a few weeks."

"I recognize the situation presents some challenges, and I don't have any answers about how to resolve the logistical problems. But I know how I feel, Lily Susan."

She didn't reply, was silent so long that he would have thought she'd fallen asleep if not for the sidelong gaze that didn't waver. "It's a fantasy, Max. Fantasy doesn't translate into reality. Trust me, I know. That's my area of expertise."

"You create fantasies."

"I do. But they only last a day then my couples have

to go off and live their real lives. They have to live their vows. Or choose not to. That's the reality."

"You can bring fantasy into reality, Lily Susan. Look at what you've done with your work. When you want something, you make it happen."

"I don't know what I want anymore."

"You do. You want me."

She blinked, once, twice, looked so startled that for a split second he questioned whether he'd imagined the awareness between them, made it up because he wanted her so much.

"Oh, God, who told you?" She sat upright. He didn't get a chance to reply. "It was Joey. I know it was. That rat. No wonder Mom is all like, 'Oh, you've always had a crush on him and he knows it so be nice to him, Lily Susan. Don't hurt him, Lily Susan.' She thinks I'm a Brazilian runway model with no moral center."

Alcohol-fueled passion animated her beautiful features. Max wasn't interested in the vulnerable part—except to appreciate Rosie's concern for him. Or the moral part, either. But the crush part… "You've always had a crush on me?"

"Nothing is sacred anymore, honestly. You'd think family counted for something, wouldn't you?"

"You'd think." He brought the glass to his lips, taking a swig that singed like acid all the way down.

Her family secret had been safe because he hadn't a clue, hadn't once suspected. He'd thought this awareness was a purely adult occurrence, but it didn't really matter when it had begun. He was right, and that was all he was interested in. She wanted him. He wanted her.

No matter how hard she tried to avoid him, the simple fact was that she did feel something for him. And had for a lot longer than he'd realized.

There was hope.

His phone vibrated and he glanced quickly at the display, knowing he would ignore anyone but his daughter right now.

Scott.

He glanced at the wild blond beauty staring daggers at him and knew he couldn't ignore this call. He couldn't help smiling when he said, "I'll be right back."

He had the phone to his ear before the door shut behind him. "I thought you were supposed to be honeymooning."

Scott laughed. "Yeah, well, made the mistake of checking my email. Joey told me she's with you. How's she holding up?"

"Fairly well, all things considered."

"Riley will be relieved. Listen, Max, there's not much I can do from up here, so I've called the chief. He's going to start the wheels turning. Someone has been leaking Lily Susan's whereabouts since she got back to town. Now there's this accusation she's the blogger. The woman who had a cease-and-desist letter drafted got information from somewhere."

Max leaned against the wall, grateful for this family that looked out for each other, grateful to be a part of it. Maybe not a real part like Scott was. The thought made him smile. "What can I do?"

"If you want protection for Lily Susan, we can do that. But the rest, well, we're talking FBI. Internet crime is their jurisdiction. The chief is on the phone now getting things rolling."

Max tried to put aside everything he felt—surprise, hope, worry. He needed to think clearly. "I don't have any indicator that she's in any physical danger. I'll keep her with me for a while to be on the safe side. Sound good?"

"Sounds good. I'll be in touch when I hear something."

"Don't work too hard. This is Riley's last vacation. Ever."

Scott laughed and ended the call. Max was about to step inside the room when the doors to the bar swung open and Chick appeared.

"Thought you'd want to know that two reporters from the *Poughkeepsie Journal* showed up asking about the celebrity you're hiding in there," he said. "They heard she was driving a MINI-Cooper and wanted to know if that's hers in the back. They saw the rental plates."

Max slid the phone into the case. "Thanks for the heads-up. Can you keep them entertained while I get her out?"

"You got it."

"The bill—"

Chick waved a dish towel dismissively. "On the house. Don't keep champagne in the inventory. That was a gift someone left one Christmas."

A decade or so ago from the taste of it. "You're a gentleman and a scholar, Chick."

Chick furrowed his bristly brows and tried to look mean. "Get her out of here. I'll keep them at the bar."

Max pushed the door open and found Lily Susan leaning back in the chair with her eyes closed. "We've got company," he said. "The press."

Her expression melted into one of pure horror and she was pushing away from the table. Even tipsy she knew this drill. "Can we get out the back?"

Slipping a hand around her elbow, he steadied her. "Yes. I'll drive. We'll come back tomorrow and pick up your car. Chick will take care of it."

She hurried along beside him down the hallway, all humor gone. It wasn't until she was safely inside his car, hunkered down in the seat, that she asked, "Are you taking me home?"

"No. You're still a little looped on bad champagne."

"I'm an adult, Max, not fifteen. You can't threaten to tell my parents."

He remembered that incident, but before he got a chance to respond, she pressed a hand to her forehead. "Oh, dang. The twins are there. You're right. I shouldn't go home. They might notice I'm not right, and what kind of example would I be setting for them?"

Max liked that she'd considered that. But he was actually more worried about the press. They could easily find her parents' address online.

"Don't worry, Lily Susan, you're coming with me. I know the perfect place to hide."

"Overlook?"

He glanced at this woman who'd come to mean everything to him—a woman who, by her own admission, had had feelings for him for a very long time. "I want you to trust me."

Meeting his gaze, she considered him. "Are you sure you have my best interests at heart?"

"I do." And he'd never meant anything more.

He'd known he wanted to pursue how he felt for her, hadn't known where that pursuit would lead, since she'd soon be leaving town. But Max was going to figure out how to make this work, because what he wanted from Lily Susan had nothing to do with temporary. And what Lily Susan wanted—whether or not she was willing to be honest—had everything to do with him.

CHAPTER TWENTY-FOUR

"LILY SUSAN, we're here."

Max's voice roused Lily. She must have dozed because she opened her eyes to find the car coming to a stop. The faint glow of the dashboard gave way to darkness when he turned off the ignition. He turned toward her, his face all pale angles in the shadows, somehow unfamiliar. Or maybe it was drowsiness that made her feel this way.

"Where are we?" She had to force the words out, her voice so faint it barely penetrated the quiet intimacy, the fact she'd fallen asleep during his rescue.

"The guest house."

Overlook. She wasn't surprised. Where else would he bring her? He got out and reappeared at her door, wrapping an arm securely around her to help her out of the car. The cold air roused her a little and some barely functioning part of her brain knew it couldn't be all that late. But the sun had set completely. She could see the lights from Overlook twinkling in the distance through the trees.

Max unlocked the door and helped her inside. It was warmer in here, but to her surprise, he didn't turn on any lights, simply guided her through the dark house, his body so warm against hers, so close.

He led her to a bedroom.

They were playing with fire. Lily had no ability to reason right now, her self-control was weakened by anxiety and bad champagne. The Max of her fantasies had melted into the reality of a caring man with his arm around her, a man who'd made it loud and clear that he wanted her. And Lily knew, she knew with every fiber of her being, that all her sane, solid arguments against being with this man would never hold up against the strength of their chemistry.

He wanted her. She'd always wanted him.

It should have been so simple.

He must have sensed that she was about to object because he pressed a warm finger to her lips and said, "Shh. Trust me."

She trusted him more than she did herself.

Lily didn't resist as he slid the coat down her arms, tossed it onto a chair. He guided her to the bed, yanked back the comforter. She sank to the edge bonelessly, and he didn't say a word as he slid his own coat off then bent to pull off her shoes.

His hands were warm against her skin, his fingers strong as he brushed them along her ankle, a deceptively casual touch that sent a tremor of awareness through her.

Right now she didn't want to think about resisting the way she felt about Max. She didn't want to think about what had happened today. That had been the whole point of stopping at Chick's. She wanted to forget. For a few minutes, she wanted to forget everything and feel good, pretend all was right in her world. Was that really so much to ask?

"Go on, lay down." His voice was a husky whisper in the quiet.

She sank against the pillows, into the softness of the luxurious bed, her senses still heightened from the champagne and drowsy from sleep. She sighed as he pulled the comforter over her, cocooning her in warmth.

"Lay with me," she said.

He hadn't expected that. She could tell by the way his eyes widened so she could see them, a pale blur in the darkness. Stretching languorously, she inched toward the center of the bed to give him room to climb in. And without a word, he kicked off his shoes and slid in beside her, all hard muscle and hot strength as he wrapped his arms around her and pulled her close. She snuggled against him and burrowed her face in the crook of his neck and shoulder.

She wanted to feel good.

And in his arms she did.

The last thing she remembered was the feathery touch of his fingers against her cheek, his soft breaths against her hair.

LILY WASN'T SURE how long she slept but when she opened her eyes again, she found Max watching her. She didn't think he'd slept. Knowing this man, he'd simply laid here and held her. That was Max. Solid. Caring. Her mom was right about that.

She wondered what came next. Should she get up? Fall back asleep? Not worry about the consequences, tip her head back and kiss the man she had wanted forever?

Awareness swallowed up the moment. She was so completely aware of him, of the strength of his body, the way she nestled against every hard hollow as if she'd been designed to fit.

"Thanks for saving me," she finally said, playing it safe, her voice a hushed whisper in the quiet.

"My pleasure."

She didn't doubt that. He'd made what he wanted clear. She remembered that much. "How did you find me?"

"Luck mainly. I thought you might have gone to Riley's for some peace and quiet and saw your car."

"Wish I'd have thought about going there. It was so stupid to go to Chick's. Thank goodness those journalists didn't catch me. I have you to thank for that. My hero."

He liked that. She could tell in his soft exhalation of breath, almost a chuckle, not quite.

"So why did you go?" he asked.

"Impulse. No real reason. I needed to come down off what had happened, didn't feel I could do that at home with Mom and the kids. I wasn't ready to start answering questions or reassuring everyone. I saw Chick's and pulled in."

"You okay?"

"Didn't you ask me that already?"

"You were loopy."

"I'm still not right."

She felt rather than saw his smile. "Then I guess I'll be asking you again later."

She smiled at that, remembering once a long time ago when he'd threatened to tell on her for drinking. He'd driven her home then, too. Such an honorable man.

The darkness didn't hide the intensity of his gaze, and she grew flushed and dazed. Maybe it was the aftereffects of the champagne. She wasn't much of a drinker on the best of days. Today hadn't even come close.

Or maybe it was the power of his look that held her because in that moment there was nothing but her, him and this incredible awareness.

He felt it, too. She could tell. Even the air between them crackled with expectation.

They didn't speak. There was nothing to say. She had no answers. She couldn't even think of all the questions, not with this crazy excitement stealing through her, with the feel of his arms around her, the length of his body against her, the chemistry so unique to them swallowing her whole, making fantasy and reality collide.

This was Max.

She'd wanted him forever. The man of her wildest dreams, the perfect groom, the only constant in her ever-changing wedding fantasies.

This was *Max*.

And he was in her arms.

Tipping her face, she met his gaze and what she saw in his handsome face stole her breath. Those striking eyes that seemed to cut through the darkness, a trick so unique to him, revealed everything he felt.

Had she ever been wanted this much?

Lily never felt as if she had.

"Max." His name slipped from her lips on a sigh, their faces so close they shared an expectant breath.

She sensed his movement before his hand rose, fingers spearing into her hair, anchoring her close as his mouth came down on hers, all warm excitement, all insistent need.

The whole world stopped in that moment, a moment where everything vanished but the feel of his mouth on hers, the taste of his desire, the reality of giving in to forbidden pleasure against every shred of reason, all control gone.

Threading her arms around his neck, she couldn't stop from exploring, feeling the glossy hair beneath her fingertips, the stubbled curve of his chiseled jaw, the strong cords of his neck, the pulse that throbbed in time with hers.

His tongue swept boldly inside her mouth, and she tasted the silken whisper of his breaths, the impatience of his need. And Lily knew, somehow had always known, that if she ever kissed him, she'd never want to stop.

She didn't want to stop. Her body shot from drowsy to eager in one aching heartbeat. Their kiss demanded a response from the deepest parts of her. And got it, in the way her body pressed close to his, impossibly close, so eager. There was no hesitation, no unfamiliarity of a first kiss. There was only greedy appreciation and raging chemistry.

Lily wanted to unfold underneath him, drag her hands over his warm skin, explore every hard muscle and learn him by heart.

Had she ever felt this way, so needy?

No.

There would have been no forgetting.

Not the way his tongue tangled with hers, not the way his heavy body pressed her into the soft mattress when he shifted again to deepen their kiss.

His arms braced her on both sides, and suddenly she could slide her hands over his broad shoulders, feel the strength beneath the fabric of his shirt. She traced the flexing biceps that still balanced most of his weight, dragged her hands down the sweep of his back until he exhaled what sounded suspiciously like a moan.

"Tell me this isn't real, Lily Susan," he whispered. "Tell me you don't want to keep kissing me."

"I do." She couldn't lie. Not to Max.

He kissed her again then, his mouth meeting hers hard, demanding a response that she knew she shouldn't give.

But Lily was drowning in him. She allowed herself to be sucked in, kissing him with abandon, pressing her body close to ease this growing ache inside, hips arching to cradle what was becoming a very prominent erection.

He trailed his mouth along her jaw then pressed feathery kisses along her neck, igniting fire in his wake, and her own breath slipped from her lips in tiny gasping bursts. And her hands could only trace his body, hold him close.

"Make love to me," he whispered against her mouth in between more kisses…fierce kisses, tender kisses, kisses designed to seduce away her every objection.

"What about tomorrow?"

His tongue dragged along her lower lip, a sultry move that was all challenge. "We have tonight."

Which in no way answered her question. She remembered what her mom had said about hurting him. But this man who kissed her with such hot need wasn't vulnerable. This was a man who knew exactly what he wanted. And when she thought of the way he'd held her in the cemetery, she knew he was well aware of what she did and didn't have to give, maybe even more than she was.

Would she really sacrifice tonight with him, worrying about what might come tomorrow?

This was Max.

And Lily had wanted him forever.

She replied by tugging his shirt from the waistband of his pants until she could get her hands against his skin. He growled against her mouth, such a needy sound, and his arms came around her with whipcord strength. Suddenly he was pulling her up onto her knees, facing her with such a look of hot desire that she trembled beneath his gaze.

Their hands tangled in their eagerness to unbutton and pull off, to push down and tug away, until they were both kneeling in the middle of the bed, naked and breathless and oh, so greedy.

And there was nothing in the world but Max and this moment in his arms and the melting heat between her thighs.

She touched him freely, exploring the man who had

been a fantasy for so long. She dragged her hands along his ribs, reveled in this urgency, the heat of this need and the honesty of his passion. He wanted her and didn't hold back.

Nibbling his way down her throat, he explored her breasts with tiny kisses, the receptive peaks, the sensitive undersides, making her tremble against him.

And when he finally pulled her to the bed in his arms, their legs twined together as he pinned her against him, and she rocked her hips to cradle his erection, sank her fingers into his tight bottom. Their time together was too sweet to hurry, but Lily couldn't stop touching him.

Their bodies fit so neatly, and she felt surrounded by him, hard muscle and warm skin. His mouth met hers again and it was Lily who moaned against his lips, who sought out his hard heat and eased him inside, savoring the way his muscles coiled tight in reply, the way he practically vibrated at her touch when she rode him the smallest bit, pleasure sharpening his features, a look she'd only imagined, the look of a man about to lose control.

"Lily Susan." There was no more restraint. He drove in deep and all Lily could do was hang on, meeting him thrust for aching thrust, forgetting everything but the feel of him inside her and the pleasure that had been a long time in the making.

CHAPTER TWENTY-FIVE

Today is a grand and glorious day, *mes amis*. The sun is shining, the vacation has refreshed me, the past is about to be finally laid to rest so I can move on with my exciting future. And, *no*, I am *not* the All About Angel blogger. Cross my heart.

LILY SENT THE POST off to her Twitter account and, for a change, what she wrote was really how she felt. She could have added: The afterglow was as glorious as the sex. There was some exhausted sleep then more kissing and more cuddling and more sex. More exhausted sleep. Then a shower together, more kissing and more cuddling and even more sex.

Of course, that tweet would have been too long to post and entirely too personal. So she kept her feelings about their romantic interlude all to herself, perfectly shiny and new feelings, ones she didn't want reality to tarnish.

Max seemed content to leave their night as the lovely romantic interlude it was. He didn't say one word about what the morning would bring, and when the sun rose and the morning was upon them, he didn't try to convince her to discuss the future.

All he did was kiss her, tell her how much he enjoyed their night together, then kiss her again. Lily was relieved.

No worries about the future. No weirdness. No complications. Just two adults who'd shared something special.

He was pleasant as he drove her to Chick's to collect her car, stealing another kiss in the parking lot before they parted ways—him to get home to Madeleine and Lily to get back to reality, which meant not only work, but also dealing with the fallout of yesterday's events.

She had to talk with Elaine and put in a call to Chief Levering. Max had relayed the details about Scott's phone call, and while she hated that he'd been interrupted on the final days of his honeymoon, she appreciated the help. The cease-and-desist letter in itself was no problem as *she* wasn't the blogger. But, of course, the situation dominated the internet.

Lily was in such a great mood that she didn't care.

She got home in time for breakfast with the twinnies— homemade pancakes drowned in butter and maple syrup. She spent a few hours making her phone calls and gathering requested information, which she took down to the local FBI headquarters to Chief Levering's friend, who was personally investigating the case and working on a Saturday to boot.

So, instead of counting down the days to the wedding—twelve to be exact—Lily found herself counting the days since *that night,* Lily told herself she was content with their one romantic interlude and Max was a gentleman to respect the limitations. Still, when her phone vibrated and she saw his name on the display, she thought it sweet of him to call.

"Hey," she said, breathlessly.

"Bonsoir, belle." His deep voice hinted at shared intimacies and evoked a physical response low in her tummy, memories of all the things they'd shared in the dark.

"Bonsoir, beau," she replied with a smile, heading out

to the back porch to speak without being overheard. "I didn't think you knew how to speak French."

"I have a kindergarten kid coaching me."

Dropping onto the love seat, she curled her legs beneath her and stared out into the dusky backyard. "Well, tell her she's doing a fine job. If she keeps it up, you'll be able to take her to Paris in springtime by the time she graduates high school."

"You're a comedienne, too. I had no idea."

"There are many things you don't know about me."

"Maybe I should do an internet search about who the *real* Lily Susan is."

That made her laugh.

He'd called to find out what she'd worked out with the FBI. As far as he was concerned, he had a vested interest in the resolution of her situation, not only because he'd rescued her last night, but also because he was a publisher who intended to keep the story factual. At least the news he controlled.

"I do appreciate your efforts on my behalf," she told him and brought him up to date on what the FBI was doing.

On day two after *that night,* Max and Madeleine showed up at Lily's parents' house for Sunday dinner as usual. The meal was the same noisy Angelica family affair that it always was. And Lily had been so concerned about weirdness between them.

Of course, he'd caught her outside behind the garage while they were playing hide-and-seek with the kids. Pulling her into his arms, he stole a kiss that left Lily clinging to him and weak in the knees.

And still no mention of tomorrow or the future.

Which was a perfectly good thing, Lily told herself,

since she would be leaving town in less than two weeks and would be dead busy between now and then.

And she was.

On the third day after *that night,* Lily hit the ground running to wrap up wedding preparations. When she wasn't in her office on the phone, she was picking up gowns and tuxedoes and accessories and spare items to replenish her emergency kit.

She never once heard from Max that day.

On the fourth day after *that night,* she headed to Overlook to check out all Ginger's preparations in the house and on the grounds. Lily was finalizing menus and guest lists and wine lists and song lists and picking up china and silver and glassware—she didn't like what the caterers could supply—and decorations enough to fill not one but four rooms. Not to mention the hallways leading to each room because she preferred to carry her themes throughout her fantasy settings.

She was pleased when Max showed up unexpectedly in the middle of his workday, looking so dashing and handsome in his business suit and wool duster. Lily spotted him immediately, those long-legged strides reminding her of what his legs had felt like twined between hers, all hard muscle and thrusting strength.

By the time he got to the place where she and Ginger had been debating the merits of the various sites for formal photos, Lily was feeling a flush that started in her toes and worked its way steadily up her body, until she was opening her own jacket to let the chilly November air cool her off.

So much for no weirdness.

Max, however, didn't seem similarly affected. He kissed his mother's cheek, flashed a dimpled smile at

Lily, his gaze raking over her as if he appreciated the very sight of her.

When Ginger had to go to the house to take a call, Max took Lily's hand in his and they strolled along the riverbank together as if he they were two lovers.

"I thought you'd be working." She needed to put something normal between them. He acted as if he had every right to touch her, and she didn't pull her hand away because she liked the way their fingers twined together, such a simple, easy gesture, but one that felt so right.

"Riley's back. I told her absolutely no more vacations. She has that newsroom running like a clock. I've never seen anything like it. Even my grandfather is impressed."

"She's something. That's for sure. But you've known that all along, haven't you?"

"I have." He thumbed her knuckles idly as they walked along, another simple gesture that felt right.

Max had stuck with Riley through weddings and babies, through death and the grieving process. It said so much about the man Max was. So caring and loyal. No wonder Mom and Dad would approve of him.

Lucas hadn't even come close.

When Ginger reappeared on the piazza, Max let his hand slide from Lily's, leaving her missing his warm touch and wondering if he would continue with these small intimacies for as long as she was home. She intended to ask him.

On the fifth day after *that night,* Lily had lots and lots of invoices to pay, which meant lots and lots of money changing hands. She recruited Mara to help her double-check the figures. Then Max brought Madeleine by after school for their final fittings—his and hers, since she'd picked up his tux.

"As Raymond's best man, you need to look dapper,"

she told him while unzipping the garment bag on his tux with the double-breasted satin lapels. "And there's no sense saving this until the last week to fit when you're already here."

He took the hanger from her, brushing her fingers as he did, his gaze raking over her with a look of such possessiveness that Lily's breath caught in her throat. And he knew just how he impacted her, Lily didn't doubt for one second. He vanished into the dressing room smiling, leaving her to assist Madeleine, whose gown fit perfectly.

She twirled in front of the mirror, but her handsome father didn't look similarly thrilled as he tugged at his sleeves. "Don't you have anything you can put on this to dress it up?"

"A boutonniere?"

He scowled. "I'm going to look seriously underdressed next to Raymond in his decorated uniform."

"You won't be the only groomsman not in uniform. There's one other."

"Should have gone into officer training," he grumbled.

Lily laughed. "I had no idea you were a clotheshorse, Max. How come you didn't share this about your daddy, Madeleine?"

But Madeleine didn't reply. She had gone to the wardrobe and was staring at the gown hanging inside, the adult version of her own, the clear plastic garment bag revealing the luxurious tufted folds and the simple but exquisite lace of the bodice. "Is that Aunt Jamilyn's dress?" she asked reverently.

"It is. Just like yours only bigger."

"It would look beautiful on you, *madame.* Will you try it on, and we can pretend it's the wedding?"

"*Merci, petite jeune fille,* but I cannot. This is your

aunt's lovely gown and the bride should always be the first to try it on for good luck."

Madeleine accepted disappointment gracefully, her doleful expression leaving no doubt as to her opinion of having to wait until the bride arrived to see the dress.

As a consolation, Lily lifted the gown from the garment bag, shook out the satin tufts and held it in front of her. "I think this dress is beautiful and I'm a very tough sell. Isn't it gorgeous?"

"Oui, madame."

Max leaned in behind her, startling Lily with his sudden nearness, as he whispered for her alone, "You'd be the most beautiful bride."

His warm breath tickled her ear and sent a thrill straight to her toes.

"If you decide you want to be a bride, of course." Then he headed to the dressing room, leaving Lily staring after him wondering what he meant by *that.*

"Excusez-moi pour un moment, Madeleine." She followed Max and flipped aside the privacy curtain.

He glanced around at her in surprise, and she was treated to an amazing display of his bare chest reflected in the mirrors from all angles.

"Max, I have a question."

Hanging the dress shirt on the wall hook, he turned to face her, giving her his undivided attention.

"If I decide to be a bride? What does that mean?" she whispered, keeping one eye on Madeleine to make sure she wasn't within earshot. "What's going on with you? Every time I turn around, I'm caught off guard. Should I expect you to steal kisses every time I run into you for the rest of our lives or are you trying to show me what I'm missing?"

Lily wasn't sure what she expected, but it wasn't for

him to take her hand and press his mouth to her skin in the most romantic of all gestures, while his gaze poured over her with a hungry, somewhat amused look that made her heart throb a hard beat.

"Yes," he said.

"Yes, I can expect you to keep stealing kisses or, yes, you're trying to show me what I'm missing?"

"Yes to both." His warm mouth moved against her hand again, a sensual touch that evoked a response so deep inside.

"You said you'd be content with just a night."

A dark eyebrow lifted quizzically. "When did I say that?"

"That night."

He shook his head slowly, the dimple winking in his cheek. "I said we had the night. I never said I'd be content with one."

"But we've discussed this already," she hissed quietly. Madeleine was at the worktable grabbing her basket. "There's nothing about our lives that meshes. The logistics don't work remotely. You know that."

"Which is why you have to decide what you want." Another kiss. This one he brushed across her knuckles. "I'm going to keep trying to tempt you. And show you what you're missing. It's all on you now, Lily Susan. I know what I want."

She had to force herself to ask the question, brace herself for the answer even though she already knew what he would say. "And what's that?"

"You."

ON THE SIXTH day after *that night,* Lily found herself with a muscle twitching underneath her left eye as she put the finishing touches on her makeup and prepared to head into the office for another busy day.

Her anxiety had nothing to do with the wedding, which was coming together, thankfully, and everything to do with the man who completely consumed her thoughts.

But distraction came in the form of her vibrating cell phone and a call from Scott.

"I have news. You'll have to decide whether or not it's good."

Lily held her breath.

"We've identified your blogger."

She leaned against the bathroom vanity, physically overcome by a sense of relief so strong her eyes fluttered shut and she forced herself to inhale deeply, to wrap her brain around this information, prepare herself for the rest. To hope that maybe this nightmare would soon be over.

"Okay. I'm good. I'm ready. Who is it? Please tell me what's going on."

Lily had to force a calm detachment as Scott explained the chain of events that started with a fraudulent registration on the free blog.ging.com website and posts from IP addresses that pinged all over the globe to mask the originating location.

"The FBI pinpointed the location of the posts. They were sent from a public internet café here in Poughkeepsie," he explained, still not telling her who the blogger was.

Which told her to brace herself.

Sinking to her knees, Lily concentrated on Scott's explanation. The café owners were cooperating with the investigation. An FBI tech team had spent the night scouring the hard drives to see if they could find evidence on any of the public computers. According to Scott, even if someone deleted a file, there would still be a record that a knowledgeable hardware technician could get to.

They'd hit pay dirt sometime after midnight. Not only had they found files containing several of the All About Angel blog posts, but they'd also discovered a document accusing Lily of being the blogger that had been sent via email attachment through the café's server, along with financial transactions paying for the internet time that corroborated the identity of the blogger with the times the posts had been written.

"Agent Callahan wants you to swing by the field office this morning," Scott said. "He'll advise you about how to proceed from here. I'm not sure what he's going to tell you. File a lawsuit, press criminal charges or both. He'll know what you can do legally and then you talk to your attorney. Once you get a lock on all that, you'll be able to have your publicist make a formal statement or do whatever you want to handle the press. So, you okay?"

"I'm okay. Are you going to tell me who it is? Wait. First let me say thank you for all your help. And please tell the chief, too. I'll give him a call later but I don't want to forget to say thanks now because I suspect I'm going to be reeling as soon as you tell me who the blogger is."

And Lily was dead right about that.

CHAPTER TWENTY-SIX

AFTER HANGING UP the phone with Scott, Max left the *Herald* and drove toward Lily Susan's office. He had no way of knowing if she'd be there since she wasn't answering her cell, but it seemed the logical place to begin tracking her down.

He needed to keep moving right now, needed to act. How had she handled the news? He hated thinking of her in the FBI field office alone. But Lily Susan lived her life that way.

He wanted so much more than that for her.

And from her.

Turning onto her street, he immediately caught sight of her slim figure. She was sitting on the steps in front of her office, bundled up in a peacoat, arms wrapped around her knees.

He'd half expected to find a crowd of reporters around her place, but there was just Lily Susan. A huge part of him gave an inward sigh at the sight of her, looking no worse for the wear, merely contemplative.

And so beautiful. He seemed to have gone from widower to lover in one giant step. He couldn't explain why—he only knew, as he steered the car into a spot on the street, that she had come to mean everything to him.

She watched him cross the street and unlatch the iron gate that led to her office.

"Hello, Max. What brings you by today?" A smile played around that beautiful mouth.

So far, so good. "Talked to Scott a little while ago. Wanted to find out how you were holding up."

She inclined her head and patted the stone stoop beside her. "I'm good. Enjoying the fresh air. I hope we have a day like this for the wedding."

"I'll put in a request." He wasn't sure what to make of her mood, so he climbed the steps and sat beside her.

"Do you know that when I first bought this place, I used to love to sit here and listen to the traffic? This top step felt like my own place in the world. Of course, that was back when I had time to sit and listen to the traffic. I didn't have all that many clients."

"I had no clue," he admitted. "But it turns out that I like learning things about you."

She rested her face on her arm, slanted her gaze his way. "Did Scott tell you about Mara?"

He nodded.

"I never suspected. Not even for a second."

Max could relate. He'd felt the same way when he'd learned she'd had a crush on him for half her life.

"Have you talked to her? Is she inside?"

"I fired her. Told her to clean out her desk and get out. She tried playing stupid at first but with FBI field agents contradicting her story…" She gave a shrug.

"I'm surprised there's no media around. Nothing came through the *Herald.*"

"I know. Amazing, isn't it? That was Chief Levering's doing. He and Scott kept everything under wraps. You can have the exclusive, if you want it."

"Absolutely. You give me the details and I'll write it up. You know I'll present the unbiased facts."

She smiled at that. "I know. It's all that integrity. That's why my parents approve of you."

He brought her hand to his mouth and kissed it. There weren't any words for the love he'd found with her family. The same kind of love that he wanted to share with her.

Her eyes grew liquid as their gazes met, and that melting expression on her face convinced him he still stood a chance at persuading her to take a chance on them.

"So is Mara the one who leaked your travel arrangements to the press, then?"

"And to others who shall remain nameless."

The ex-fling.

"Did she tell you why?" There had to be a reason for such unstable, underhanded behavior.

"Not really. Then again, I didn't really give her much of a chance. Told her to pack up and move on. I'd have human resources send her termination papers. I suppose a severance package, too, if legal says I need to. I don't really care. Whatever it takes to put this behind me. Looks like there will be formal charges against her. Fraud, I think."

"And a lawsuit?"

"Not unless my attorney gives me a seriously compelling reason why I should. All I'm interested in is clearing my reputation. The FBI can deal with Mara."

"How long has she worked for you?"

"Over eight years. I sent her to run this office about four years ago because she was such a strong employee. The weddings planned here demanded a lot of autonomy since I wasn't running the crews."

Four years. Since Mike.

Max understood, and, twining his fingers through hers, he held on.

"Your mother thinks that was part of the problem," she said. "I guess Mara had made some comments about why your mother would be content to be carved out of World-wide Weddings Unlimited. Ginger thinks Mara had so much freedom up here that she started seeing the place as hers and didn't like being forced to live in my shadow."

"I can see that. You're pretty overshadowing."

She chuckled.

"But I can't believe you've already spoken to my mother and I had to hear everything from Scott." He tried not to sound incredulous, didn't think he managed. But, come on, they were lovers, even casual ones.

"She's my business partner in this venture," she said as if that explained everything.

What had he expected? This was Lily Susan. Getting her to broaden her focus from work into a more balanced life wasn't going to happen overnight. Unfortunately he was operating on a time limit.

"I wanted to talk with your mother before I talked with you."

"Got that part. Loud and clear."

Lifting their clasped hands, she pressed her soft mouth to his knuckles, lingered over the kiss until his pulse started to pound thickly behind his ears, a purely physical reaction to their closeness. And how much he wanted to get her naked again.

"There was a method to my madness." She finally lowered their hands, but still cradled them in her lap. "Once

I found out what was going on with Mara, I knew exactly how I wanted to handle the situation."

"Really?"

"I considered Mara a friend. Not a personal friend, but a business friend, someone I enjoyed working with and thought I could trust. I have a lot of relationships like that in my life, and I've decided I want more than that. I think I've sacrificed quite enough to achieve my goals, and I'm not willing to give up any more."

For a second Max couldn't believe what he was hearing. His pulse was rushing hard in his ears. But he agreed with her. She had sacrificed what should have been most important in her life—the people she loved.

"So, I've decided that I'm going to move the main office here and run it myself. With your mother."

"Well, she'll definitely like that, which means I'll like that. And the rest of my family, too. My mother's at her best when she's busy. But what about Worldwide Weddings Unlimited?"

"It'll still be my company, but every wedding won't necessarily be a Wedding Angel original. I've got a lot of really talented people on my staff, so I'm going to subtly shift the focus off Wedding Angel original events and onto establishing Worldwide Weddings Unlimited as a business that puts out quality events."

"You think you'll be happy scaling things back?" He had to ask, had to know how much of a chance he stood. "You've spent a lot of time away from here." A lot of time trying to get away.

"Can't say for sure, but I didn't say there wouldn't ever be another Wedding Angel original wedding. And I'll still have to visit my offices. We'll see. The one thing I do know is that I want to give *us* a chance."

The only reply Max had was to pull her into his arms and kiss her, again.

THE BEST PART of being five days out on the big wedding—without a local office manager and an assistant working from a bed—was that Lily was too busy to pay attention when the press went berserk over the identity of the All About Angel blogger.

Being in Poughkeepsie, of course, helped. Had she been in L.A. or Manhattan, the press would have been more visible.

By giving Max the exclusive, she further chopped off the story at the knees. The *Herald* had a jump on all the media outlets, and after speaking to her publicist, Lily had given a press conference to contain the damage.

Wedding preparations also kept her from getting too overwhelmed by her family, who wanted to be involved. And while she had shared the news about shifting the focus of operations back to this office, which pleased her parents to no end, she hadn't been around to deal with the fallout.

No, there wasn't time for a big celebration until after the wedding.

No, she didn't have any idea where she would live.

No, she had no earthly idea how long the restructuring would take and if she'd be in the country for Christmas.

These busy days proved to be a comfortable transition time.

But the absolute best part of the wedding preparations involved Max. Now that they were down to the wire, there were lots of phone calls and fast meetings where they wound up grabbing lunches or dinners. There were drive-bys at her office or his house and always there were stolen kisses.

She felt they were dating in the middle of a whirlwind because she was always excited to see him, always pleased when he called. They hadn't had any more glorious nights together. The simple fact was there weren't enough hours in the day to accomplish all that needed to be done.

Lily should have known things were *too* good. She was too happy with the media blowing up all around, too content for something dramatic not to go wrong. That's the way her luck had been running lately.

When Max showed up at her office unannounced at noon on Friday, she knew something was wrong. He didn't kiss her. He didn't smile. And to think about it, he hadn't called or texted her since his drive into the office this morning, which should have been her first clue that something was up.

"Max, what's wrong?"

"Have you listened to the news today?"

No hug. No smile.

Lily braced herself.

"No."

"A terror attack in Afghanistan."

Lily gasped, reached out to place a hand on his arm. "Your brother-in-law?"

"No, Raymond's okay. He wasn't in the village where the bombing took place. But there are civilian casualties, and he's an officer. They canceled his leave."

"But he's okay?"

"Life on the front in war. We're all praying." Max exhaled heavily. "I don't know how my in-laws do it."

"Are they okay?" They couldn't be young. Lily ushered him into the viewing room, urged him to sit. He looked shell-shocked. "What about you? Let me get you something to drink."

She hadn't taken the first step when it hit her.

The wedding.

"Oh, my god!" She stared at him, saw the truth reflected in his face. "Oh, my god."

The words poured from her mouth unbidden as her brain tried to process. Would she have to try to salvage some good from the wreckage, turn another wedding event into a charity function? Two in the span of a year?

The media would go berserk.

Max must have known she was about to freak because he was on his feet, arms around her, guiding her to the sofa.

"Seems we've hit a snag."

She sank to the sofa. A snag? *A snag?* Her chest seized around her lungs, making her fight for breath. She was going to hyperventilate. She knew it. Leaning forward, she put her head between her legs, commanded herself to calm down.

Max sat beside her, stroked her back, her hair. He kept whispering something, but she couldn't make out what he was saying past the thoughts rushing at breakneck speed through her head.

The wedding. All that work…*the media.*

Her eyes fluttered closed as if she could block out reality. Simply shut it down.

The media was already going berserk. On the heels of

everything with Mara, which some sources were spin-
ning as internal trouble at Worldwide Weddings Unlimited and others were playing up raging jealousy like a
daytime television storyline, this would be like the last
nail in the lid of Worldwide Weddings Unlimited's coffin.
Okay, maybe not the last nail.

"Don't despair, *mon bel amant*."

My beautiful lover.

Lily didn't think he got *that* from his kindergarten
tutor.

Opening her eyes, she found him watching her, looking tender and somewhat amused. Although she had no
idea what he could possibly find amusing.

"Take a deep breath and listen to me," he said. "I've
got an idea."

She couldn't seem to manage the breath yet, kept telling herself that the most important thing was that Raymond was alive when other innocent people weren't. A
wedding was a wedding. They could plan another. No big
deal.

Max pressed a kiss to the top of her head. "Listen to
me. We've got a perfectly good wedding planned. We've
got everything we need except for a bride and groom. I'll
be the groom."

It took a moment to wrap her brain around *that*. Surely
he wasn't suggesting... But Max was already on his feet,
staring at her with that dimple flashing.

"Take a chance, Lily Susan. I love you. You've loved
me forever. You just have to decide what you want then
everything else will fall into place. I'm heading down to
the clerk's office right now to get the license." He held
his hand out to her. "Are you coming?"

His expression was all expectation, and Lily's heart throbbed a single hard beat at the hope on his face, the love.

This definitely wasn't the romantic proposal she'd dreamed about in her youth, but she was learning that there were times when reality beat fantasy hands down.

She exhaled hard, willed herself to calm down. Then, slipping her fingers into his, she said, "I'm coming."

EPILOGUE

Happy Thanksgiving, my friends. Surprise! Today is my wedding day, so send good thoughts my way. I have so much to be thankful for and I promise to post *lots* of photos. Peace and blessings to all;-)

LILY SENT THE POST to her Twitter account then tucked her BlackBerry away in her purse. She wouldn't need it for a while. She glanced in the mirror of the powder room, and was amazed at the reflection.

A bride who looked exactly as a bride should look, with a natural flush in her cheeks and sparkling eyes. The gown... Well, the gown would have made anyone look amazing.

Lily might not have chosen it for herself, but she honestly couldn't love this gown more, especially since there was a little girl wearing a miniversion right outside the door. An adorable little girl who had already started calling her *Maman*.

Taking a deep, steadying breath, she turned and caught sight of the wrap she'd had made to winterize the gown so Jamilyn would get photos outside after the ceremony.

And in that moment, Lily knew how she would make this wedding truly hers.

She didn't care that there were musicians set up in the music room. She didn't even care that it was too cold to be outside comfortably for long. *Her* fantasy wedding at Overlook had always involved being married on the grounds of the Hudson River.

And this was *her* fantasy wedding.

It didn't matter that she'd turned Mom, Caroline, Riley and Camille into her last-minute attendants with gowns that didn't quite fit. It didn't matter that Camille was wearing the dress she'd worn as Riley's maid of honor. It didn't matter that she'd never met many of the guests before because she and Max had told Jamilyn and Raymond's guests who still wanted to attend a big Thanksgiving event to join the celebration.

All that mattered was the love.

So when she asked Ginger to direct the guests to grab their coats and head outside, everyone went without complaint. Because there was so much love at Overlook today.

The change of venue took approximately ten minutes, and then Lily was following her wedding party onto the grounds that she'd dreamed about, her lace veil fluttering in the breeze.

And when she saw Max standing on the bank of the river, waiting for her, watching her with that striking gaze that turned her insides into marshmallow—a familiar phenomenon from her youth—Lily knew this was exactly the turn she'd wanted her life to take, exactly the life she wanted forever.

A life with Max.

And Lily's wedding turned out to be exactly what a wedding should be, a fantasy day that promised a lifetime of real.

* * * * *

Harlequin *Super Romance*

COMING NEXT MONTH

Available November 8, 2011

#1740 CHRISTMAS IN MONTANA
North Star, Montana
Kay Stockham

#1741 TEMPORARY RANCHER
Home on the Ranch
Ann Evans

#1742 ALL THEY NEED
Sarah Mayberry

#1743 THESE TIES THAT BIND
Hometown U.S.A.
Mary Sullivan

#1744 THE SON HE NEVER KNEW
Delta Secrets
Kristi Gold

#1745 THE CHRISTMAS GIFT
Going Back
Darlene Gardner

You can find more information on upcoming
Harlequin® titles, free excerpts and more at
www.HarlequinInsideRomance.com.

HSRCNM1011

Harlequin® Special Edition® is thrilled to present a new installment in USA TODAY *bestselling author RaeAnne Thayne's reader-favorite miniseries,* THE COWBOYS OF COLD CREEK.

Join the excitement as we meet the Bowmans—four siblings who lost their parents but keep family ties alive in Pine Gulch. First up is Trace. Only two things get under this rugged lawman's skin: beautiful women and secrets. And in Rebecca Parsons, he finds both!

Read on for a sneak peek of CHRISTMAS IN COLD CREEK. *Available November 2011 from Harlequin® Special Edition®.*

On impulse, he unfolded himself from the bar stool. "Need a hand?"

"Thank you! I…" She lifted her gaze from the floor to his jeans and then raised her eyes. When she identified him her hazel eyes turned from grateful to unfriendly and cold, as if he'd somehow thrown the broken glasses at her head.

He also thought he saw a glimmer of panic in those interesting depths, which instantly stirred his curiosity like cream swirling through coffee.

"I've got it, Officer. Thank you." Her voice was several degrees colder than the whirl of sleet outside the windows.

Despite her protests, he knelt down beside her and began to pick up shards of broken glass. "No problem. Those trays can be slippery."

This close, he picked up the scent of her, something fresh and flowery that made him think of a mountain meadow on a July afternoon. She had a soft, lush mouth and for one brief, insane moment, he wanted to push aside that stray lock of hair slipping from her ponytail and taste her. Apparently he needed to spend a lot less time working and a great deal *more* time recreating with the opposite sex if he could have sudden random fantasies about a woman he wasn't even inclined to like, pretty or not.

"I'm Trace Bowman. You must be new in town."

She didn't answer immediately and he could almost see the wheels turning in her head. Why the hesitancy? And why that little hint of unease he could see clouding the edge of her gaze? His presence was obviously making her uncomfortable and Trace couldn't help wondering why.

"Yes. We've been here a few weeks."

"Well, I'm just up the road about four lots, in the white house with the cedar shake roof, if you or your daughter need anything." He smiled at her as he picked up the last shard of glass and set it on her tray.

Definitely a story there, he thought as she hurried away. He just might need to dig a little into her background to find out why someone with fine clothes and nice jewelry, and who so obviously didn't have experience as a waitress, would be here slinging hash at The Gulch. Was she running away from someone? A bad marriage?

So…Rebecca Parsons. Not Becky. An intriguing woman. It had been a long time since one of those had crossed his path here in Pine Gulch.

Trace won't rest until he finds out Rebecca's secret, but will he still have that same attraction to her once he does? Find out in CHRISTMAS IN COLD CREEK. Available November 2011 from Harlequin® Special Edition®.

HSEEXP1111

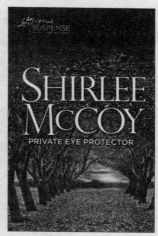

ROMANTIC
SUSPENSE

CARLA CASSIDY

Cowboy's Triplet Trouble

Jake Johnson, the eldest of his triplet brothers, is stunned
when Grace Sinclair turns up on his family's ranch declaring
Jake's younger and irresponsible brother as the father of her
triplets. When Grace's life is threatened, Jake finds himself
fighting a powerful attraction and a need to protect. But as
the threats hit closer to home, Jake begins to wonder
if someone on the ranch is out to kill Grace....

A brand-new Top Secret Deliveries story!

TOP SECRET
DELIVERIES

Available in November wherever books are sold!